THE
RICE
THIEVES

Best Wishes
Enjoy the Read –
Bill Clapson
Oct 18

THE RICE THIEVES

WILLIAM CLAYPOOL

MEADOW
LANE
PRESS

The Rice Thieves

Cover design by eBookLaunch.com

ISBN 978-0-9860637-8-7 (sc)
ISBN 978-0-9860637-7-0 (e-book)

Published by:

Meadow Lane Press
King of Prussia, PA 19406

Printed in the United States of America

OTHER NOVELS BY
WILLIAM CLAYPOOL

Windfall Nights

The Cocaspore Project

The House Beneath the Damen Off-Ramp

NOTE

There are no real people represented as characters in this work. The names and personalities are fictitious. Any resemblance of any character to any person, living or dead, is entirely coincidental and completely unintended.

Kill with a borrowed knife.
Tan Daoji
High General, Liu Song Dynasty

PROLOGUE

The day was very hot and humid, even for Augusta, Georgia. Shelly, the short New Yorker, and Buddy, the tall Texan, were drenched in sweat from the previous seventeen holes. Both men were ready for the long round of golf to end, although there was still the issue of the nine carryovers on their bet. The bet on the last hole would be for ten skins, and if they failed to decide it on the course, they would cast their fate to the golf gods and cut cards to settle accounts.

On the eighteenth tee, Buddy said to Shelly, "I know we said 'no presses,' but this match has gotten very interesting. I might make back all the money I've lost to you over the years. How about we double the skins value now?"

Shelly looked at him and shook his head. "Sorry, pal, that's too rich for my blood. I'm just a two-comma guy, not a three-comma guy like you."

Shelly stuck his tee into the ground and placed his ball. As he addressed the ball, Buddy said faintly, "And that's why you'll stay a two-comma guy."

Shelly stepped away from the ball and glared at Buddy.

Buddy raised his hands in mock surrender.

Shelly took another practice swing, addressed the teed ball and then ripped his drive. The shot threaded the narrow chute to the eighteenth fairway and it just kept going. It was by far his best drive of the day.

"Nice drive. Any seller's remorse?" asked Buddy. "My offer is still on the table."

"You seriously want to play this for 200?"

"I'm willing if you are."

"You're nuts."

"I know, but I only see you down here once a year, and I think it ought to be memorable."

"It's already been memorable; still, no double."

"Suit yourself. No guts, no glory."

Buddy took the tee, placed his ball on the peg, and hit. His drive also found the fairway through the chute of trees, yet it was short, about sixty yards behind Shelly's.

Buddy watched the ball come to rest and turned to his friend. "I'll give you one more chance to change your mind."

Shelly shook his head slightly, and looked carefully at the two balls down the fairway. He turned to Buddy. "Okay, we'll double."

Buddy said. "Good. Nice to see you have a little spunk left in you. Let's play golf." He started walking down the fairway.

The men, both tired, slowly walked the uphill finishing hole without saying another word.

Buddy's next shot, a fairway wood, was redemptive, and it almost made up for his short drive, although he was still well short of the green. Shelly's second shot veered off the side of the elevated green, and landed without further trouble.

Buddy hit a wedge for his third shot, although not well. His ball came to rest on the green fifty feet away from the hole.

As Shelly addressed his third shot, Buddy yelled out to him. "Remember, we said 200. Right?"

Shelly said nothing as he looked down on his ball. He was fifteen yards from the fringe of the green. He addressed the ball and made his swing. His club caught the ground well behind the ball and it traveled only five yards.

Buddy saw the shot and yelled, "Ouch! You're not feeling any pressure, now, are you? Do you want to re-double?"

Shelly didn't look at Buddy. He just cursed to himself and set up for his fourth shot with the same club after the caddy toweled off the mud.

Shelly took a deep breath and made his swing. He clipped the ball cleanly. The ball cleared the fringe and released beautifully on the undulating surface, keeping just enough speed to power through the breaks. It came to rest momentarily on the lip of the cup and then dropped in.

"Yes!" he screamed. "We call that par where I come from. Do you want to re-double now?"

"No, not right now," said Buddy quietly, as he and his caddy set up his putt.

Buddy finally chose the line and addressed the ball. He made a smooth stroke, and the ball took off. The first break was right followed by a small downhill ride to a left break. The ball was on course. The last ten feet were straight. It rimed half the cup before it dribbled beautifully into the hole.

Buddy let out a loud scream, "Yes! We call that a par, too!"

He came over and shook Shelly's hand. "Great round of golf."

Shelly said, "Yes, but our business isn't finished yet."

"No, it's not." Buddy turned to glance over his shoulder. "Let's do it here; there's no one playing behind us."

"Okay," said Shelly. "Do you have the cards?"

"Yes, in my bag." He turned to his caddy. "The cards are in the top pocket."

The caddy walked to the bag and returned with a deck of playing cards. Buddy handed them to Shelly. "You look them over and decide who cuts."

Shelly looked over the cards. "Roy cuts for me, and Charlie cuts for you."

"Okay," said Buddy.

Shelly held the cards in his hand and looked at the caddies, who understood their game.

"Do you know how much you're cutting for?" Shelly asked.

"200 dollars," said Roy.

"I wish," said Shelly. "Cut a good one for me."

Roy took his card and held it. Charlie followed.

"Let's show 'em boys," said Buddy. "What did you find me?"

Charlie showed a ten. "Good job," said Buddy. "Okay, Roy, let's see that little card; make it a five for my friend from New York."

Roy turned his card and showed a queen.

"Damn!" said Buddy. Shelly let out a whoop and hugged Roy before shaking Buddy's outstretched hand.

"We'll settle up in the clubhouse," said Buddy, walking away from the others.

* * *

After showering, dressing, and now sitting over an iced tea at a table in the clubhouse, Buddy gave Shelly the check for $200,000.

"I enjoy spending these afternoons with you. However, you're becoming an expensive date," Buddy said.

Shelly smiled at him, the check in his hand. "I could almost retire and just come down here once a year to play you in golf. You've been a steady annuity for the last five years."

"I did beat you six years ago."

"Yes, but it was only for ten grand. Dollar for dollar, you're way behind."

"I know exactly how far behind I am, and I'm going to make it my life's work to even it up. I'll figure out a way to get my money back from you."

"Well, I wouldn't count on golf for that. I don't like playing poker or pool, and I sure as hell won't play basketball with you. How are you going to do it?"

"I don't know. It's sure gonna be fun to figure it out. Are we on for next year?"

"Our eighth anniversary in the club. It's on the calendar. Are we going to see one another in New York?"

"We'll see." Buddy looked at his watch. "I gotta go. I have a dinner date in Houston. Believe me, I'll be thinking about you, my friend."

"I'm flattered. Safe travels home."

"Thank you, you too, Shelly. I promise that somehow, some-day, you will pay."

"I'm curious as to how you'll make that happen."

"So am I. It may take a while, but I guarantee we'll come back to this in the future."

CHAPTER 1

Despite the persistent cold rain and the inviting comfort of the small bar, there were few patrons enjoying the warm fire and quiet music within. In Oban, rain and cold were no strangers and people understood it; actually, they embraced it. It was their way of life. Lying in what sailors knew as the "roaring forties," the climate and setting of Oban, New Zealand was not for everyone. In truth, it was not for very many people at all, with only about 400 hardy souls calling Stewart Island their home.

Oban was the jewel of Halfmoon Bay on Stewart, the southernmost inhabited island in New Zealand. Unlike its Scottish namesake, Stewart's Oban was better known for its great white sharks than its single malt scotch. However, it was beautiful, friendly, quiet, and that suited him just fine.

Mike Franco had arrived three months before. It took only a short time before he learned his way around the little village and met everyone in the town's small service industry—barber, grocer, wine store owner, and bartender in ascending order of importance to him. His small rented house was working out perfectly, and he had extended his visitor visa for the full twelve months of his lease. It was all generally going as planned—the plan he had made throughout his long rehabilitation for a shattered femur. He didn't enjoy thinking about his injury or the circumstances around it, and he tried not to look back.

The plan was simple. Leave the Navy, put his financial house in order, throw away his cell phone, and go to where he could quietly discern what he should do with the rest of his life. However, a small variation to the plan occurred with the appearance of Ani, a striking Maori beauty he met during one of the ferry runs back to the mainland.

Ani's reasons for coming to Stewart were largely the same as his—R&R for TBD. She left the North Island early in life and grew up in Melbourne and went to university there. She returned to Wellington after college and worked for a few years, became tired of it, put her cash aside, and went south, far south to Stewart, to glide for a while on her savings. That wasn't exactly his story, although the gliding part was the important overlap.

She was cold to him at first, then she gradually thawed, moving from almost hostile, to formal. It got interesting when she continued to warm to friendly and then to very friendly. After a month of sharing wildlife tours, park hikes, seeing the Kiwis and making the obligatory shark dive, their relationship became much more involved, and she now spent more time at his place than she did at her own. The plan had changed, and he was happy it had.

They sat in a back booth nursing drinks before dinner. In deference to the cold night, she was wearing a cable knit sweater, a departure from her collection of deep V-neck shells. It suited her, but then again, anything suited her.

The gentle light of the pub shaded her face in a soft, mysterious way that reminded him of a beautiful background figure found in a classical painting. She could be the old master's mistress and would have been captured on canvas as a secret known only to them. The painting would have ensured her beauty was preserved for as much of forever as the artist could control.

Of the mixed genes that formed the ancient Maori, the Polynesian and the Melanesian, Ani was the lucky receiver of a breathtaking mix of both. Her long dark hair was an auburn blend, falling in soft waves over her shoulders. She had unblemished hazel-toned skin, full lips, and a fine straight nose that all worked together for a devastating effect on him. As he took it all in, he studied her, noticing again that she had the most alluring blue eyes.

They had been exploring family; her parents were still in Melbourne, and her brothers had come back to New Zealand and were working in Auckland. It was his turn, and he deftly changed the subject.

"Your eyes are so beautiful," he said. "How do you come to have blue eyes?"

"Is this is the first time you've noticed my eyes are blue?"

"No, of course not," he said uncomfortably. "Your eyes just knock me out tonight. I just mean...they look radiant. Isn't that rare?"

"What do you mean 'rare'? You mean blue eyes for a Maori?"

"Yes."

"I'm not sure. It's not that rare among my relatives. I think it might be convict blood in me from generations back."

"Pirates in your past?"

"Maybe."

They both reached for their glasses and took a drink.

She laughed.

"Is this truly the first time you've noticed my eyes are blue?"

"Oh no, certainly not. They just seem to shine tonight."

"Maybe it's because I'm wearing this sweater." She gently pulled at the heavy garment on her shoulder.

"I don't follow."

"Perhaps your focus tonight is on my face, rather than my chest."

He stalled. "My attention is always on your face."

She looked amused as she took another sip of her drink. "No, it's not," she said quietly.

He shrugged his shoulders. "Sorry, I guess it's in my genes."

"It's okay," she reached across the table to pat his hand. "I think my boobs are my best feature."

"Your 'boobs?'" he repeated.

She grinned and made a sweeping gesture looking down her chest. "Yes, these," she said, and added, "You know 'boobs'... knockers, jugs, titties, gigglies, hooters, et cetera, et cetera, et cetera." She looked up to meet his eyes and broke into laughter.

He was laughing too, but managed to say, "I do think your eyes are lovely."

After she stopped laughing, she said, "Yeah, thanks." She held his hand now, still smiling at him. "You know, you weren't supposed to be this cute."

He looked puzzled. "What does that mean?"

"Take it on its face."

"Did you have an interesting premonition about me? Did my mauri come to you in a dream, or was I foretold to you by a wise ancestor?"

She laughed. "Right, maybe. Anyway, you are cute."

"Thank you, so are you."

They were quiet for a moment, then he looked toward the kitchen, hungry, and ready to move on to his meal.

He turned back to her. "Well, I think your eyes are your best feature," he said emphatically. "And, as they might say in a court of law, I've seen all the evidence and it would be hard to say your eyes are more or less beautiful than your breasts. It's like asking a parent who their favorite child is. They're different, yet you love them all."

He took a sip of his drink before adding, "I also like it that you don't have a tattoo on your face."

"Oh, my ta moko. We moved to Melbourne before I got to the age where I would have jumped into that. Maybe I'm not a good Maori, but that idea never appealed to me."

"Well, I think it becomes you to not have a tattoo on your chin."

"That's because you're not Maori."

"I think I'd have support on this from a lot of your people."

"Maybe," she said casually. "What else do you like?"

He thought about the question and realized no good would come of this if he gave a clumsy answer.

When he decided on the answer that would give him the least trouble, the wall-mounted telephone on the back wall of the bar rang loudly. He waited until the bartender answered and waited longer when he saw the bartender suddenly looking his way.

The bartender laid the phone on the counter, and walked toward them speaking almost in a whisper. "Mike, there's a woman on the line with an American accent calling for a Michael Franco on behalf of some bloke named Pauling. You want to take the call here?"

Mike, surprised, hesitated before speaking. "Oh, shit," he murmured quietly. "No, tell her I'm not here and that you haven't seen me for a week or two." Franco reached into his pocket and pulled out a bill, handing it to the bartender as he said it.

As the bartender walked away, Ani asked. "What was that all about?"

Mike didn't answer her until he heard the bartender finish with the caller. "You don't want to know. It's about a guy I worked for a while ago. I don't know why he's calling. Let's just say I don't need to hear from him right now." Mike took a drink. "Now, we were talking about your other parts…"

"Yes," teased Ani. "What other anatomical feature of mine sets me off… or should I say, gets you off?"

Franco quickly said, "I love your hair—the length, the color, the way you wear it."

"Okay. Anything else?"

"You have those beautiful legs; toned, long, and perfectly proportioned."

She was enjoying the conversation. "Thank you. Anything else? This is interesting."

"Well, there's your…"

Franco stopped in midsentence when the telephone rang again. He listened to the bartender take the call. The bartender said, "Just a minute, I'll check," and walked back to their booth.

"Mike, it's a grumpy man with an American accent who says you damn well better take his call."

Franco reached back into his pocket and fetched another bill. He handed it to the barman. "Tell him I just left."

The barman put the bill in his pocket, shrugged his shoulders, and said, "Okay," as he walked back to the phone and brusquely told the caller that Franco had just left. He switched off the telephone and winked at Franco. He pointed to the fact that he killed the phone and he laid it on the bar, off the receiver. Franco waved from across the room.

"Sorry about that," Franco said to Ani.

"No worries," she said. "This is a persistent fellow, it seems."

"You have no idea."

"Now, where were we?" she asked, with a smile.

"I think I was complimenting your legs."

"Yes, we've covered that. Are there any other parts you'd like to discuss?"

"If I must, I'd love to tell you how much I enjoy your…"

He was stopped from completing his sentence by the cell phone ringing from inside her purse.

She gave Mike a quizzical look. "Could it be him?"

"Yes, probably."

"Should I answer it?" she asked.

"I suppose you should if we're ever going to finish this conversation."

"Are you here, if it's for you?"

"Yes," he said reluctantly.

She pulled the mobile phone from her purse.

"Hello?" she said into the phone.

She handed Mike the cell phone.

He said, "Hello, Admiral."

"Franco," said the voice on the other end, without a greeting, "take this call outside where you won't be overheard."

"I don't work for you anymore," said Mike.

"I know," the gruff voice replied. "We're going to fix that. Go outside."

"It's cold."

"Wear a coat," demanded the Admiral without missing a beat.

"It's wet."

"Hell, it's always wet there. Grab an umbrella if you need it."

Franco hesitated before he made up his mind.

"Just a minute," said Franco to his caller.

Franco whispered to Ani, "I'll be right back."

He pulled his coat off the booth, draped it over his shoulders and went out the door.

"All right, I'm outside," he said into the phone.

"Good, here's what I want you to do. I'll have transportation ready for you tomorrow at that airstrip on Stewart at 1000 hours local. We'll have lunch in Dunedin and I'll tell you what I need from you."

"What's this about?"

"You'll hear all about it tomorrow. Basically, it's a case of theft from a U.S. government facility. I think you're the right guy to help me with it."

"With respect, sir, I'm retired now. Why would I risk my neck again?"

"No, Franco. No risks. No heavy lifting for you on this one. I have a team of investigators who will be doing all the hard work. I just need you to keep me up to date as to what's going on."

"I don't think I want to be involved with you again, Admiral. I'm enjoying a nice peaceful life here. By the way, how did you find me? I thought I was off the grid. I don't even have a cell phone."

"Being 'off the grid' is a relative term, Mike. Remember, I still have friends at the NSA. Unless you pay cash for everything and always hide indoors, we can usually locate you. It takes a lot of work to completely drop off the grid these days."

Franco waited before speaking. "Sir, I think I unconsciously thought of that when I came here with all the cloud cover for those damned satellites."

"Well, the optics are amazing these days," said the Admiral enthusiastically. "I can tell if you've shaved in the morning, so don't worry about hiding behind a little cloud cover. Just be at the airstrip at 1000 tomorrow."

"What's in it for me? Why should I interrupt my happy holiday?"

"I'll give you $10,000 to have lunch with me, and another $100,000 if you take the job I'm going to offer you."

"How long will the job take?"

"One month, tops. If it goes any longer, I'll give you $100,000 a month for each month over."

"Are you serious?"

"Have you ever known me not to be serious?" barked the old man.

"No, sir, but that's a lot of money."

"You're not in the Navy anymore. You were a lot cheaper when you wore the uniform," explained the Admiral.

"Yes, sir," said Franco. "Okay, 1000 local, just lunch, and $10,000."

"Correct, and we'll bring you back right after lunch."

"What kind of transportation am I looking for?"

"I'm calling in a favor from a friend in the Royal New Zealand Air Force. It's what we'll call a training mission for them. I imagine they'll show up for you in a King Air. They'll bring you to me when you arrive in Dunedin."

"All right, sir. I'll be there. Bring your checkbook."

"The check will be here waiting for you."

"One other thing, sir."

"What is that Franco?"

"You are a nasty old man to track me down here."

"I know that, son. But you still love me. Tomorrow."

The line went dead.

It was raining even harder now, and Franco hurried back into the bar with numerous thoughts racing through his mind. Most of those thoughts were memories of his last adventure with the Admiral. It had not turned out well and mostly he remembered the painful six months he spent recovering from his wounds.

* * *

Ani gave Franco a hard time when they returned to his house. She demanded to know who the caller was, what had gone on between them, and what he was involved in. Except for telling her that he had to make a quick business trip the next day, he said nothing else. It frustrated her tremendously, and she carried on for a long time, although she calmed down when they went to bed. They went to bed relatively early, and to Franco's relief, they stayed up very late.

They slept until eight and Franco made breakfast for them. After eating, she lounged in her short robe while he dressed. He tried to discuss what they would do for dinner that evening. She was vague, not wanting to make a decision.

"How do you think that man got my cell phone number?" she asked, changing the subject from dinner back to the previous evening's phone call.

"Well, I'm guessing if he knew I was here, and could identify me by satellite, he could identify you as well. If you were seen making a call by the satellite, he could trace the number to the cell station for the same time and bingo, you're caught."

"Aren't there all sorts of laws stopping that?"

"I'm not so naïve as to think that a few laws will slow him down if he thinks he needs to find something."

"This man is that important?" she asked.

"Yes, and he has all the connections he needs to do whatever he wants." Franco turned away to continue cleaning the kitchen.

She was still in the living room in her robe reading. "You know, Mike, I should have returned the favor," she said, putting down her newspaper.

"What's that?"

"I should list all the things I find attractive about you."

"That's sweet of you, but it's really not necessary."

"No, it is. I want to tell you."

"Okay," he said, walking over to her chair. "Tell me."

"I will," she said, smiling as he settled into the chair beside her. "Mike, I love your dark brown hair and black-brown eyes. I love the fact that you're tall and fit. I love your dimples, and the way your eyes kind of slant up when you laugh."

"Thank you. As you might say, 'anything else?'"

"Yes, I love..."

Before she could finish, the taxi beeped its horn in front of the house.

"Yes, Mike, lots of other things," she said, looking out the window. "I guess you have to go."

As Franco walked to the door, she blocked his way, dropped her robe to the floor and kissed him passionately. "Have a great trip," she murmured.

He thought about her lovely eyes and looked down at her body. She was probably right about her best feature. He kissed her again. The cab beeped a longer blast and he broke off the kiss.

"Duty calls," he said.

She lifted her robe from the carpet and put it on as he started to open the door.

"Mike," she called, as he walked down the first step to the street.

He turned. "What?"

"Do me a favor."

"Sure."

"Say hello to Admiral Pauling for me. It's been a while."

Franco stopped dead in his tracks and thought about what he had just heard. He took a deep breath before speaking. "You're not going to be here when I come back, are you?"

"I don't know. Remember, you weren't supposed to be this cute. Have a good lunch." She waved and gently closed the door.

Franco turned to the idling cab and didn't know whether to curse or thank Pauling when he saw him.

CHAPTER 2

One Year Earlier

The package began its journey in the early evening, as the botanist had meticulously planned. He had always been what employers call a "difficult" employee who didn't interact well with his peers and he preferred to work odd hours. Given the job's wage scale and the island's labor pool, his supervisors were happy to have him despite his often prickly behavior. On this day, he arrived at the facility shortly after lunch, as was his custom. He bid goodbye to his co-workers at five o'clock and enjoyed the quiet of the building while he waited for sunset. He tended his plants, adjusted the humidity controls, tested the soil, and carefully logged his entries into the computer notebooks. After he finished his usual rounds, he went outside for a cigarette. He watched the sun drop slightly lower while he waited to finish what he had recently been paid so well to do.

He relaxed on the bench outside the large, enclosed greenhouse, catching glimpses of the orange-blue splash of sun sinking into the Pacific horizon. The glow from the lights of Honolulu would also soon be visible in the western sky across the choppy water of the Kaiwi channel. It was a paradisal setting, quiet, with just the tropical breeze rustling in the palm fronds to fracture the total peace and the rhythmic, breathtaking beauty of the ocean beyond.

The western plain of Molokai was dry and would not have been terribly hospitable for most of the test crops in the building. However, the outside weather didn't really matter because this facility was the department's quarantine station, and it could manage any plant's requirements. When Honolulu customs found an inbound plant they didn't like or didn't understand, it was sent here for observation. When the Hawaiian Department of Agriculture field agents found an unfamiliar or newly invasive species, it was also brought here for study. It was a very fascinating job for a botanist, but it definitely didn't pay well. That part would change after tonight, he thought.

He finished his cigarette and returned to the facility. He was alone in the giant greenhouse looking over almost five acres of enclosed foliage. Several plots were shielded with large plastic screens. The plots housed varieties of blooming and non-blooming plants. The plots were generally small beds, with about three hundred species under watch for one reason or another. The sprinkler system was a work of technologic art with each plot receiving a computer-programmed amount of water. The high humidity plants were also isolated from the temperate plants and the arid species by divider walls. This evening his focus was not on the plants, but on the seed storage room beyond the plots.

Seeds were isolated from the plants of particular interest. The seeds were stored in a special room and each seed bin in the room was labeled and marked for individual treatment. Access to the seed room, like access to the entire facility, was controlled with a punch combination lock rather than key card access. It was old school, but the mechanical punch keys were reliable, easier to maintain than a computer card system and, since they spent the big money on the sprinklers, they scrimped on the locks. This was plant security, not national security, and access would never be highly controlled. The Department of Agriculture was not among the leading beneficiaries of cabinet level funding, and when you stripped out the pork barrel funding for farmer subsidies, and food stamps, it was barely scraping by.

The seed room was set at the same temperature as the rest of the greenhouse, although each of the seed bins was individually controlled for heat and humidity. The seeds he was seeking were stored in a large bin. He carried a special briefcase into the room, opened it, and removed the zip lock plastic bags from the double seal sheltering of the inner case. He opened the seed bin that housed the seeds that would create the treasured plants. The scoop in the bins made it easy to fill the eight bags and, because of the volume of the seeds in the bin, the eight bags barely made a dent in the total.

After carefully filling the bags, resealing the case, and double-checking the floor to make sure there was no spillage, he left the room. The door snapped locked behind him and he was on his way. He checked the grounds around him and was satisfied there was no one to observe him. He left the greenhouse and the USDA complex, driving happily to the pre-arranged meeting on a quiet road near the beach.

After a short drive with virtually no other cars on the two-lane road, he turned off to an even less traveled dusty lane. As outlined in their plan, the other car was parked in front of him on the dirt road. The party of one sat on the car hood, anticipating the thief's approach. They were surrounded on both sides by a heavy growth of the scrub kiawe trees that made their meeting seem even more intimate. The moon was not yet high and the lane was already very dark in the early evening

The botanist thief, who had met the smuggler several times before, surrendered the case and the smuggler gave him an envelope containing the bank confirmation of the last installment of the payment they had agreed. No words were exchanged. The botanist pulled out a small flashlight and examined the contents of the envelope. Satisfied, he turned away from the other man. Each man was pleased with the transaction, and they parted as night fully engulfed the island.

The final drop of a beautiful full moon gave way to a perfect dawn. In its soft glow, the fading skyscraper lights of Hong Kong Island and Kowloon framed the final path into Victoria Harbor; only the smuggler, whose name was Liu Chao, wouldn't be finishing the trip. He mused about the long voyage from the mid-Pacific, and he was happy to be home. It had been expensive and the risks had been enormous but it was almost over. He would leave the ship soon.

The huge container transport was in an anchorage south of Hong Kong Island waiting its turn to unload at the terminal. With dawn approaching, signs of activity were heard from all over the waking ship. Chao thought about his long trip and the pleasures of dry land. The sun climbed gently up the eastern horizon on the open sea, as he nervously anticipated the last leg.

Their morning berthing was scheduled at the Kwai Tsing terminal and, in the emerging day's light, he could see what was likely the pilot boat approaching in the distance. He was ready to join it. His pilot uniform shirt was too small for him, and it stretched tight beneath his life jacket. It was uncomfortable; thankfully, he would not have to wear it for long.

Chao's only luggage was a backpack and the briefcase by his side, which was now more valuable than gold. He had carried the briefcase on the small boat from Molokai to the rusting tramp freighter out of Honolulu, and then to the huge container ship in the mid-Pacific. The cost of this trip home was about $400,000 U.S. dollars—all payments for helping him carry this case discreetly back to Hong Kong Island. With the rest of the bribery and procurement payments, the all-in costs of the project were close to a million, however, those costs would easily be recouped within the first year. After that, the profits would be enormous, assuming the usual cooperation from the government.

The boat was clearly visible now. Chao could see the pilot on board who was dressed identically to him. The pilot stood amidships while crew members came on the forward deck to ensure their passenger's smooth transfer to the giant ship and Chao's own transfer in the opposite direction. The crew barked instructions back and forth and he felt even more at home with the Hong Kong dialects he heard. The experienced helmsman of the pilot boat had no difficulty broadsiding the cargo ship and holding position for the transfer.

The pilot came aboard first. He also wore a life vest and the same company shirt. He carried a briefcase on board similar to Chao's, and the ship's crew held the pilot's case as he passed it up the ladder to the entry bay in the cargo ship's hull. In the briefcase were charts the pilot would use to help bring the vessel into port—not that a seasoned pilot would need them—and the supporting paperwork for the terminal arrival. Chao thought about the relative value of the two briefcases and laughed to himself.

Their ship was fully loaded and she rode low in the water. There were only three rungs up the ladder to the platform. The true pilot hopped off the small boat and was on the boarding platform in a few moments. On the platform, he barely made eye contact with Chao. The newcomer collected his case and entered the giant ship on his way to the bridge.

Although the crew seemed to notice the snub, they said nothing and helped Chao onto the pilot shuttle. Chao was reluctant to give up his case, but did so, needing both hands for the ladder. He thanked the crew for handing the case down to him when he was securely on-board the bobbing boat.

Once aboard, he immediately went below to the small cabin as the pilot boat pulled away from the giant ship. Chao removed his life vest, and placed his case and backpack on the berth. He pulled out a nylon duffle bag from the backpack and expanded it on the berth. Turning to the briefcase, he popped the latches, and opened the cover. Eight double zip-lock bags with reddish green contents were carefully arranged in the case. Chao placed them carefully in the duffle bag and zipped the layer of waterproof plastic between the bags and the nylon duffle. He removed his pilot shirt and put on a simple black pullover. After he finished, he took a deep breath... and waited.

Rather than head for Victoria Harbor, the pilot shuttle turned out to the open water toward the back of Hong Kong Island. There were a few fishing boats out in the pre-dawn hour, and no visible harbor police. The customs patrols were not strict on their own people and they would not stop a clearly identified pilot boat. The pilot crews were usually Hong Kong nationals, not mainlanders. So were most of the customs agents, and they would not interfere if a small black market trade went on outside of the meddling arms of the central government. It was a code that nothing would be imported that would hurt their people—no guns, no explosives, and no manufactured drugs. The currency, diamonds, or gold that might be smuggled in were good for the economy, and the bribery proceeds were certainly good for the cash flow of the pilot boat crews. The shift supervisor said he had known their traveler since school days, and it was not necessary to evaluate his motives or to inspect his materials. There was no reason to doubt that he would follow the code. However, if the harbor police detained them or if the crew reported him, Chao thought it would not be a tragedy. It would just be a bit more difficult as favors would have to be called in.

The last leg of the trip took about thirty minutes. In the creeping, orange light of the coming dawn, the helmsman found the small inlet on the south coast of the island. The pilot boat entered the inlet and approached the isolated dock off to the side behind an outcropping of rocks. When the boat reached the dock, Chao collected his duffle bag and backpack, and thanked the helmsman and the crew. He strode to the pulpit of the small cruiser and hopped off the bow. The pilot shuttle's engine shifted to reverse almost immediately after Chao touched down on the small dock. He walked toward the shore in the growing daylight, briefly pausing to watch the boat depart before leaving the dock. Sunlight now filtered in over the mountains behind the inlet, and to Chao, it was definitely a beautiful new day.

Fifty meters down the small path from the rickety dock was an unpaved street. A car was parked there. When the driver saw the traveler, he popped open the car's trunk before leaving the car to greet him. He ran to him and hugged him warmly. After they broke the hug, they looked at each other's happy face before entering the car.

The driver was the first to speak.

"You look so good, little brother. How was your trip?"

"Although it was long, it was much easier than I thought it would be. The accommodations on the ship were fine. I had an individual cabin. It was small, reasonably comfortable, and I only left to take meals with the crew."

"How was the weather? Any problems being seasick?"

"No. It was generally calm. Our late mother would be happy to know that I never lost my dinner. That was a good thing too, because although I had a private cabin, I did not have a private head."

"I'm sure it would please her to know that her little boy with the weak stomach crossed the Pacific without vomiting once. I am happy it went easily for you."

"Thank you for that. Even so, it is good to be home. No more Pacific crossings for me."

"It is a relief to me to have you home."

They made their way around the mountainous island on two lane roads. They drove quietly for a time, before the driver spoke.

"Was there any difficulty in bringing your package?"

"Other than the stress on my heart from the excitement, it was not difficult."

"What was the worst of it?"

"Leaving Hawaii was the most stressful. I thought the Americans would stop me at any time. I did not feel safe until we were three hundred kilometers out to sea."

"Did you think they were looking for you?"

"No," he said, smiling, "You know a guilty conscience on an honorable businessman is a heavy weight."

"Which honorable businessman were you thinking of? Surely not you."

"It was a figure of speech. This type of smuggling is new to me. My mind saw police behind every building, every bush, and every wave."

"Chao, you always had too much imagination," said the older brother.

"Yes, I don't have the right temperament to be a smuggler. Taking blueprints or computer chips doesn't feel like smuggling. This did."

"Don't underestimate your talents. You are very successful at all of it."

The traffic was building as they turned onto a major road. The morning rush was well underway. Chao closed his eyes in the now familiar setting and his brother respected the quiet and his brother's fatigue. After another half-hour of stop and start traffic, they turned off the street and into a garage. Chao awoke, looked out, and did not need to ask where they were. He opened his door and met his brother at the open trunk of the car.

"Let me carry that for you," said the driver as his brother reached in for the duffle bag.

"No," said Chao. "Father said we should always finish a job we start. I'll carry it up." He hoisted the duffle, closed the trunk, and followed his brother.

They said nothing more as they rode the elevator to the lobby of the massive building above them. They walked over the polished stone floors from the garage elevator to the building elevator banks. It was still early and very few people were in the lobby. The elevator arrived quickly.

With no other passengers, it was an express trip to the thirty-first floor. The men exited the elevator and walked down the carpeted office hallway, stopping at the door lettered in English and Chinese, "Edwards Technologies."

They opened the door and walked down a corridor past several cubicles until reaching the last office. They entered the corner office that had a commanding view of the harbor and Kowloon through two walls of glass. Closing the door behind them, Chao lifted the duffle to the desk.

"Are you ready?" asked Chao.

"Yes. Let's see what six-million-yuan worth of rice seed looks like."

Chao unzipped the duffle. Opening the duffle wide, he unzipped the inner cover and took out his clothing, placing it to one side. When the clothing was stacked neatly away from the duffle, he looked at his brother for dramatic effect before starting to remove the rest of the contents.

One by one, he laid the sealed plastic bags on the table. The other man was wordless as he watched.

When Chao finished, his brother looked delighted as he counted the bags in front of him.

"Well done. Eight liters of seeds. This is more than I was expecting."

"Remember, Mother told us that happy surprises are the best sweets life gives us. Happy surprise, Jun."

"Well done. Our ancestors must be proud of you this day."

"Yes, a happy day. Should we drive out to Uncle's farm now?"

"No, you are tired from the long journey. You need to rest. I'll drive out to Lantau later today and bring these to him. I heard that rain is on the way so it is a perfect time."

"You know our associate in Hawaii says they do not need as much rain as normal rice. Their roots grow quickly, and they are much more efficient than the roots of normal plants."

"And they produce a crop in 90 days?"

"That is what he said. He said that if the conditions are perfect, we can produce a crop in 60 days."

"60 days? That is amazing, two or three times as many crops in a year than normal if the weather is right."

"Yes. They are very hardy, and self-propagate, so less labor is needed to plant them."

"That is amazing. I think the Americans were wrong to keep this to themselves."

"They have their corn and wheat farmers to please. We must concentrate on rice."

"We need to celebrate your success, brother." Jun walked to a cabinet behind his desk. "I've been saving this for a very special event," he said, pulling out a bottle.

"It's only 7:30," said Chao, as his brother poured two glasses from the bottle.

"That doesn't matter. We need to toast your success and our future. We have done a wonderful thing for China."

Jun turned to Chao, handing him his glass. "To China," Jun said. "May you never see hunger again. May you never need to import food again."

"To China," answered Chao. "Gan Bei."

CHAPTER 3

Franco's plane was waiting when his cab arrived at the single runway airstrip on the outskirts of Oban. There was little other activity and only a few people took any interest in seeing Franco board the King Air turboprop.

Without much fanfare, a pilot in a Royal Air Force uniform welcomed him aboard, pulled up the air stairs, and closed the cabin door. Franco took one of the seats in the back and the crewman took his own seat as the co-pilot. Franco was consumed with trying to understand how Pauling had planted Ani, and he spent most of the next airborne hours working this out in his head.

He remembered the last time he saw Pauling and it brought back memories he would rather have kept buried. The old man had visited him in intensive care after the last mission. It seemed like a hundred years ago. He had still been intubated and his leg was in traction. The chest tube in his side made any movement even more painful than the bullets that had caused the problem. Those unpleasant images were coming back all too clearly.

Why was he making this trip? Hadn't he learned that nearly dying for the Admiral the last time was enough? Well, at least the money he was being paid for this trip was attractive; that couldn't be said for the last time.

The cloud cover continued, and there was little to see below until they settled into the approach at Dunedin. The ceiling was such that the harbor and surrounding low mountains came into view only on their final approach. It was a terrible sightseeing tour for such a picturesque town.

The pilots taxied the plane down to the general aviation area and pulled up to the large Gulfstream business jet on the tarmac. The co-pilot popped the cabin door and lowered the stairs before speaking to Franco.

"The Admiral's waiting for you, mate. He lives in the big, white house." The pilot pointed at the Gulfstream. "We'll be here when you finish, Commander, and we'll take you back to Stewart."

Franco thanked the young officer and deplaned. He took a few short steps on the tarmac to the foot of the Gulfstream's steps. A large man in a dark suit stood at the bottom of the steps. The man looked at Franco and said, "Welcome aboard, Commander Franco. The Admiral is expecting you."

After Franco boarded the big jet, another man in a suit who had been posted at the cabin door, excused himself as Franco entered.

Sitting at a desk, alone in the large cabin, Pauling had a folder in front of him and was reading a document. "Good to see you, Franco," said the older man, without looking up. "Hold on a minute while I finish this. Have some water or coffee." He pointed to the jet's galley. "The coffee's fresh."

"Do you need anything?" Franco asked the old man. Receiving no reply, Franco walked to the alcove and helped himself to a cup of coffee.

He carried the coffee back to the couch opposite the desk, and sat, waiting another minute or two while the Admiral completed his reading.

Eventually, the old man looked at Franco. "How was the trip up?"

"Just fine," said Franco. "Before we have any other conversations, I want to know how you set me up with Ani. By the way, she says 'hello.'"

Pauling said, "Oh, thanks. Ani's a great kid. I've known her for a while. I asked her to keep an eye on you."

"And does that mean pimping her out to keep me interested?"

"Hell, Franco, I don't know anything about that. I have nothing to do with anything between you two beyond a little basic intel." The Admiral added with a smirk, "Give yourself a little credit, son. I just asked her to watch you and to tell me if you left Stewart Island. Frankly, I didn't care if she even met you—probably would have been better if she hadn't."

Franco thought about what he had just heard. "Okay, why am I so special to you? What's on your mind, sir?"

The old man arranged his folders and launched into the briefing. "I'm involved with a case of theft—big time industrial theft, that has expanded to stealing from the federal government. The theft is particularly embarrassing since it involves stealing assets we were supposed to be keeping in safe custody for a prominent citizen." The old man paused before saying, "I know you're going to love the fact that this theft involves plants."

"Plants? You must be joking."

"I'm not a joker. You know that," quickly replied the Admiral.

"Yes, sir," said Franco, and then continued, "My last encounter with plants didn't turn out very well."

The Admiral spoke slowly. "I understand your reluctance. However, this time it's going to be different in that you're not on the point. I need you because I need a person whose judgment I can trust to keep me informed on the progress of finding these thieves. I need information I can trust and I want you to be there. You'll be in the rear—just talking with me, and only if I call you, which I probably won't. No guns, no rough stuff, just observation. The front team is being run by Sam Rorke, who's just perfect for this job. I'm sure it will all go very smoothly."

"The numbers you mentioned earlier are a lot of money for just chatting with you."

"Call it payback. I owe you from the last outing. On that last mission, you had to deal with a lot more than I expected and you paid a price for it. Since neither of us are in the Navy anymore, I have a little more flexibility to take care of you and I don't mind paying you well."

"I assume I'll get paid when the job is done," said Franco.

"That's right. Rorke will tell you when your services are no longer needed and I'll manage to get the money to you."

"So, I'm working for Rorke?"

"Well, you're working for me but this is Rorke's show. So, it's probably good to think you're working for Rorke."

"I suppose I can do that for that kind of cash."

"Good. Franco, this is a very important project. Here's why..." The Admiral paused again.

"This operation involves two brothers from Hong Kong who have done rather well by stealing western technology—mostly U.S. technology. They're fairly broad-minded in what they choose to steal, and they've made a lot of money. We think they've taken out sensitive and proprietary technologies from our computer industry that are both hardware and software related. They front these technologies through their Hong Kong company and sell to the highest bidder, with Chinese government-connected companies usually being the highest bidder. This time we think they pilfered rice seed stocks from a Department of Agriculture station in Hawaii."

"Really?" said Franco. "You're telling me they stole rice? Stealing rice seed for China? Isn't that a little like bringing snow to the North Pole? I would guess that they have plenty of rice seed in China."

The Admiral said. "You might think that, and that's the important part I'm coming to. Yes, the Chinese are the world's biggest producers of rice, but they're also the world's greatest consumers. Over the last few years, they haven't been able to grow enough of it to be comfortably assured that they'll have enough for their domestic consumption. They are now big rice importers, mostly from other countries in southeast Asia. They also have other problems. The provinces that are the rice bowl of the country are being taken over by residential and industrial development. The clean water supply there is always a little tenuous depending on the rain, and they've even found cadmium contamination in their rice, not that anyone will talk about that. Their government is always nervous that their domestic rice production will actually decline. The Peoples Liberation Army hates the idea of China being forced to import food. The U.S. could supply all their grain needs—rice, corn, and wheat—but the PLA doesn't want to rely on us."

"I can certainly understand that," Franco said thoughtfully. "How is this stolen seed going to help them with their production issues?"

"This seed is a super strain of rice that increases the rice yield per unit of planted land. It might also make marginal growing areas more productive. This rice is quite different from the usual strain and its properties were discovered completely by accident. Let me explain."

The Admiral took a sip of water before speaking again.

"Rice is truly a source of protein. Its protein content is about eight percent. We don't think of rice much beyond its carbohydrates because in the west, we have other sources of protein. Anyway, people have been playing around with rice genetics for years trying to increase the grain's protein content, or to make the plants drought resistant, or to increase the yield. Well, a U.S. company hit the jackpot in the rice modification game and they did it while trying to do something unrelated."

The Admiral continued, "A group of plant scientists from Houston was playing around with these rice genes to make a very specific protein. They wanted to use rice to make a protein for pharmaceutical purposes. Interestingly, they didn't have the patent on the medicine; a New York based biotech company had that. They reviewed the protein's structure in the inventor's patents and with genetic modifications, engineered their rice plants to make it. The rice guys in Houston decided they could be the lowest cost manufacturer so that when the medicine was a big success, the originator company would want to come to them. Their idea was to grow this rice, mash it up, and pull out this protein from the mix. It would be a very low cost production method. It turned out they succeeded in doing this and they wanted to scale up production rapidly in facilities outside of their laboratories. They planted a lot of this stuff in Hawaii on Kauai."

"Let me guess," interjected Franco. "There was a problem."

"Yes and no," said the Admiral. "They took these modified seeds and brought them out to the company's test farm on Kauai. They were in such a rush to conduct field experiments that they didn't declare what they were doing or obtain clearance to bring in their plants. That is against the law, and the Hawaii Department of Agriculture takes that law very seriously. The HDOA found out about this relatively early on in their plan and, with the help of the USDA, they shut down the whole farm. The state laid a big fine on the company, which the company paid in a quick settlement so none of them would go to jail. They also voluntarily surrendered all their plants, seed stocks, and records of the project kept in Houston. They gave them to the USDA on condition that they would be returned to them if this protein became a commercial product and that the USDA would keep them updated on all issues related to the quarantine. All in all, it was a reasonable settlement for the company.

"The USDA took the plants to their quarantine facility on Molokai and destroyed the rest of the plants in the field on Kauai. What the USDA found with these plants was nothing short of spectacular. This strain of rice is not only drought resistant, and has about a 20 percent protein content, it also grows like a weed, and self-propagates. It's very invasive. Instead of the usual rice growing cycle of 120 days, this rice matures in no more than 90 days and under the best conditions, as quickly as 60 days. It's almost a completely different plant."

"Okay, what's the problem?" asked Franco.

"The problem is that the USDA seed stocks were stolen and smuggled out of the country. This super rice could make the sellers super rich and once again, this is U.S. technology being pirated."

Franco asked, "Why do you think it's this group in Hong Kong?"

"Rorke will tell you more of the story when you take the job."

"I thought this was all private enterprise. Obviously, Rorke is government, right?"

The Admiral said, "Let's just say that Rorke's team works for me."

"The warning bells are starting to go off now," said Franco.

"No, Franco, listen to me, and remember you are just a rear echelon observer. Trust me."

"Who do you work for these days, Admiral? I thought you were out of the Navy and settling into a quiet private life."

"I still work for the American people. I retired from the Navy. I didn't retire my patriotism. I do what I can when I'm asked."

Franco changed the subject. "Okay, sir, let's go back to the crime."

"Sure," said the Admiral. "Rorke's team investigated the whole story of the theft and we think we have it all worked out."

"When did all this happen?" asked Franco.

"We think the theft was about a year ago. We only recently confirmed a lot of the details. We figured out that an employee at the USDA facility was in on the theft. We determined that one of the Hong Kong brothers was the smuggler. By the way, the passport we think he used to come in to the U.S. never left.

That helps to make the case that he smuggled himself and the seeds out of the country."

"All right, where does your team fit in?"

"Very simply, we want to see if we can find out where the seeds went and who owns them now. Rorke's team will be going to China to see if they can learn more about what the brothers have done. I want you to join that team in Hawaii and go to Hong Kong with them. It shouldn't take long. Either we find the rice or the trail runs cold quickly. Any questions so far?"

"No, sir."

"Are you in?"

Franco said, "It sounds too easy to me. Is there a catch?"

"I hope not," said the Admiral. "I have to tell you this is getting under my skin. Although I don't imagine we'll be able to extradite the thieves from China, if a company imports Chinese rice with the same genetic signature as the USDA seeds, the owners will be able to make a case for patent infringement. It would be useful to know where they're growing it so we can be better prepared for the long international legal harangue that will surely come."

The old man shook his head and added, "This industrial theft has to stop, and we have to put these guys out of business."

Franco listened and the old man began again. "Right now though, we are flying a little blind. When we have a better idea of the situation, we can make plans to deal with it."

Franco kept quiet.

"Well?" asked the old man. "What's your answer?"

"Sir, I have a hard time saying 'no' to you.'"

"Good. Welcome aboard."

"Thanks," said Franco, without much enthusiasm.

The Admiral took another sip of water before speaking. "There is another person involved in this who you need to know about."

"Okay."

"Remember your old friend from Chicago, Dr. Paul Sloan?"

"Yeah, I remember everything about that trip—mostly, very bad memories."

"I understand. Well, Sloan is involved in this, too."

Franco groaned. "I don't know why, but I'm not surprised."

"Sloan had serious personal problems after his Chicago project. He started to drink, then became a steady drinker, and then became a drunk. He sank pretty low."

"That's a shame," said Franco.

"Yes, although the story doesn't end there for the good professor," continued the Admiral. "He woke up one day and saw what a shambles his life had become, and he took the cure. Apparently, he's been dry since."

"How is he involved in this?"

"I don't know if you knew this... Sloan had a big job at the USDA after the Chicago situation. He was a very capable guy, and for the time before he crashed, he was well regarded. When he went on the skids, they were going to fire him, then he took the pledge, did the rehab, and they kept him on. They still didn't trust him, though, and they gave him a window seat since he screwed up so badly. When he dried out, they arranged for him to be a "special assistant" to the USDA station chief in Hawaii. They figured it was a nice way to ease him into retirement. However, we need Sloan on this project. Evidently, if you know what you're looking for, you can tell the super rice plants from normal rice by the veins in their leaves. It's extremely subtle, particularly in the field. I've looked and I can't tell the difference, although Sloan can determine which are the modified rice plants. Because we need his expertise, even with the security risk that he's a recovering alcoholic, he'll be attached to the team."

"All right," said Franco. "Let's hope this turns out differently than the Chicago mission."

"It will," affirmed the Admiral.

"One other thing," said Franco.

"What?"

"Why did they make this rice protein anyway? What was it going to do?"

"As far as I know," said the Admiral, "it was going to be for an ulcer healing product. You eat the medicine and the ulcer quickly disappears."

"It sounds interesting."

"It was interesting enough for the rice genetics company to leap into production before the medicine was even tested in people."

"The person making that decision must enjoy taking big risks."

"He does. You'll meet him in Hawaii."

"I hope this assignment is as easy as you think it will be."

"I'm sure it will be," said the Admiral. He pointed out the opposite window. "The catering truck is here. Let's have lunch. Before we eat, I have your check for coming here today."

The Admiral removed an envelope from a seat pocket next to the desk.

"I'll do my best for you, Admiral."

"You've never let me down yet. You're going to enjoy working with Rorke, and I need you to stay close to Sloan."

"How close?" asked Franco.

"Not that close. Not surveillance," said the Admiral. "I just need you to be available if Sloan needs a friend to talk to. I don't want Sloan speaking to anyone about the stolen rice. He knows that, but I figure if he's interested in having a conversation with someone he shouldn't, it would be good if he had an old friend available to talk him out of it. You saved his life once and there's no doubt in my mind that he'll trust you if he happens to have any doubts about tracking down these Chinese thieves."

"I'll do what I can, sir."

"You'll do fine. Sloan is absolutely critical to this investigation and I need for him to know you're there for him if he wavers in any way in his commitment to helping us and his country. That is your main job."

"It sounds easy enough. Is there any reason he wouldn't help?"

"I hope not," said the Admiral.

"Okay, then. I'm in."

"There is one other thing," said Pauling.

"Yes, sir?"

"Keep an eye on Rorke for me. I don't expect any problems, but let me know if you see anything that bothers you."

"Can you be more specific?"

"No, Franco, but I trust your judgment. Just let me know if you have any concerns."

"Very well."

"Good, your tickets and travel itinerary are in this envelope. I also included a cell phone with my private number for you to contact me if there's an emergency. Otherwise, all communications will go through Rorke."

"Yes, sir," said Franco.

"Good. Welcome to the team. I'm happy we're working together again," said the Admiral. "Let's eat."

"Yes, I look forward to working with you again... I guess," said Franco reluctantly. He left the couch to follow the Admiral to the table as the sandwiches were brought to the cabin.

* * *

Franco left after eating half a sandwich. Pauling said goodbye to him and as soon as he left, the Admiral picked up the phone on his desk. He dialed, and spoke.

"Are you going to be okay having my friend Franco on the team?" he asked.

The old man listened to the brief reply and said, "Franco is a very steady hand. He can keep his mouth shut, and he'll be more than willing to take risks if you need him to. Above all, Sloan owes him his life and if things ever start to unravel, Franco might be invaluable in helping you bring the professor back to the fold. Besides, I owe Franco from the last time I used him, and I like being able to pay him back."

After a few moments, the Admiral responded, "Good. Franco will join your team in Hawaii. Play nice."

* * *

Franco's return flight was uneventful and, on approach, the pilots called down to Stewart to arrange a taxi for him. The cab was at the airstrip when Franco arrived and it drove him back to his home. Franco entered and saw that Ani had moved everything of hers out. She left no trace, only a note.

"Be happy, be careful, and don't let anything happen to that cute face. – Good-bye, Ani."

Franco sighed as he realized that a chapter in his life had just been completed. He packed his bags, and checked the travel itinerary and tickets the Admiral had included in his payment envelope. The commuter flight out to Invercargill and the connections to Auckland and Honolulu were not until tomorrow. He would say an indefinite goodbye to his barman, have dinner and a couple of drinks, and think about all he was about to leave behind.

CHAPTER 4

Nine Months Earlier

L antau Island, at the mouth of the Pearl River, was a short drive from the mainland over the Ma Wan Channel and surprisingly rural compared to the congestion of Hong Kong Island and Kowloon. The island was best known for two attractions—the Giant Buddha statue and Hong Kong Disneyland. Away from these tourist magnets, the low green mountains of the island, the ancient fishing villages, and the secluded beaches provided a welcome retreat from the crush of the city. The only reminder of the urban congestion was the constant flow of jets to and from the international airport on a landfill island off to the north.

Liu Jun and Liu Chao drove without speaking in the light, late morning traffic. The tunnel traffic off Hong Kong Island was mild, and the congestion across the Tsing Ma Bridge from the mainland was minimal. They exited the highway near the airport and crossed the spine of the island toward the south coast by a

43

winding secondary road. Close to the island's southern coastal plain, they turned onto a less traveled lane that led to a private road blocked by a steel chain-linked gate. Chao was driving, and he stopped the car to pull open the gate. He drove the car past the gate, returned to close the gate, and continued driving down the private lane lined with rows of bushes and flanked by the densely growing low scrub that was common on the island. After a few bends, the land cleared and a cultivated field came into view. Two small buildings, a modest house and a tool shed, stood close to the lane. Rice was growing in the paddy fields. A hand-lettered sign on a broken board hung on the shed. Written in traditional script, the sign read "Happy Stream Farm."

Standing between the buildings, an old man wearing a large straw hat and tall rubber boots stood with a rake watching the car approach. As it neared, he leaned his rake against the shed and walked toward the visitors. The car stopped and the two passengers opened the car doors.

Jun walked to the old man and bowed. The farmer returned the greeting.

"Uncle Quan, how are you?" asked Liu Jun.

"Very well, and how are you? Was your trip difficult?" asked the old man.

"No. It was very easy today. Chao is an excellent driver, and he made the trip in good time."

"I am happy to hear that," said Uncle Quan. "I hope young Chao didn't speed too much."

Chao walked over to the two men. "Uncle, I am careful not to upset my older brother. I took very good care of him today."

"I would expect nothing less, Chao," said the old man, grinning.

Chao gestured to the paddy. "How are the children growing?"

Quan looked pleased. "You won't believe it. I planted two mu with the seeds you gave me and the rice is doing amazingly well. Let's have tea first, and then I will show you."

Quan left the two without further words and they followed him to the small house.

They climbed a single wooden step onto a narrow porch and walked into the house. The simple kitchen was the entrance room and it contained a worn wooden table and four chairs off to the side. A small bedroom with a bed and a grass mat on the floor was off the kitchen. A kettle rested on the small propane cooktop. Quan warmed the kettle and prepared the tea while his visitors spoke quietly to each other.

He placed the small teacups on the table and invited his visitors to join him there.

"How is the city?" asked Quan. "Is there any exciting news?"

"There's always exciting news," said Chao. "Between business and the government, the newspapers are full. We have no shortage of things to talk about."

"Is there anything that will bother an old farmer like me?"

"Probably not."

"Good. I don't need any extra information. My old head is too full these days to remember much anyway." He tapped a finger against his bald scalp.

Jun spoke, "We don't worry about that. We just need your memory to remember the family stories and to remember how to grow rice."

Quan took a sip of his tea. "I just wish your father could have lived to be here with us to see this. It is almost too easy to grow this rice. It seems to grow itself."

"Please explain, Uncle. What do you mean?" asked Chao.

"I've not seen anything like it. I plant it in water and a few weeks later I see other shoots nearby where I didn't touch. This rice has a mind of its own."

"Is there any problem with that?" asked Chao.

The old man spoke. "There's no problem except that old peasants like me who only know how to grow rice will not be needed."

"We'll always need you, dear uncle," said Jun.

"Maybe for the stories of the old days when your father and I were children," said Quan, "but not to grow rice from the seeds you gave me. They will make me even more obsolete."

"I'm sure that is not true. Do you think we could grow this rice?"

"Well, that would be a good test for these special seeds," replied the old man. "I'm sure your Father would be surprised in the afterlife if his two city boy sons were growing rice."

"You could be a farmer," said Jun to his brother.

Chao took a sip of his tea. "No, it is always the first son who receives the land. You should be the farmer."

"Let me tell you a few other things about your seeds," said Uncle Quan. "Not only does your rice grow almost on its own, it grows very fast and it makes flowers in weeks. The grain comes rapidly and you can see it much earlier than normal rice. These seeds are quite impressive."

"Those are Chao's magic seeds," said Jun to the old man. "He found them and brought them to their rightful home."

"Yes, we are the home of rice," agreed the old man. He looked at Chao, "What were the Americans going to do with these seeds before you found them?"

"I don't know. I think they were hoarding them because with their corn and wheat, they do not need rice like we do. I think their agricultural lobby of wheat and corn growers may have put pressure on their government to withhold these seeds."

"That seems foolish," said the old man.

"It's foolish unless someone is making money, and over there someone is always making money," answered Chao.

The trio let that statement stand without further comment until Quan spoke. "Young Chao," said Quan, "your rice does one other thing that seems remarkable to me, and I think this is the most interesting."

The brothers waited while the old man took another sip of his tea.

"Two weeks ago, when we had not had rain for ten days, one of my paddies was leaking and it ran dry. All other rice would have been dead at that stage of the planting and I would have had to replant them. It was not so with this rice. It seemed to find water on its own. Its main roots go very deep and it doesn't need much rain to survive. It thrives in our usual weather, however, it can also survive in drier conditions."

"Does that open the possibility of growing rice in other areas of the country?" asked Jun.

"Yes," said Quan. "I think so. Chao's magic seeds could expand our rice fields to places we would not have thought possible."

The two younger men smiled at one another.

"Uncle Quan, do you think it is too early to share our findings with our friends in the government?" asked Jun.

"If you want to make money on this, you must tell them eventually. You know they will want to grow this at their own facilities.

I know you have excellent government connections. Right now, I think you should not tell them too much about what we have learned. I would like to finish a crop here before you discuss it very widely. It would be very bad to over-promise."

"What about putting the seeds in our own fields at the other farm?" asked Chao.

"What other farm?" asked Quan.

"It is up in Guangdong Province, a few hours from here, north of Shenzhen," said Jun.

"Why have you never showed me this other farm?"

"You told us you don't like to leave Happy Stream Farm."

"No," said the old man. "I don't like going to the city, but I would like to go to see my nephews' farm."

"Well," said Jun, "let's do this. We'll grow a crop of the new seeds at our test farm and when they are growing and looking beautiful, we'll drive you out."

"Good. How much will you plant?"

Jun had thought about this earlier and quickly replied, "I think we'll be able to plant three hectares."

"All right, you plant that much and I will want to see it growing. I will also have more seeds for you from my first plants here. Will you promise to take me there when the sprouts are up?"

"Yes, we will," said Jun. "Tell me; does the new rice look any different from the usual rice you grow?"

"I can't see any differences."

"Well, if you can't see any difference, no regional inspector from the Ministry will be able to see any difference either."

"I'm sure that's true," said the old man. "Even so, promise me that you will not tell the government too much about these new seeds until another test crop is harvested. Your father would never approve of being impulsive and discussing this with them in detail until you are sure of what you have."

"Yes, Uncle," said Jun. "We will wait until we have three hectares of beautiful rice before we make any conclusions."

"This is very exciting," said Chao. "Perhaps we should toast with something other than tea."

"Too early in the day for me," said Quan. "I'll sleep all day if I do any celebration before afternoon tea."

Chao was smiling and said to his uncle, "If the new rice does not need as much water, you won't have as many leaches in the paddies. You can retire your large rubber boots."

Quan said. "You should stay in the city and not tend the farm. You might not do very well in the fields. The boots are not for leaches in the paddy, young nephew. They are for snakes in the brush outside of the paddies."

"Perhaps Chao's magic seeds will keep the snakes away, too," said Jun.

"That is a theory I will not test," said Quan. "I'm comfortable in my boots, and I've seen too many snakes here over my many years to abandon them."

They each finished their cups. Quan spoke. "Let's go to the paddies and visit my children. Chao, please watch where you walk."

CHAPTER 5

Franco took the nine-hour day flight to Hawaii after traveling to Auckland from Stewart Island. He arrived at his hotel after midnight. After the long flight, he didn't sleep well. He was to join the team in the morning at an office in Honolulu near the airport. The attendees were to be two people from the Rorke team and Paul Sloan. The meeting was an orientation, mostly for him, he assumed, and would be followed by a flight to Molokai. Later, they would meet the owner of the rice genetics company for dinner back on Oahu.

Franco had mixed feelings about seeing Sloan again. That was a large part of why he had trouble sleeping. He remembered vividly all he had done for the man, and hated hearing that Sloan seemed to have squandered most of that effort. Between trying to clear his mind of these flashbacks and adjusting to the time change, he only managed to fall asleep at 5:00 am. He slept though the alarm he had set for 6:30. When he looked at the clock and it read 7:15, he bolted out of the bed and rushed to make the 8:00 meeting. He hurried through a shower, dressed, and dashed to the street via the hotel coffee shop. He made it to a taxi with a bagel and coffee in hand and had just enough time to finish them both before the cab arrived at the office address.

The address was for a mid-rise rundown building stuck in a neighborhood of warehouses. The building was on the flight path of Honolulu's airport, and as he left the taxi, the sidewalk trembled while a jumbo jet screamed overhead on its final approach. He paid the fare and quickly entered the building. The elevator took him to the third floor, where he found the office at the end of a darkened hallway. There was no name on its door to suggest the activity within. It was 7:59.

He opened the door and saw a receptionist's cubicle on the right. A few tired chairs were in the open reception area and old tourist posters of Hawaii hung on the drab walls. A woman was at the copy machine in the cubicle and she turned when he arrived. If she wasn't the most beautiful woman he had ever seen, he couldn't name the other contenders. She smiled as he closed the door behind him. He guessed she was in her early thirties and she was dressed in a tasteful dress that fit her 5'9" frame perfectly. Her red hair was shoulder length, framing her ivory skin and striking green eyes. She was absolute perfection. When he realized his mouth was hanging open, he quickly attempted to recover.

"Where is the meeting?" he asked her. "I'm a little late."

"The conference room is at the end of that hall. They're expecting you," she said, pointing down a narrow corridor.

Franco thanked her. He couldn't place her accent. It was British, or maybe South African, he guessed. He wondered who this Sam Rorke was, to be able to hire such an amazingly beautiful assistant.

He found the conference room after walking past several offices, all furnished with the same distressed furniture and all unoccupied.

The conference room décor was similarly dated and worn. The table and eight chairs showed scratches on the former and rips in the latter. Two men sat at the long table and looked up as he entered. One man was Asian, the other man, the one he knew, was Anglo. The man Franco recognized, Paul Sloan, jumped to his feet as he entered.

"It's good to see you again," he exclaimed. "I never knew what happened to you in Chicago, except I heard you were hurt there. I just learned a few minutes ago that you were joining us. I never had the chance to thank you for all you did."

Franco took Sloan's outstretched hand. "I was happy to serve," he said. "I heard a few things didn't turn out too well after that mission."

"Right," said Sloan quietly. "The project didn't work out the way we expected."

"I was talking about what happened to you," said Franco.

"Yeah, uh…" stammered Sloan. "My life just kind of fell apart for a while. It was a rough time."

Franco didn't offer a response.

"Everything is much better now," Sloan continued. "I love Hawaii. It's a wonderful playground for a botanist, and I'm flying again. It's all good. If I last here another five or ten years, I won't have to move anywhere to retire."

"I'm glad it's working out for you," said Franco. He turned to the other man. "I assume you're Sam Rorke?"

The man rose and took Franco's hand. "No, I'm Harold Chen. Welcome to the team, Commander."

From behind Franco, he heard, "I'm Samantha Rorke." The beauty from the copy machine extended her hand to him. "It's nice to meet you, Commander. Admiral Pauling has told me a lot about you. Welcome." She turned to the others. "Let's start. We have a hard stop at 10:30 since we're flying to Molokai to see the quarantine station." She sat at the head of the table and began to distribute the papers she carried.

"Before we dive into the details, I'd like us all to introduce ourselves to make sure we know why we're all here. I'll start.

"My background is that my mother was from Hong Kong from an old English family that was three generations on the island. My father was an American. My parents met and married when my father was stationed in Hong Kong and attached to the State Department. He brought my mother back with him to the States, and I was born in Fayetteville, North Carolina, when my dad was stationed at Fort Bragg. When I was two, my father left the Army and joined a company headquartered in Hong Kong. We moved there and stayed until I was 16, when we moved back to the states. I went to college at Yale as an art major. Two years into college I had a financial wake-up call and realized I wouldn't make a living as an artist. That epiphany eventually led me to an MBA in finance at Wharton, and I was happily on my way to a career in international banking. I did that for a few years before I was tapped on the shoulder by a friendly CIA recruiter who thought he could give me a more interesting life with my Hong Kong background and international finance experience. Long story short, I said yes, started working for the Company, and subsequently met Admiral Pauling. The Admiral asked me to start working on special projects for him and that's what brought me here." She looked around at the group, "Any questions?"

"That's pretty top line and sterile. Are there any fun facts about you?" asked Franco, thinking about how Pauling had not really prepared him for Sam Rorke. He didn't know if he was happy or angry about it.

She said, "We're not here to have 'fun,' Franco, but I will tell you one interesting fact. Perhaps it's my art major background, or maybe it's more sinister—I am an excellent forger. Seriously, I'm very good. Just a little practice and I'm a real menace. Don't leave your checkbook out."

"Thanks for the warning."

She turned to her colleague. "Hal, tell them a little bit about yourself."

Hal turned toward Franco and Sloan. "I consider myself a real California guy, although I was born in Hong Kong. I moved to San Francisco when I was two. I went to public schools there before going to Stanford. I majored in Asian Studies and Computer Science. When I was a senior, I was tapped by a Company recruiter to come work with them in Langley as an analyst and as a pre-emptive computer security specialist, which means 'friendly hacker.' I did that for a few years before I asked about going into the field. I was approved for fieldwork and went to the CIA's 'Farm' for training. After that, I was dispatched and spent a few years in Hong Kong, which was easy for me, since I had been going there every summer I can remember to stay with my grandparents. Even though I was enjoying that, Sam asked me to be part of a team for Admiral Pauling's special projects group. I thought about it and it sounded interesting. So, here I am."

Hal turned to Sam.

"Thanks, Hal," she said. "Any questions?"

"How big is this special team and what do you do for the Admiral?" asked Franco.

"The answer to the first question is easy," said Rorke. "The team's standing members are just Hal and I. We have contractors in our areas of operation, which are Japan, Korea, and China. We've done projects in Taiwan and Singapore, only as a part of larger operations. Because of our cultural and language skills—Hal and I both speak Japanese, Korean, Mandarin, and Cantonese—we focus on that part of the world. What we do is largely investigative and it usually involves an angle of industrial, rather than direct governmental, espionage. Does that help?"

"Thanks," said Franco. "How long has Pauling been involved in this? He just retired from the Navy a few years ago."

"I think you just answered your own question, Commander," she said. "Why don't you tell us all a little about yourself?"

"Sam, by now, I expect you know more about me than I know about myself. Is that correct?"

Rorke replied, "I think our information on you is probably current and correct, nevertheless, please humor us and enlighten Dr. Sloan."

Franco looked at Sloan and began. "After college, I joined the Navy and became a carrier pilot. I met Admiral Pauling, who was, at that time, Captain Pauling, on my first deployment. I did four cruises before they took away my medical qualifications because of an eye injury. After that, Pauling, who had rocketed up the ranks to Admiral, convinced me to stay in the Navy and transfer to Naval Intelligence. For better or worse, I followed his advice."

Sloan turned to Hal and Sam. "As part of my transition to the Intelligence community, the CIA let me spend a few months down at Camp Peary. We might have to share our stories about the 'Farm.'"

Franco turned back to Sloan. "I stayed in the Navy until I retired a few months back. The little exercise in Chicago, where I met Dr. Sloan, culminated with me spending months in rehab. During rehab, I decided I didn't need the Navy anymore. I thought I'd done enough and I decided to hang up my blues. It was the right decision. Until a few days ago, I was having a peaceful life in a quiet place where no one could find me, until Pauling did find me, and asked me to join this team."

"Why did you agree to join us?" asked Rorke.

"Frankly, because the money was good. Also, Pauling did a few favors for me over the years that made it hard for me to tell him 'no.'"

"What exactly did happen to you in Chicago, Commander Franco?" asked Sloan.

Franco hesitated, seeming to momentarily relive the scene in his head before he answered. "Paul, I took two bullets in tender spots. Eventually I healed up okay and like they say, you should see the other guy. Anyway, that experience was enough for me to re-think my priorities. By the way, please just call me Mike. I don't need to hear the title 'Commander' any more in my lifetime."

"You saved my life, and the lives of my wife and daughter," said Sloan with difficulty. "Thank you again."

"Yes, that was the job," said Franco quietly.

Neither man spoke until finally Rorke broke the silence.

"Dr. Sloan, we each know a lot about you for different reasons. Would you like to tell us a little about yourself in your own words?"

"Sure," said Sloan. "I also flew jets in the service. I was on the Marine side, and after the Corps, I went back to school to study botany. My grandfather was a corn farmer and I think he gave me a reverence for plants. I did a Ph.D. in botany and taught at the university level for over twenty years. After the experience that Mike described in Chicago, I left the university and started working at the USDA in Washington. I became a very accomplished alcoholic there and lost my wife, my job, and pretty much everything else I cared about except my daughter. Finally, with her help and AA, I dried out."

Sloan seemed to think carefully about his next words before continuing. "Unfortunately, it was all a little too late. My wife didn't want me anymore. My daughter went off to college. The Department no longer trusted me, although instead of firing me, they gave me the option of being an assistant to the station chief in Hawaii in charge of special projects. That sounded pretty good to me, although I still lose sleep thinking that in a dark view of the future, I'll be lying in the sand with an umbrella drink in my hand and it will start all over again. Anyway, I'm dry now, and that's how I came to be here, and the rice species we're talking about is my 'special project.'"

"Thanks, Paul," said Rorke. "Do you have any questions, Franco?"

"No," said Franco. "It's all pretty clear."

"If you have any questions or wisdom to impart at any time, please don't hesitate to speak up," said Rorke. " I believe the Admiral wants you to feel free to advise me if you think I need it or if I ask for it."

"Samantha, I don't know you very well, yet I already think the idea of you asking advice from me or anyone else is kind of a stretch. I believe you have a crystal clear idea of what you want to do all the time."

She said, "Of course, although I'll certainly value your judgment since Pauling thinks as highly of you as he does." She turned to Sloan. "Paul, would you tell us the story behind the rice plants?"

Sloan cleared his throat. "When I came on station, I heard this excitement from a couple of guys in the quarantine greenhouse. They said one of the plants brought in by the HDOA was running wild. They were right. It was a new strain of Oryza sativa or typical Asian rice and it looked very similar to all the other strains seen throughout South Asia. It was hard to tell the difference from regular rice just by looking at it, although there were subtle differences in the leaf structure. However, its rate of growth and time to maturity were remarkable. We had edible grain-sized seeds in as early as eight weeks under optimal soil and moisture conditions. None of the guys knew much about it except that it was quarantined from a private farm and that there were legal proceedings involved.

"I decided to look into it a little further, and learned that the farm was owned by an agriculture research company based out of Houston. After a few calls, I learned this was only one company within a much larger corporation. It's part of the financial empire of William "Buddy" Jerome, whose name you may have heard before. I managed to reach Mr. Jerome and he told me how he came into the rice genetics business and specifically how this strain came about."

"I have to say that Buddy is a very nice guy. I've now met with him many times over the last several months. We're going to have dinner with him tonight and I'm sure he'll tell you the full story about his rice then. The short story is that Buddy had his people engineer this rice strain as a means of producing a protein a biotech company is developing for human use. The rice production is a clever way to make this protein cheaply. Buddy is looking to settle a score with the CEO of the biotech company with this rice product."

Sloan looked at Franco to see if he had any questions. Seeing none, he continued. "None of the biotech angle was documented at the quarantine station. They only know where the rice was grown in Hawaii, not why it was put there. That doesn't matter. What matters to them is that this is a super strain of rice. It grows fast and produces about two to two and a half times as much protein as regular rice. It grows like a weed and pops up all over. It self-germinates like no other rice anyone has ever seen.

"Now we haven't told Buddy's people all that we learned about their rice. I suspect they were only interested in the protein yield since that's what they made it for. The speed of growth plus the invasiveness of the plant may not be important to them. Oh, and we also found that it's drought resistant as long as the air is humid enough. Anyway, I'm sure you'll learn more tonight when we meet with Buddy. I think you'll find him entertaining. By the way, we haven't told him about the theft and, as I understand it, we don't intend to tell him until we learn more about it. Isn't that right, Sam?"

"Yes," she said. "Buddy still thinks we're holding his plants at the station and he doesn't know anything about what happened to his seeds. We shut down his rice operation in Houston until our investigation is completed."

Franco asked Sloan, "Why don't your Department of Agriculture people know about the biotech angle of this, and how did Jerome take to shutting down his Houston rice operation?"

Sloan answered. "For your first question, I just learned about this biotech motive a month ago and I hadn't filed any paperwork on it. Admiral Pauling called me and told me to keep it quiet. Remember, the theft had already taken place. All the USDA knew is that they had a super strain of rice that grew like crazy and could be an enormous crop."

"They know even less now," interrupted Rorke. "We destroyed the remaining plants."

Sloan spoke again. "Mike, to answer your other question, Buddy didn't really mind the USDA shutdown of his Houston rice project. This was the only ongoing rice project he had. As I understand it, he set it up, as you heard, to complement a biotech project of a golfing friend of his, and, just as importantly to him, as a business excuse to come to Hawaii more often. The major commercial interest of his company is in developing different corn and wheat strains for U.S. growers."

Sloan continued. "Buddy voluntarily surrendered everything his company has done on the rice project, and they have conveyed all their seed stocks to us."

"Why would they do that?" asked Franco.

"Buddy is all red-white-and-blue. He's a trusting soul—sort of. We keep him up to date on our work with his project on a regular basis. It's informal, he wants to hear what's going on." Sloan paused. "To be clear, he wants Sam to keep him up to date on the project."

"It's not all that friendly, Franco," Rorke added. "Buddy's company entered into a consent decree for the criminal charges of illegally planting this rice. Yes, he thinks I travel from the USDA in Washington to update him on the progress of our activities with his rice as per our friendly agreement under the consent decree. Remember, he broke the law. We asked him to surrender all the records of the project, both hardcopy and electronic, and to give us custody of the materials. He has done this voluntarily and without a legal battle."

Sloan looked at her. "I'm not sure that's the only reason he wants Sam to keep him informed."

She waved him off.

"How many people know the full story?" asked Franco.

"If by 'the full story' you mean who made the rice, why it was made, what its properties are, and that it was stolen," Sam said, "it's just the people in this room, the Admiral, and whomever the Admiral decides to share it with. Quite a few people know a little bit of the story. We're the only ones who know the full story."

"That's a pretty exclusive club."

"Yes," said Rorke, "And I expect everyone here to keep it that way."

She looked at her watch and said, "We should have a van waiting outside now, ready to take us to the airport for our trip to Molokai. Let's go to the scene of the crime. We'll talk more there."

CHAPTER 6

Six Months Earlier

Quan did not enjoy leaving the island. Truthfully, he did not even enjoy leaving Happy Stream Farm. He complained he was too old to fill his mind with new ideas and too tired to fill his day with traveling, but he agreed when his nephews wanted to take him to their farm in Guangdong Province.

The car drove up the dusty lane just as he finished his breakfast. His nephews told him it would be a hired car, so he was not surprised to see it. He took his last sip of tea when the car stopped and Chao opened the front passenger door, left the car, and walked to the house. Quan placed the teacup in his kitchen sink and met his nephew on his small porch. He patted Chao on the shoulder, walked to the car, and took his seat in the back with Jun.

"This is a big day, Uncle," said Jun.

"It is very unusual for me. That is for certain," said the old man.

The car turned around in front of the small house and drove back down the lane. Chao got out of the front seat to close the gate. As soon as he returned to the car, they were moving again.

"When did you last leave the island?" Jun asked.

"It was many years ago," replied the old man. "You were just a boy. I went to meet you, Chao, and your father in the city."

"What did we do?"

"I don't remember much about the day except that the argument I had with your father wasn't worth my time to make the trip. Travel was harder in those days, and I had to spend the night before coming home. That was good in a way, because I saw your father in the morning at breakfast and we reconciled our issues."

"What did you argue about?"

"Your father wanted me to sell the farm on the island and move to the city to be near your family. He said living alone there was unhealthy and I would die alone and lonely on the farm. He worried that if I ever became ill, I would not reach a doctor in time."

"You didn't agree with him?"

"No," the old man said. "Remember, it is your father who is now with our ancestors, and he was three years younger. I guess his doctors weren't all he was expecting them to be. He was right about one thing, though. I do intend to die here."

The old man said nothing more. The car weaved through the lush low mountains that formed the spine of the island and eventually turned onto the highway near the northern coast.

Although the traffic was heavy, they moved along quickly. The new bridge off the island was a marvel to see, and despite himself, Quan found it interesting. From the Lantau Bridge, it was a short drive to the Tsing Kau Bridge leading to the mainland New Territories. The highways were wide and modern. They moved quickly out of the Special Administrative Region to the Shenzhen Bay Bridge. Theirs was one of the few private cars on the bridge, which was filled with bus traffic. On the mainland side of the bridge, the traffic was stopped at the arrivals terminal. Their driver met the customs police with the documents Jun had given him.

The boundary policeman examined the documents, took a quick look into the car, grunted to himself, and waved them along. A few minutes later, they parked next to another car with a driver. They switched cars from the right-hand drive Hong Kong car to the left-hand drive mainland car, and they were off again.

Quan had never been in an automobile that drove on the right-hand side of the road, and it felt strange to him. He had also never been in Guangdong Province. Much of it looked like parts of Lantau although the frequent rocky outcrops looked harsher than the soft green hills of his island. There were also many villages and larger towns and factories.

They veered west toward the Pearl River to miss the Shenzhen traffic, although that was almost impossible with the nearly 20 million people in this enormous metropolitan area. Farmers tended fields in areas spared by the inexorable urban creep. They crossed several small rivers with lazy brown-green water, where oxen worked the fields, although few other animals were seen. Quan took particular interest in the small paddies that popped up beyond the villages along the road. It looked as if it was going to be a good year for their rice as well.

"How often do you come here?" asked the old farmer.

"It depends on how active our computer business is," responded Jun. "We go into Shenzhen often when we are working with computer products."

"I have seen a computer. I have never owned one," said Quan.

"Unless it is made in Zhongguancun outside of Beijing city, Shenzhen is likely its home. They make the chips, the switches, the screens, the keyboards—all in Shenzhen." He pulled out his mobile phone. "This is a computer. It was made in Shenzhen."

Quan waved at it dismissively. "I would never want one of those. It looks like a leash for a badly trained dog to me. Sometimes, I'm happy to be old."

They drove a few more minutes when Quan touched his nephew's sleeve and said, "I've seen enough of this. Wake me when we come to the farm." He rested his head on the door and closed his eyes.

They drove away from the city, toward the river delta, before looping back to the east. The factories and shops were fewer and the towns gave way to villages and small farms. After a time, they drove off the main highway onto dirt roads. From there they found a path leading into the field between hectares of rice paddies. Quan awoke when the car came to a halt.

As he stirred, he saw two men coming from the field to greet the car. The farm had no house, just a group of rice paddies and a small, unpainted wood tool shed with a rusted metal roof.

Chao left the car and walked over to the men. Quan could not hear them, although their conversation looked friendly. When the old man left the car, he saw that the farm was tucked into a narrow valley of flat land between two rows of the small rocky hills. The nephews' small farm must have been part of a larger network of rice paddies that continued up the valley into a larger commercial rice growing operation.

The old man walked to the group and was struck by how well the crop was progressing. Although the air was heavy and humid, once he saw the growing rice, he walked a little quicker. Jun introduced Quan to the two workers as the man who was responsible for the plantings. The field workers were very deferential to Quan, and they complimented him on his rice. Quan enjoyed their excitement as they told him what he had already observed with this new strain.

"You will find that the rice tastes better too," said Quan with a laugh.

Quan turned to Jun. "Tell me whose land all of this is," he gestured. "You said you only had ten hectares of land."

"We bought our ten hectares from the large farm beyond. The owners worked with us on other business dealings and they were happy to sell us a small portion of their farm. They gave us a good price on this land when we became interested in agriculture. Our government connections helped with the property transfer. We have had this for almost a year."

"You will make them even happier soon," said the older of the two workmen. "Your uncle's rice almost plants itself and now they have your super rice growing in their fields. Did you want us to remove the shoots that spread over to their land?"

Jun laughed. "No, let them grow. Our neighbors will appreciate our generosity."

Jun walked his uncle to the edge of the paddy and asked him if there was anything else he wanted to see.

The old man stooped down and examined one of the plants on the margin of the field.

"They look wonderful," he said, almost to himself. "It is lovely to see them all growing here."

He turned to his nephew, "I'd go into the paddies, but I don't have my boots."

"Uncle, we don't have snakes here."

"Of course you do. It doesn't matter. I've seen enough. Thank you, Nephew. I'm ready to go back to Lantau."

"After we have lunch," said Chao.

"Yes," agreed the old man. "After lunch."

* * *

They drove to a nearby town and ate lunch in a small quiet restaurant. Over tea, the old man said to the younger two, "I have been thinking that it may be the right time to tell your government connections about your rice."

"Are you certain, Uncle? You do not think it is too soon?" asked Chao.

"No, I believe it is right to discuss it with them now. My worries of the rice not growing well outside of my farm have vanished. It seems to grow beautifully here. Since the government has not yet approved this strain, do not ever tell them we have grown it ourselves. They'll want to control it and remove all the plants from my paddies and I don't want the inspectors on my land. We should just give them seeds and let them grow the rice on government land. They will be able to harvest the seed faster and only they have the means to bring this rice to the people."

Chao turned toward his brother. "Can we make enough profit if we sell to the government this way?"

"Yes, our government people will be good partners for us. They have not let us down yet."

"That was in computers; this is food," said Chao.

"It's all just 'buy and sell,'" said Jun. "We will do fine."

"Do we tell them Uncle Quan invented the rice?"

"Absolutely not!" said the old man. "I want nothing to do with the government or any attention. I love my quiet life."

"That's fine, Uncle," said Jun. "If anyone asks, we will tell them we found this rice in Thailand."

"Why not tell them the U.S.?" Quan asked Jun.

"Our government friends would not be happy to learn that American rice was feeding our people. If they thought it was American rice, they might not grow it for us. They must never know. From now on we must always call it Thai rice."

"That is perfectly acceptable to me," said Quan. He raised his teacup in a toast. "To the mighty farmers of Thailand," he said.

"Yes," said Jun, raising his teacup. "Gan Bei for Thailand."

CHAPTER 7

The short helicopter ride over the Kaiwi Channel to Molokai was bumpy but the views were breathtaking. At Rorke's request, the pilot made a sightseeing diversion. No one complained. They flew to the windward north coast over small drop islands and then along huge ocean cliffs near the Pelekunu Valley. Where there were no sea cliffs, the valleys from the inland volcanic ridge flowed down to lava beaches like sylvan glaciers. The valleys seemed young and unspoiled. The sparkles of their waterfalls over the lava outcroppings stood separated from the lush growth of the tropical apron below them. These green basins were almost inaccessible from the land and protected by the foamy surf that crashed in from the vast ocean beyond. They were perfect in their isolation.

The helicopter flew around the island before heading back to the west. On the western side, the cliffs gave way to a plateau that gradually blended into the coastal scrubland flowing down to the sea. On this coastal plain, the helicopter flew once around a fence-enclosed compound. Franco noticed there was no guardhouse on the driveway to the compound's main entrance. He reminded himself that this was a plant facility, not a military facility. After circling once, the pilot landed gently on a helipad in the USDA quarantine facility and shut down the engines for his passengers to deplane.

To Franco's eyes, the facility wasn't impressive. It was comprised of two buildings of wooden construction that looked like aging, suburban ranch housing, and another building of steel construction that looked like an enormous industrial garage. They were all connected. In the background was a cinder block wall around what looked like a large furnace.

On the ground, Sloan led the group into the wooden buildings. He opened the door to a small reception area. A whirring old window box air conditioner was the only sign of activity. Sloan led them through the reception area to a conference room at the rear of the facility.

Rorke, Chen, and Franco arranged themselves around the table in the same order as in Honolulu. Franco assumed Rorke and Chen had seen all of this before and that the presentation was just for him. Sloan manipulated a projector and a computer while they sat. When the projector image was in focus on the white wall, Sloan spoke.

"This facility was established in the early 50's by the Hawaiian Department of Agriculture, essentially as a disposal area for any plants or fruits that were confiscated by customs."

Sloan projected old photos of the facility. Except for the connector passages between the buildings, the large greenhouse, and a few coats of paint, the facility appeared unchanged.

"After the materials were given a quick inspection, they were typically taken to the incinerator at the back of the property, which you may have noticed as we flew in."

Sloan flashed another old photo of two overly happy looking employees with baskets of fruit and plants in front of the incinerator.

"In early 1960, a few months after Hawaii's statehood, the USDA assumed responsibility for this facility and used it as much for plants found on farms as for materials stopped at customs. Currently, about half of the activities here are for observation of plants grown in Hawaii by local growers. The rest of the activities are pretty much split between various botanical research projects and inspection of materials confiscated by border agents. The facilities here consist of this luxurious office building, a small wet laboratory building, and the large greenhouse facility you saw coming in."

Sloan showed additional images of a site map of the grounds and the interiors of the buildings he described.

"As you can see from the following pictures, the greenhouse has changed a great deal over the years. It doesn't look like much from the outside, but inside it's very sophisticated. We can alter the soil, the humidity, the UV exposure—pretty much anything we want in the twenty cells of the facility. Each cell is environmentally separated if we choose, although usually, we keep it all ambient and maybe have only one or two of the cells at a time in either very high humidity or in arid conditions.

"The seed room is similarly maintained for heat and humidity in the storage lockers."

Sloan showed images of the room with rows of pullout storage bins, and additional images of a few bins containing seeds that were opened.

"That's the facility. Plants are flown in here from all over the state, and occasionally, we'll be sent materials to study from Samoa and Guam as well. We don't process any specimens from the mainland. Any questions?"

"What about security?" Franco asked.

"There's not much of that," said Sloan. "The front gate is locked. It opens with a six-number keypad without a swipe card. The same combination opens the greenhouse and the seed room locks. The security camera broke about ten months ago and we haven't been given the funds to repair the system. Seed and plant security are not at the top of Washington's funding pyramid. Any other questions? Mike?"

"Yes, who are the staff here?"

"Beside me, there are four staff members. The supervisor is a Ph.D. botanist with about a million years of experience in Hawaiian botany. There's very little she doesn't know about the plants on these islands. She has two lieutenants who are master's level botanists, and there is one other guy who is the handyman on site who knows nothing about plants, although he can keep everything running. There had been one other staff member, recently separated from the site, whom I suspect Sam will discuss."

Rorke stood and began to speak. "We've been watching our thieves' behavior for months and we think know a lot about them. We're pretty certain the thieves are two brothers. One is thirty-eight and the other is thirty-five. They are both native-born Hong Kong. Before and after the handover to China in '97, their father made a fortune by being one of the PLA's primary brokers to and from western companies. Even though the Army had, and still has, its fingers in many industries, their father specialized in technology—both software and hardware. He brought substantial amounts of high tech materials into China from all over the world, some legally, some not, and most from the West. The father had well placed friends in the government, and parlayed his profits into a sizable real estate empire both on Hong Kong Island and on Kowloon. He was right in the midst of a deal for a casino in Macau ten years ago, when he died suddenly of a stroke. The sons tried to step in, but the casino financing syndicate didn't want to deal with them and they were cut out.

"That was the start of a rough patch for the boys. They dabbled in new office space development. They judged the market poorly and took a bath there. They were over-leveraged on a few other projects and then were forced to sell most of Daddy's crown jewel properties at a fire sale to stay afloat.

"Just when the heavy storm clouds were gathering around them, Mom saved them. She married a high-level government man she and her husband had known back in the 'Pre-Return' go-go days. The official was a widower with no children, and he took pity on his dithering stepsons. He arranged for their struggling office properties to enjoy full rentals from the Red government. He made the right connections for them with other Hong Kong officials and helped them finance a few better deals. Soon they were back on their feet."

She took a sip from the water bottle on the table in front of her and then continued. "With the help of their government connections, the brothers learned, as their father had, that there was an easy market in peddling the right Western technology to Chinese interests. This line of work seemed to suit their personalities.

They both like taking risks. The older brother takes business risks and he has been the more impulsive one about the family investments. The younger brother just likes to spend money and his tastes run to hot cars, drugs, and women, lots of women. The older brother's spending tastes are more refined—fine food, expensive wines, elegant clothes."

"Do these brothers have names?" asked Franco.

"Not as far as you're concerned right now, Franco," she said curtly. "I'll tell you everything you need to know in due time."

"Yes, ma'am," he said.

She gave him a stern look, then continued. "About six years ago, the brothers formed a company. It was a front they used for the trade shows and business development conferences they'd attend. We've found that they are amazingly careful not to leave a paper trail and they never tell their buyers the source of the stolen technology. It's a plausible deniability thing. But everyone understands the game and when the technology comes to market, it's been modified enough that it seems like the buyers made it themselves. If it's a government buyer of the stolen goods, they work very hard to hide it and it never comes to market. They certainly won't admit they have to steal all their best technology from the West. We think the Chinese Red Army gives the brothers cash and the brothers make the right contacts. The brothers both speak perfect English, by the way. We were first put on to these two by a tip from a small software firm started by one of Hal's friends. They said the brothers stole a killer app from their company and Hal's friend saw it in China before they finished its development in the U.S. That was two years ago and we've been watching them on and off ever since.

"From what we've seen, the older brother usually scouts the technology and schmoozes the senior management types. When he's found a mark, the younger brother makes the mid-level management contacts, handles the payments and bribes, and arranges for the transport of the technology. When they've stolen from a U.S. company, we think they smuggle the hardware—usually small tech prototypes—out through Mexico. We've also seen them smuggle software programs via courier to Montreal and then to Hong Kong.

"As I said, they are very good at covering their tracks, although with the help of the NSA and the folks at Langley, we think we know their M.O. very well. They don't send software over the wire. They never talk business on cell phones, and, except for their government contacts, it's only the two of them. Everyone else they use is either an outside contractor or temporary help. We were able to hack into their office and home computers, and there are no records of any business transactions. We think they funnel their smuggling money out of China through banks owned by the PLA. These banks probably wire the funds to banks in Switzerland and the Caymans. We have not been able to hack into their accounts on the bank computers and we only think Switzerland and the Caymans because of trips the brothers went on last year. We have no real proof yet."

She took a sip of water.

"When did they decide to become rice thieves?" Franco asked. "It's a long way from computers."

"That's a very interesting question," said Rorke. "We learned that they have an uncle. Our local contacts surveilled him. The old man lives a very modest life; he's kind of a hermit. He bought into that whole Cultural Revolution thing when he was younger. He was raised with our thieves' father in a middle-class family in Kowloon. As I mentioned, their father went into business. Their uncle chose the agrarian nirvana ideal and got close to the land. He works about a half-acre on his farm, growing his own rice and vegetables. He never married. The brothers look in on him from time to time.

"We've watched the old man try to convince his nephews that China's future is in farming and that people should be encouraged to grow their own food and forget about all this manufacturing. Obviously, that message didn't resonate terribly well with our boys and their big city lifestyles. I do think the old man is a patriot, and he's convinced them to steal rice for the good of China. I think the brothers just learned on their own that they can make serious money out of this."

"How did they find out about our rice seeds?" asked Franco.

Rorke chose her words carefully. "As we piece it together, the USDA staff member who knew about this fast-growing rice was at an agri-tech conference, and was first approached by the younger brother. A few drinks later, they were good friends. As the younger brother kept buying the drinks, we assumed they became business partners. We only know this in retrospect from the surveillance system at the bar near the conference and from security cameras around Molokai. We backed out the employee's travel locations from his expense reports.

"When another USDA employee found that the rice seed bin seemed a little light, he suspected the seeds were stolen. We were called to look into the matter."

"Why would the USDA call you?" interrupted Franco. "Are rice seeds part of the CIA jurisdiction these days?"

"How we cooperate with other investigative branches is not your problem, Franco. Just know that we've had our eyes on this for a while," she said firmly.

She continued to address Franco, "We don't exactly know when the theft occurred. However, we did a little forensic accounting and learned that the employee accomplice bought a $250,000 fishing boat on his $60,000 a year salary. He paid cash for the boat from large wire transfers that were recently deposited from offshore banks. He wasn't exactly discreet. After we looked at security camera images from coffee shops and bars on the island, we noticed the younger brother was in town again buying drinks for our USDA employee. We assume he made the deal and smuggled the seeds off the island."

"Did the employee confess to this?" asked Franco.

"No," said Rorke.

"Why not?"

"Because he drowned in the Kaiwi channel before we could speak with him. He must have fallen off his new boat. It was found drifting about ten miles from where they found most of the body floating."

"'Most of the body?'" said Franco.

"Yes," said Rorke. "There are a lot of sharks in that channel."

After a pause while everyone absorbed that grisly thought, she said. "Okay, Paul will walk through the facility with us. We'll catch our ride back to Honolulu when he's done. Franco, you and Paul and I are going to Buddy's home for dinner this evening. As far as he'll know, you work with me at the USDA in Washington, and we're out here for a review of the quarantine station. I want you to pay attention on Paul's tour. Jerome may ask you a few agriculture questions and I don't want you to blow our cover with him."

"No problem," said Franco. "I just love learning about plants."

"That's wonderful. Because tomorrow, we're leaving for a growers' convention in San Francisco and we'll meet with two of Jerome's people there. You'll have more time to learn about rice before we visit our thieves in Hong Kong."

"Wonderful," said Franco. "Sorry, Paul, but all this plant science is way over my head. I'll have to leave it to geeks like you and Jerome to explain it to me."

Rorke said. "I don't know that I'd put Buddy Jerome in the geek category."

"Okay, I'll reserve my opinion until I meet him."

"I think you'll be able to make your mind up about Buddy very quickly."

"If you say so."

"I do," and after a moment's hesitation, she said, "Paul and Hal, would you give me a minute or two alone with Mike?"

"Sure," said Sloan. "We're done in here. I'll meet you in the greenhouse." They both stood and walked out of the conference room.

Rorke waited for them to leave and the door to click shut before turning to Franco.

"I want to be very clear with you that this is my operation and it's going to be run on a strictly 'need to know' basis." She let her eyes linger on Franco before continuing. "There's a lot of information here that you don't need to know, and to be completely honest with you, it's information you don't want to know. You don't have to ask a lot of questions to try to find out every detail. You're going to have to trust my judgment on this. Can you live with that?"

"I don't even know you. How can I trust your judgment?"

"Look, Pauling brought you here for a reason. He also put me here for a reason. It's really a matter of your trusting Pauling."

Franco thought about it. "Okay, I guess I'll have to."

"That's the right answer. Only if I ask you again, say it like you mean it."

She expected a reply. He said nothing.

"One other thing, Franco. You have one job on this operation and that's to ensure that your friend Sloan behaves and that he doesn't talk to strangers about where the seeds came from or what they do."

"How am I going to do that?"

"Look, I'll be watching him, too. Just remember that if Sloan needs someone to talk with, make sure you're available to him. I'd rather prevent a security breach than have to deal with one. That's why Pauling brought you here. Just do your job."

Franco felt his temper rising.

"Let's go take the tour," she said. "After that, we'll fly back to Honolulu and meet Buddy." She turned and left without another word. He stood there unsure of whether he wanted to stay on this mission or go directly back to Stewart Island. He followed her reluctantly, thinking of the fee Pauling had promised him.

CHAPTER 8

Three Months Earlier

R ather than at his government office, they met him in a small quiet restaurant in Hunan Province on a back street in Changsha city near the river. It was hot and humid and the noisy air conditioner in the window strained to keep the few patrons comfortable. The frayed, red, floor-length curtains were held far back with chairs to give the struggling machine room to operate. It wasn't helping and tiny sweat streams made slow rolls down the faces of both men.

Jun sat behind his half-finished lunch, watching his brother eat. "Why do these people make their food this hot?" he said, between deep drags on the cigarette in his hand. "The weather is hot enough. Why make it worse on your insides?"

"Your stomach is too old, brother. You should stick with congee and bread sticks."

Jun took another deep drag on his cigarette. "I didn't work this hard to eat jook, or the fire they serve for food in this province," he said, exhaling in Chao's direction.

"You have no taste. Maybe your stomach is not too old, just too western," Chao said between bites.

It was after one in the afternoon, and the lunch crowd had cleared. The secretary of the ministry official had called to say he was running late, and that was an hour ago.

Jun crushed his cigarette and immediately lit another.

"You know we have a law against smoking in restaurants now," said Chao.

"Yes, but we'll both be as old as Quan before they enforce it."

"If you stay out of Beijing; they do enforce it there."

"I have no plans to go to Beijing anytime soon."

"I heard they're also enforcing the law in Shanghai."

"I heard it's like Hong Kong, very selective."

"Perhaps we can ask the Assistant Minister why that is."

"If the bastard ever comes. We came all the way here to meet him, and he can't be on time."

"I thought you said he was doing us a favor with the seeds."

"It doesn't excuse the little worm for making us sit here for an hour."

Jun considered switching from tea to beer, but he did not want to give the Assistant Minister of Agriculture a poor impression. He had met Zhang Wei only once before, and it was a brief encounter. They met at a technology conference in Shenzhen when Zhang was a much lower grade official. Jun remembered thinking that he was an ambitious young man with good family connections and that he would do well. The family connections were stronger than Jun appreciated and Zhang Wei progressed even faster than he had predicted.

After two more cigarettes and another cup of tea, the official walked through the door. Jun and Chao were the only two patrons left in the restaurant, and Zhang Wei walked quickly to their table. Jun tamped out his cigarette and placed the ashtray on the table behind him.

Both men stood to meet the guest.

"I'm very sorry I am late. I was required to stay on a conference call to Beijing for much longer than was scheduled," said Zhang after bowing to them.

"It was no trouble. We completely understand that government business is more important than two small importers," said Jun, as he introduced his brother.

"It is wonderful to meet you," Zhang told Chao, "and to see you again," he said to Jun. "Again, I am so sorry to be so late. The work you do is very important for the People's Republic, and we are excited about it."

"Thank you," said Jun. "We try to do our part for China."

"Yes, and you do it very well," said Zhang.

Jun waved to the waiter in the corner and Zhang Wei ordered tea when he approached the table.

After the waiter left, Zhang spoke. "You know the ministry is quite focused on improving our rice production methods. With many young farmers moving to the cities and the expansion of our factories on farmland, it is more and more difficult to maintain our harvest quotas. When you add in soil erosion, and soil depletion in addition to the usual weeds and insects, it is a challenge now, and it will be a greater challenge in the future. We are importing more rice every year, and that is not a position the ministry finds acceptable. We are under a lot of pressure to increase our domestic rice output."

"We understand the situation, and we hope that our efforts will help," said Jun.

"Mr. Liu, when you brought our attention to this strain of rice you found in Thailand, it was a most timely surprise. Please tell me how you found it."

Jun looked to see that there were still no other patrons in the restaurant and that the waiter was out of earshot. "Chao and I were in Bangkok on a business trip investigating a new computer technology when our colleague approached us about this new strain of rice he had found. The rice came from a very sophisticated grower there who, over many years, had an interest in crossing strains. Our colleague said he was willing to broker the deal if we wished to license these seeds. The only condition was that we could not know who the grower was, particularly if we were selling the seed technology to China. As you well know, rice exports here from Thailand have become a large part of the Thai economy and our contact did not wish any trouble from his government. After a few more meetings, we agreed on the price and through our contacts, managed to bring the seeds out of the country. I'm sure you don't want to know all the particulars of that."

Zhang nodded knowingly.

"We, of course, brought the seeds straight to your ministry for testing since Chao and I know nothing about rice. It sounded like an interesting product for China. Please, tell me, are these seeds any good?"

Zhang smiled broadly. "Yes, yes, they look very promising. I am happy to tell you now that we are very excited by their performance in our test paddies. We grew a few trial plants in a small paddy and were so impressed with them, we expanded our test to a government farm not too far from here. That is why I asked you to meet me here in Hunan Province."

Zhang sipped his tea while the brothers watched. "It should please you to know that because of your outstanding reputation for bringing many successful technologies into China, we had given your seeds our highest priority."

Zhang watched their reaction.

"In fact," he continued, "we have planted all the seeds near our major production farms. We wanted to see how your Thailand rice would grow in the best of conditions. We generated additional seeds in our test paddies and combined them with your original seeds. We planted the maximum we could, about 20 hectares. It is our hope that if these plants continue to look promising, we will take the seeds and quickly ramp up production on government farms in several provinces."

Jun responded to him. "That is wonderful news for us."

"The Minister in Beijing could not have been more excited when I discussed this new hybrid strain of plants with him," said Zhang. "I was so bold as to predict that we might double China's rice production in a decade."

Zhang motioned the two men to lean in closer to him. "It will be a great irony that Thailand super rice will reduce and hopefully eliminate our Thai rice imports."

The Liu brothers smiled at each other.

Zhang continued. "I assume you will trust the Ministry to arrange the appropriate financial compensation for you at a later time."

"Of course," said Jun, as if he had an alternative. "The government has been very generous to us in the past. That is certainly acceptable."

"Good," said Zhang. "I insist that you use the same discretion with this project as you have exercised with your previous computer technology projects."

"There will be no records of this anywhere," said Jun.

"Excellent, we all understand what we need," said Zhang. "Now, come, let's go see how your rice grows. This will be greatly rewarding for all of us."

CHAPTER 9

Franco met Sloan in the hotel lobby. Sloan was dressed in blue jeans and a button-down shirt. Franco had changed into dress slacks and a sports coat.

"You seem pretty casual for a business dinner," said Franco, looking at Sloan's jeans.

Sloan replied, "You haven't met Buddy."

"He's a casual guy?"

"Let me just say that in the seven or eight times we've met, he's always worn blue jeans."

"Am I overdressed?" asked Franco.

"No, you'll be all right," said Sloan and pointed to a car entering the portico. "There's Sam."

The men walked to the approaching town car. Hal was driving, and Sloan opened the passenger door in the front. Sam sat in the back seat, wearing a very low cut black dress. Her hair was up, and her face had a beauty pageant's worth of eye shadow, mascara, and lipstick.

Franco looked at her and at Sloan. "Are we all going to the same party?"

"Franco, it's part of the job. You haven't met Buddy," she said.

"No, I haven't. I'm certainly looking forward to it," Franco said, as Hal pulled out into the evening traffic flow.

"He's not a personality you'll meet every day," added Rorke.

"Why?"

"Let me just say he's a self-made billionaire who's very satisfied with himself. You'll see he puts on this simple oil patch, country boy act. Don't be fooled. He doesn't miss anything, and he has an amazing memory. I've met with him half a dozen times. The first time he asked me about my family and we had a long talk. The last time, he still remembered the street where I had lived in Hong Kong and asked several very specific things about my residential college at Yale. I didn't even remember talking about that. I was impressed."

"Maybe he just likes you."

"Possibly, but I've seen him this way on other topics too. He owns a dozen or so companies and I have the impression he's on top of each one of them. Just don't be fooled by his hayseed routine when you meet him."

"I'll try not to."

Hal drove down to the waterfront past a group of mixed-use high-rise buildings, then past a few cruise ships and the cruise ship terminal, ending up at a large modern high-rise in the Kakaako neighborhood. Hal pulled up, and the doorman opened the back door.

"Welcome back, Ms. Rorke," said the doorman, as she slid out in front of Franco. The doorman took her hand to help her out and added, "Hello, Professor," as Sloan left the front seat. "Good evening," he said to Franco, not bothering to ask his name. Hal was apparently not coming with them, and he drove off as they entered the building.

The doorman led them into the entrance hall. The man at the wide reception desk greeted Sloan and Rorke and pointed them to a far elevator. A very large man stood by the elevator door.

When they approached, the man said, "Good evening, Ms. Rorke. Good evening, Professor. Welcome, Mr. Franco."

The sentry entered the open elevator door and they followed him in. The guard placed both his thumbs on the security pad until the light flashed green. There was only a single button to push. The guard pushed the button and left the elevator.

"I guess that must be our floor," said Franco, as the lift's doors closed.

Sloan said, "Buddy owns the whole building. He lives and works on the top four floors. I don't think he has any other tenants or residents here."

The elevator began to move. The indicator panel above the door showed them going to the 35th floor.

The elevator opened to a small entryway with a large open double door behind it. A slight man in his twenties was there to greet them. The man was Asian and wore a black peci on his head.

"Hello again, Ms. Rorke and Professor Sloan. It's very nice to have you back." He spoke with a pure English accent that could have come from the West End of London.

He turned to Franco and bowed slightly. "Hello, welcome. My name is Paku. You must be Mr. Franco."

"Yes," said Franco.

"Please come in. Mr. Jerome is excited to see you all. He is waiting for you on the roof deck. The escalators are to the left. Please follow me," he said, and turned into the apartment.

They walked after him to see a large open plan design with spacious rooms that opened to reveal 180-degree views of the ocean and Diamond Head. The escalator was as described and they followed Paku up one floor. The rooms were a smaller scale here, with a kitchen, living room with an adjoining covered outside deck, and a hallway that Franco assumed led to the bedrooms. They took another escalator that emptied out into a greenhouse on the roof.

Outside of the greenhouse, a single man stood speaking on a telephone. He turned toward them when Paku opened the door of the greenhouse to lead the three guests out to the roof deck. The man was dressed in a Hawaiian shirt, cowboy boots, and blue jeans. He was fit and lean with graying temples on his well-cut hair. He abruptly stopped speaking and switched off the phone when he saw them. He was about six four, and moved quickly across the deck to meet them.

"Hey, nice to see y'all again."

He shook Sloan's hand and bent to kiss Rorke's cheek as he said, "Yeah, a little bit of sugar."

After he kissed her, he took a step back. "Sam, you're looking good, damned good. You been working out?"

"I'm always working, Buddy."

"I bet. You know, you smell great tonight, too. Is that a new perfume?'

"Same old stuff, Buddy."

"Well it becomes you, honey. Stick with it. You tell me what it's called, I'll buy the company for you. Then you'll never run out." He turned toward Franco and asked Rorke, "And who's this?"

"Mr. Jerome," said Franco extending his hand, "I'm Michael Franco, also from the USDA."

Jerome took the extended hand and said. "Mike, be a friend and call me 'Buddy.' Nice to meet you. I always like to meet another plant man. We couldn't live without 'em."

The big man turned toward the greenhouse and yelled out, "Paku, bring more drinks over here."

Franco had not noticed the full rooftop bar when he walked in. The houseman soon walked back to the group and handed a glass with clear fluid, ice and a lime to Jerome and a glass of white wine to Rorke.

"Is this still what you like, Ms. Rorke?"

"Yes, thank you, Paku," she said.

"Mr. Franco, what would you like?" asked Paku.

Franco looked at Paku and gestured toward Buddy and said, "I'll have what he's drinking." Sloan asked for ginger ale and Paku walked quickly back to the bar.

"Let's sit and get to know one another," said Buddy, leading them to a seating arrangement that overlooked Diamond Head.

"Did y'all just come in from D.C. today?"

"Yesterday," said Rorke. "We wanted to be rested before we saw you, Buddy."

Jerome shook his head. "Don't tease me, Sam," he said, grinning as he took a drink. He turned to Franco.

"Now, what's your story, Mike? You look ex-military to me."

Franco turned to him.

"That's right. I was in the Navy for a few years."

"What did you do for them?"

"I flew airplanes until I lost my medical clearance because of an eye injury."

"Carrier jets?'

"Yes."

"What did you do after that?'

"I was asked to..." Franco stopped midsentence when he saw Rorke's expression and immediately understood that she wanted no mention of Naval Intelligence, "to do administrative work. I got bored with that pretty quickly and so I left the Navy."

"What are you doing on this project?" continued Buddy.

Franco began to speak, then Rorke cut him off. "Mike was assigned to us because of your ongoing legal obligations. He oversees the compliance of companies with consent decrees."

Franco said nothing.

"Well, sounds important," said Buddy. "We'll definitely have to take good care of Mike." He turned to Franco, "I'll make sure we keep you well informed."

"I trust you will," said Franco.

"Now I gotta ask," said Buddy, "Is the USDA any better than the Navy?"

Franco stammered a little, "I think so. I'm able to meet interesting people like you."

"That's bullshit, Franco. There's damned few like me," Buddy laughed.

"You're right, Buddy. I've never met anyone like you."

"Damned straight. You know, to me, you don't look too blind to fly. If you want, you can come out and fly my Gulfstream with me. The offer's open. We can do a little island tour. My pilots would be happy to give you a check ride."

"Maybe I can ask my boss for a little time off."

"Sam, how about that? You can come too. You too, Professor."

"We'll let you know," said Rorke dryly.

Buddy lowered his voice and spoke to Franco. "That doesn't sound too promising."

"No," agreed Franco, taking his drink as Paku returned. "Tell me, Buddy, how did you make all your money?"

Buddy laughed. "That's a good direct question, Mike, and I'm glad you asked, because I love to tell my story. It's the American dream writ large, as they say. It couldn't happen anywhere else but here." Buddy took a small sip from his glass.

"I confess I was lucky. I grew up in a little town in Oklahoma named Chickasha. My dad was a pastor and my mother taught high school. I was a commuter student at OU and studied mechanical engineering. In my junior year, I figured out a few tricks to reduce stresses on the drilling columns they were using in Oklahoma at the time. I filed patents, got a few backers, quit school and started my own tool and dye shop to manufacture these devices. We did okay with that, and then I started looking into a corrosion problem they were having with turbine blades at the local power plants. With a few chemist friends of mine, we came up with a new coating process to extend the life of the blades, and I started another company. That one went gangbusters. I made a few more plays in energy-related companies and eventually bought my own oil company. Again, I got lucky, and that turned out real good.

"With the cash flow coming in, I started to have fun with the money. I got into real estate, and I became a partner in several development and holding companies. I financed a construction company that was able to land major municipal contracts all over the Southwest, and finally, I stumbled into agriculture, which is where you all come in."

"Yes, why did you decide to grow rice?" Franco asked.

"Just a minute," said Buddy as he turned and yelled toward the bar while lifting his glass, "Paku, fella, you're fallin' behind." Buddy lowered his voice. "He's not much of a bartender, but he's one helluva cook. He's a pretty good bodyguard—steady with a gun, and amazing with a throwing knife. Because he's a good Indonesian Muslim, though, he doesn't appreciate the finer points of keeping a glass full."

Paku came with another round.

"Rice and rice genetics…," Buddy said. "That started about five years ago. I had a few OU friends who were working at College Station. They talked me into investing in their idea to feed the world with better seeds. They hired a load of people who are so much smarter than me it's scary. We moved the labs from College Station to Houston and we have a nice little facility going there. Those boys are working on a bunch of neat projects, and they've made good progress, mostly in wheat and corn.

"A while ago, I learned they were studying rice, too. They told me all about rice and field production and rice protein and so forth. They said they could make rice with improved growth and protein production. I said 'great, go ahead'—what do I know about rice? Nothing except they serve it with fish in restaurants in Houston. Now, I have all this in my head.

"Well, I played golf at National in Augusta about two years ago with my friend Shelly Gardner. I'm a member there, and Shelly and I only see each other once a year on the date we both became members. That's a sacred date for us. We play our annual game rain or shine, course permitting. We missed last year on account of a crazy bastard who T-boned Shelly's car the day before the match and broke his leg. That was too bad, because my game was improving, and I thought I'd be able to skin him. Shelly's annoying as hell, although for reasons that elude me, I really do enjoy seeing him once a year."

Buddy took another drink before continuing. "Now Shelly's into biotech this and biotech that and he's made a lot of money at it. Anyway, two years ago Shelly told me about this new product his company was developing to cure ulcers. He said it was a special protein and he's worried it's going to cost too much to make. He won't be able to charge enough to make any money with the cost of goods.

"Now a light goes off in my head and I think why not send my seed boys off to make Shelly's protein in their rice? I talked it over with them, and they did a little research and about five, six months later, they called me. They told me they did it. They went into Shelly's patents, studied the structure of his protein, back-engineered the genes, and put them into our rice. Now Shelly's protein is expressed in our rice plants—and not just a little bit of it. Well, I was so excited about this I wanted to grow up a shitload of it before I saw Shelly again at Augusta—this year's game is coming up in a week, by the way. I don't have any patents on this protein, except for the rice parts, but I figured if I can make it for pennies on the kilo, Shelly's going to want to make a deal. Actually, he'll be desperate to make a deal. It's going to be funny as hell to have old Shelly over a barrel. He's a real smug New York bastard, and I can't wait to see the expression on his face when he comes crawling to me. It's going to come as a complete surprise to him. He has no idea I've been playing with his protein. I wish you could all be there when I tell him."

Buddy looked intently at Rorke. "I bet you Shelly's reaction would put a twinkle in your pretty eyes. It's a helluva joke, you have to admit."

Rorke said nothing.

Buddy continued, "As we all know, I made a small mistake, a little boo-boo, a little admin paperwork glitch. I cut a few regulatory corners, didn't file enough forms, and I brought my rice into Hawaii before it was cleared. We loaded up our farm with it and got busted by the HDOA and the USDA. It cost me a lot of money in lawyers, although it could have been worse." He looked back at Rorke. "At least I got to meet you."

"Was it was worth it?" asked Rorke.

"Every nickel, baby," said Buddy.

He turned to Franco, "Does that answer your question, Mike?"

"Most of it," said Franco. "What else were you growing on your farm?"

"Nothing much," said Buddy. "Having the farm was really just a good excuse to write off my trips to Hawaii. Wife number three didn't care much for Houston, although she loved it out here. We spent a lot of time in Maui.

"My philosophy is that making money is the Christian thing to do. Make the money, give a lot of cash away to people who don't know how to make it, put a lot of folks to work, and have fun with the rest. I'm having fun. Maui was fun. Man, Maui was lots of fun."

Buddy continued. "Now, as I understand it, y'all are going to California to meet with a couple of my plant scientists on the way back to Washington."

"Yes," answered Rorke. "We'll give them a full update on your rice plants and our progress with understanding their biology."

"That's good. They like to know all this stuff. Hell, the rice grows just fine. That's all I care about." Buddy turned to Franco. "Do you understand all this science stuff, Mike?"

Franco said, "I'm new to rice, but, yes, I think I understand most of it."

"Well, good for you. I guess it's also good for you to have the professor here to guide you through the tricky parts."

"That's my purpose here," said Sloan.

"That almost sounds philosophical," said Buddy, and he took another sip from his drink. "Let's leave the plants for now. Do you have family, Mike?"

"No, I'm single. Never married," said Franco.

"That's a much more economical approach to the institution of marriage than I have pursued in my oft-wayward life," said Buddy, gravely. "Still, I don't think I could have done it any other way. Just my nature."

"Are you still married?" asked Franco.

"No, I'm between wives," said Buddy. "I'm currently looking for number four." He looked to Rorke. "Sam, you might want to think about pursuing that assignment. We could hold the auditions any time you want."

"I'll give it serious thought," said Rorke.

"Now, honey, I'm serious about this. The pre-nup is the worst part. All the rest is upside, I promise you. You know, even with the damned pre-nup, the other gals made out just fine. I left number three that beach house in Maui and believe me, she's fixed for life. Now, you know number three and I were getting along great until she went a little bit nuts after reading too many lady magazines. She went vegan on me. She also became a teetotaler and an exercise freak. I think she went a little Buddhist, too. Eventually, she said I needed to change many of my behaviors, if you can believe that. It went downhill from there." Buddy took another drink before adding, "I know that wouldn't happen with you."

Rorke smiled and then quietly agreed, "I'm sure you're right, Buddy."

Buddy turned away from Rorke and lowered his voice. "Mike and Professor, you might appreciate this. That Maui beach house is in a very private setting; its beach is totally secluded. Number three liked to come out and reduce her tan lines, if you follow me. Now, I'll never see that wonderful sight again. It makes me happy just to know she's out in the world with an even tan. I think it's a generous gift I've been able to give to some lucky bastard, although I know not who."

Buddy took another long drink and drained his glass. He motioned for Paku to hand him a waiting refill. "Did I offend you, Sam?" he asked.

"No, Buddy. I'm okay."

"Good. By the way, we got to find you a different name if you're coming on the payroll as number four. You just can't look like you do and be a 'Sam.' That's a shop foreman's name. That don't work when you look the way you do in a dress like that."

Buddy took another drink before continuing. "And I tell you, 'Samantha,' doesn't cut it either. That just strikes me as an uptight Brit. Even with that half-English accent, you're no Samantha, either."

"Do you have any ideas for another name?" she asked.

"No," Buddy said. "We should work on that. We'll have to give it lots of time to do it right."

He looked at the sunset and said, "Hey, let's go down and eat. I think Paku's got us set up on the terrace." Buddy rose, offered a hand to Rorke, and led the way to the down escalator.

The table on the terrace was set for four. Wine was on the table, candles were lit, and a soft jazz piece was playing in the background. Looking through the terrace into the next room, Franco noticed a large portrait of Winston Churchill surrounded on the wall by several smaller oil paintings. "Buddy, do you like Sir Winston?" he asked, after they sat down.

Buddy suddenly became even more animated. "You bet. He's a distant cousin. Lady Randolph, his mom, was American and she was a Jerome before she was a pretend Brit. In the best Jerome tradition, Sir Winston was a love child and he came up with the finest combination of brains and brass the world has ever seen. In my opinion, he saved the whole damned western civilization and made sure that Roosevelt found the balls to help him do it. He was my cousin, Sir Winston, a distant cousin, but still family. As a matter of fact, my middle name is Winston."

Paku walked around the table serving, as Buddy told the group, "Help yourself to more wine."

Buddy started to eat and the others followed.

"Another thing," Buddy said between bites. "See those other six paintings? Sir Winston did those. He painted about 500 oils and I own 22 of them. I have most of them in Houston, although I keep five in my office in New York. I'm looking to max out at 100 and I have my art scouts looking. I've been averaging only three new ones a year. I'm going to have to up the pace a little if I want to hit my goal while I still have enough friends to brag about it."

Buddy took a sip of wine and turned back to Franco. "Do you like art, Mike?" asked Buddy.

"No, not very much," said Franco.

"That's an honest answer," said Buddy. "Maybe the wrong answer, but still an honest one."

Buddy focused his attention on his meal for a few bites before asking, "Professor, how are my plants doing?"

He caught Sloan chewing and had to wait a moment before he swallowed and answered.

"Everything is looking fine so far. We've put them in with other flora and have seen no problems. We had to expose them to local insects, and they're okay too."

"How much longer you going to keep them?"

"Oh," said Sloan, "it will still be a few months."

"I see," said Buddy. "I have one other thing to say, and this will be the end of the business talk tonight. After that I can drink a little more wine and enjoy a bottle of 50-year-old Macallan I've been waiting to crack."

Buddy hesitated, then said, "Professor, you know I've turned all of my documents over to the USDA voluntarily. Now, while I've enjoyed our talks over the last few months, y'all are going to have to start moving a little faster on this project. It's been a while, and I'm seeing Shelly again at Augusta in about a week.

Buddy turned and looked directly at Rorke. "Sam, you might be the prettiest gal west of Houston. I admit that because you are just so delightful to be around, I might have been a little too generous, giving over all our materials for you government types to hold. However, understand this: if Shelly Gardner tells me he's going to make a product out of this protein, and I don't have my rice back, there'll be hell to pay. I mean it. Do we all understand that? This is business."

The three visitors nodded.

"Good," said Buddy. He shouted to the kitchen. "Paku, come on fella, we need another bottle of wine here and bring that scotch I've been saving." He looked at his guests. "Who needs a drink?"

CHAPTER 10

One Month Earlier

Zhang Wei was excited as he walked off the plane in Beijing after his flight from Hunan. Today would be one of the highlight days of his government career. He would remember this as the day he finally achieved his promotion.

He exited the terminal and looked to the street for his government car, hoping he would not have to stand long in the acrid, hazy air. Zhang was delighted when the car pulled up to the curb within a minute of his arrival, and further pleased the car was one of the newer Dongfeng models. Since the government banned foreign cars for state officials, the days of Mercedes-Benz vehicles were gone, but the newer Dongfengs were comfortable enough. He wondered if the Mercedes cars would ever be approved again. He had always dreamed that when he began government service, he might one day be chauffeured in them.

Zhang was not a fan of the capital city. When the Beijing smog hit his eyes, they started to water and itch. He knew he would start coughing if he had to spend much time on the street. However, on this trip he was lucky to be staying inside and not have to deal with the air pollution. He promised himself that if he were ever to become Minister, he would work hard to move the Ministry to Shanghai or perhaps even to Hong Kong.

On a good day, the Beijing Capital International Airport was only about forty minutes to the Ministry offices. The Airport Expressway led directly to the city, and the Ministry building was just off the expressway. Today it was an hour's trip, and all things considered, the trip thus far was one of his better ones.

His car pulled up to the curb in front of The Ministry of Agriculture. It was a stately grey building with a long apron of steps rising from the sidewalk to the three giant archways of the entrance vestibule. Inside, he checked in at the security desk in the great hall before making his way to the elevators to the Minister's suite of offices on the top floor.

Outside the suite, he showed his identification to another security guard and was admitted to the well-appointed reception area. Zhang very much liked this office arrangement and believed that when he became Minister, if he had to stay in Beijing, he would not change the suite at all.

He sat for only a few minutes when a young woman approached him and asked him to follow her to the large conference room down the hall. Two old men were seated at the table and a middle-aged man was helping himself to tea.

Zhang Wei bowed to the group. "Good morning," he said. "I am Zhang Wei, Assistant Minister of Agriculture from Hunan Province." He went from man to man to present his business card.

"Good morning," said the first old man. "I am Professor Fu."

The other old man, sitting across from him added, "And I am Professor Han."

"I am honored to meet you," said Zhang, knowing well that both professors were senior and distinguished members of the Chinese Academy of Agricultural Sciences.

"I am Mr. Ma," the third man said. "I am the Director of the Plant Protection and Quarantine Division in the Department of Crop Production."

Zhang knew of this man and gave him a reserved bow. Zhang outranked him by several rungs up the bureaucratic ladder, and was appropriately unimpressed. "It is very good to meet you, Mr. Ma," he said without conviction.

When all four men were seated at the table, Zhang and Ma listened to the two professors discuss a recent scientific meeting that both had attended, then the two professors quickly ran out of small talk. It seemed to Zhang that the two scientists did not enjoy one another's company. The four men were uncomfortably quiet until the Minister and a younger man entered. Zhang and Ma stood, although neither of the two old men left their chairs.

"Please be seated," said the Minister. He gestured to the younger man who had come in with him. "This is Dr. Gao, who will be helping us with this very important discussion."

Gao bowed, and the Minister began again. "I very much appreciate your attendance here, Professors Fu and Han. Your input on the Ministry's decision will be critical. Your wisdom and advice are incredibly valuable to us."

The two academics said nothing. They were used to being complimented and seemed very comfortable with the Minister's characterization of their importance.

The Minister spoke again. "Although we are all aware of the issues, it is important to remind everyone that at the last meeting of the National People's Congress, food security was the very top priority. This was stated again to me by the Presidium at their meeting last month. Our five-year plan has very clear directives for our food production and this is one objective in the five-year plan upon which all our government leaders agree. We must be self-sufficient in our own food supply."

He waited for his audience to signal their agreement before continuing.

"Unfortunately, our rice production has not met our planned goals. We had a drought in many parts of the country last year. This year, the long spells of stormy weather have caused many of the farms to delay their planting and we may suffer yet another poor harvest. I have had to accelerate my discussions with my counterparts at our trading partners to secure rice imports, should we need them again. This is not a good situation for us.

"As you all know, the five-year plan is quite specific on rice production, and we are well behind our projections. Now it seems we have an interesting opportunity with this new strain of rice from Thailand."

The Minister paused to gauge the reaction of the two old men, who remained expressionless. "I will now ask Dr. Gao to share his report with us."

Gao rose from his chair and walked to the front of the room.

"Thank you, Minister," he said, and turned to the others. "As you know, we have planted the Thailand strains on test plots in our farms in Hunan, and we have requested that the licensors of this technology bring in samples of rice from Thailand. I would summarize the results in a single word—'spectacular.'

"The licensors told us that this rice is fast-growing. Our Hunan test plots are only a few months old, and the rice is, indeed, growing much faster than we would have expected. The mature samples provided to us suggest forty percent higher yields per plant, and the protein content of the rice has been close to twenty percent in all the samples tested."

Gao scanned his audience to see if there were any questions, and continued. "As you have heard, this strain is said to be drought resistant and the early specimens show that it develops a root system deeper than our usual rice. Finally, the idea that the rice is 'self-planting'—which the licensors have claimed—is not entirely correct, yet we do see many satellite plants off the planted rows."

Dr. Gao waited for questions from his audience. When there were none, he spoke again. "I know that you have seen the written materials I prepared earlier, and I am ready for any questions you might have on the analyses performed."

Professor Han asked the first question. "Who are these importers? Have they worked with the Ministry in the past?"

The Minister pointed at Zhang to answer the question. Zhang began to explain. "Professor Han, the two importers are Liu Jun and Liu Chao. They are brothers from Hong Kong, and they have worked with the government on many licensing deals over the years. They have dealt almost exclusively with the Ministry of Science and Technology on both computer software and computer hardware. They have not worked previously with the Ministry of Agriculture. The benefits of their prior licensing arrangements have been enormous, according to our contacts in that Ministry. They are held in very high regard and their love of China is unquestioned."

"How did they discover this remarkable rice?" Fu asked.

"These two individuals have many contacts around the world and they were able to connect, through their intermediaries, with a small rice breeder in Thailand who sold them this technology for what they said would be a mutually profitable deal. That is really all we know about this."

"And the Ministry chooses not to ask too many questions. Is that correct?" said Han.

The Minster stepped in to answer. "Professor, in these matters, the government recognizes the need for discretion with our licensors. We ask as many questions as we need to ask, and acknowledge that there are questions better left unasked."

Professor Fu was the first to break the rather uncomfortable pause that followed the Minister's comment. "Let me add to Dr. Gao's comments. Mr. Zhang allowed me to travel to Hunan to see the plants in the test plots. I was thoroughly surprised and delighted with what I saw. For the age of the plants and the density they achieved in the plot, they look quite special. The biochemical analysis of the protein content is also remarkable. This strain seems to be high yield, fast growing, and with a great nutritional value. This rice seems remarkable in every way."

Professor Han was next to speak. "Minister, perhaps I am too cautious by my nature, but I have seen nothing like this before. I would urge us to be careful before we implement any widespread planting of this strain."

"What bothers you, Professor?" asked the Minister.

"Let's be clear," said the professor. "This is an invasive plant and we should watch how it behaves before we expose our major farms to it."

"What kind of observation period would you recommend?"

"Several crop cycles anyway. It will take time before I am comfortable with this strain, although I cannot give you a precise time, Minister."

"How do you feel about this, Mr. Ma?" asked the Minister.

"Our group at the Plant Protection Division discussed this earlier. We also feel that several crop cycles should pass before we introduce this too widely."

"How long will that take, Mr. Ma?" pressed the Minister.

"I would estimate at least 18 months before we are comfortable with the new strain."

"I see," said the Minister. The disappointment was heavy in his voice.

"What are we afraid of here?" Professor Fu quickly chimed in. "If the plant is invasive or just throws out a few satellites, it is still rice. Are we worried that we may grow too much food?"

"We don't know what we don't know, Professor," said Han.

"No, we don't, and we never will," countered Fu. "In the end, it's all rice. It's what our people need."

Fu's last comment sounded angry and the others chose not to add any further remarks.

The Minister broke the silence. "Gentlemen, do any of you have any further comments for me about this matter?"

No one offered any additional comments.

"I cannot tell you how much I appreciate your coming today. Dr. Gao will stay to lead a further discussion on the technical issues. This is an important decision for the Ministry, and your input is invaluable. I ask for your written opinions at your earliest convenience. I will take my leave now. Thank you again for your time."

The Minister bowed slightly to the guests and said, "Zhang, please come with me."

Zhang Wei also bowed to the others and he followed the Minister down the hall, past the Minister's secretarial staff and into his inner office. Zhang had been in the office once before, when he received his appointment. He admired the office with the large desk, paneled walls, and comfortable sitting area. There was very little he would change when he became Minister, he thought.

The Minster faced him and gestured to the comfortable chairs flanking the couch. "Sit, please," he said.

The Minister waited until Zhang was seated. "What did you think of the meeting?"

"I would describe it as spirited, honest, and a bit controversial."

"Did you hear a consensus opinion?"

"No, Minister. I did not."

"Do you agree with Professor Fu's worst case scenario—that we might grow too much rice and in areas where it wasn't planted?"

"I don't know. Han and Ma didn't seem to know what they were anxious about. They didn't articulate their worst case."

"Many people are just afraid of change," said the Minister.

Zhang did not respond.

"These academics have no understanding of the pressure we are under to increase our rice production. Last year's harvest was down and this year, it looks like it may be worse, particularly along the Yangtze basin. The Hunan farms are not doing much better."

The Minister stood and walked over to gaze out the window while he spoke. "I am very worried that the late start for planting will reduce our rice yield this year."

Zhang realized his place was to listen and not to speak.

The Minister continued. "The General Secretary called me last week to ask how much money I thought we would need for rice imports. I hated to give him our estimates. Although he is usually a courteous man, it was a terrible telephone conversation as he ranted about our poor results."

The Minister looked out the window overlooking the capital. "We simply have to increase our domestic production." He looked at Zhang, "Your results in Hunan with this new rice are very encouraging."

"Yes, Minister."

"I believe the Liu brothers may have given us a wonderful opportunity to care for our people."

"Yes."

"I have you to thank for making the connection, Zhang. The government will remember your service for helping with this."

Zhang felt himself smiling without intending to. "Thank you, Minister."

"I have made my decision. I will listen to Professor Fu. We can't tolerate another year's poor harvest. I will allow the new strain to be planted extensively on our government farms. It is our only hope for accomplishing the objective in the five-year plan of being self-sufficient in our rice harvest."

"Excellent, Minister. I completely agree with your decision."

"Yes, Zhang, I believe that fortune is smiling on us and that we have been given a wonderful gift. We cannot waste it."

CHAPTER 11

Franco awoke with a hangover as big as, well, as big as Texas. He and Buddy stayed up late after Rorke and Sloan left. Buddy claimed that 50-year-old scotch didn't cause hangovers. They decided to test the theory and the issue was settled definitively in the morning. It had been after midnight when Buddy called his driver to take them on a quick tour of the city. Franco was relieved that Buddy didn't stop to sample any of the nightlife he pointed out, although they did have a few more drinks in the back of the limo while driving.

Franco slept late, but not late enough for it to be curative. He had an early afternoon flight that he was dreading. With great effort, he managed to drag himself to the airport on time. He tried to sleep on the plane, only achieving success during the last hour of the flight. The brief nap hadn't helped his headache and he felt only slightly better as he walked off the plane to the concourse.

Sloan was on the same flight and they shared a cab into the city. Rorke was planning to take a different flight and would meet them in the morning. Sloan seemed to be in a pensive mood and quietly stared out the window as their cab worked its way up the peninsula from San Francisco International to the city. That lack of conversation suited Franco.

The drive north to the city was easy in the post-rush hour traffic. The convention was in the St. Francis Hotel, across from Union Square. The cab discharged them at the hotel, and Sloan suggested a late evening dinner. Franco wasn't hungry, but found Sloan's sudden enthusiasm hard to resist.

They checked in and left their bags with the bellman. Sloan seemed to know San Francisco well and wanted to walk up Powell Street to a brasserie style restaurant he remembered.

Although climbing up any hill was not Franco's preferred activity in his current condition, he agreed. He was relieved that the walk covered only a few blocks.

The restaurant crowd was winding down from a long day, and there were just a few tables filled with diners when they arrived. The hostess ushered them to a quiet booth and a young waitress, still perky at the end of her shift, distributed menus.

After a quick glance at the menu, Franco laid it back on the table. Sloan studied his a little longer before asking, "What are you having?"

"Just soup. My stomach isn't ready for much else tonight," said Franco.

"You had a long night with Buddy?"

"Yeah," said Franco, "Much too long."

"I thought I saw you looking a little green when I got on the plane."

"I'm still green on the inside. I'll feel better tomorrow. If I don't, call a doctor or a mortician."

"I'm glad it was you who spent the time with Buddy. I can't be his playmate since I don't drink. It was generous of you to fill the role. I guess it's not easy being a billionaire. It's hard to find friends."

"I don't think Buddy is looking for friendship," said Franco, taking a drink from the water glass in front of him. "He's just looking for an excuse to spend his money."

The peppy waitress returned and they ordered. She punctuated each of their orders with a "Good choice" affirmation. When the orders were duly recorded on her order slip, she retreated to the kitchen.

Franco changed the subject. "How's your wife doing?"

Sloan said slowly. "I don't hear too much from her anymore. After Chicago, things changed between us. The marriage was falling apart even before I started drinking. She blamed me for everything and, truthfully, I think she had a point."

Franco asked. "What about your daughter?"

"I'm a little luckier there," said Sloan. "She's in college, and she's proud I've been dry. It's because of her I make it through each day. I speak with her at least once a week and she e-mails me about three times a week. She's my little angel."

"I'm happy for you that she keeps in touch."

"Thanks," said Sloan. "It's hard sometimes, and she makes it better. You know, though, it's still 'one day at a time,' and 'fake it, 'til you make it,' and 'let go, let God.' I go to as many AA meetings as I can, and pray a lot. I'll go to an AA meeting here tomorrow. In a few years, they say, it becomes a little easier."

"Good luck with it," said Franco.

"Pray for me."

"I can do that."

The waitress returned with their drink orders; both had just asked for water. She served them quickly and left.

"How long have you known Rorke?" asked Franco.

After taking a sip of water, Sloan answered, "She came on the scene about nine, ten months ago, about the same time the station noticed the rice seeds were missing."

"Did the USDA contact Pauling or whoever she works for?"

"Not as far as I know. I had always assumed the station chief mentioned it to his boss or it made its way to a report. I don't know what Pauling monitors for this industrial espionage problem he's after. I have the impression he's watching many industries and he's primarily focused on any technologies going to China. I think he's had his eyes on the brothers for a while."

"Did it ever strike you as a little funny that the brothers would go from stealing tech secrets to stealing seeds?"

Sloan shrugged. "Money's money and there would certainly be a market for a new hybrid seed in China. Their scientists have been working with hybrid rice strains for years and haven't come up with anything like Buddy's rice."

"How well did you know this guy who stole the rice from the Molokai facility, the drowned employee?" asked Franco.

"Not well at all. I arrived in Hawaii just before he had the accident. They said he was kind of an odd duck, and worked unusual hours. I rarely saw him and never spent any time with him."

Franco changed the subject. "Tell me more about our beautiful redheaded leader. What is Sam Rorke like when you really get to know her?"

Sloan answered, "I guess the first thing to understand is that Sam has a work personality and a non-work personality. Her work personality is what you've seen. She's all business there. When she's in that mode, if you put her on a scale with one end being maternal and sweet and the other end being a serious ball breaker, she's way over on the ball breaker side."

"Yeah, that's what I'm seeing. It sounds like it's going to be just loads of fun to work with her," said Franco.

"Don't misunderstand me. She's not unpleasant unless she's not getting what she wants or people are not doing what she tells them to do. She's just a very tough professional lady, although she's enjoyable outside of a work environment."

"I doubt that I'll ever see that side of her," said Franco.

"It takes time." The waitress returned to the table with Franco's soup and a salad for Sloan.

They ate for a few minutes before Franco asked, "I know we're here to brief Buddy's technical people, and they're going to tell us about this rice. But what are they doing here in San Francisco?"

"They're here as part of a scientific conference on genetically modified plants. It's specific to grain producers. Obviously, in San Francisco, this conference isn't going to be very well publicized. As a matter of fact, I doubt that you'll see it noted even in the lobby of the conference hotel and it certainly won't be advertised as a conference on genetically modified foods."

"What kinds of modifications are being done to these other grains?"

"Ever since we've been growing our food, we've been looking for better plant varieties with different characteristics. We've had hybrids, or plant cross breeding, for hundreds of years. Plant science is just accelerating this with more advanced techniques of plant gene modification. People don't like to hear this... they've been eating GM foods their entire lives. Their great grandfathers were eating modified foods, too, although 'hybrids' didn't sound as scary. The techniques have changed; the idea is the same."

Sloan's attention went to his salad and Franco stayed lost in his soup. The traffic outside on Powell Street was sparse, and the restaurant was almost empty. Franco was content to maintain the silence, but Sloan started to speak again.

"You know, Buddy's rice is really amazing. The fact that it grows fast and is protein enriched is great. His people hit a trifecta with its apparent drought resistance and the way it self-propagates. It actually plants itself."

"Yeah, that's wonderful," muttered Franco, thinking to himself that he had heard enough about rice in the last few days to last him a lifetime.

They re-focused on their meals for a few minutes.

"What time are we seeing these guys tomorrow?" Franco asked.

"0900." Then Sloan continued, "You know, I understand that industrial theft is a big deal. I'm not minimizing it, but, damn, there are worse things than trying to feed more people and trying to do it more efficiently. This could be a wonderful thing for the world."

"Okay, well, that's not my worry. It's not yours either. As far as I know, all we're asked to do is to determine, if possible, where the seeds went and to confirm who took them." Franco motioned to the waitress to bring the bill.

"Well, I'm of two minds about this. On the one hand, I know Rorke and Pauling have to dig down to the bottom of this. Pauling's concern is that U.S. companies have been robbed blind by the Chinese for years, and it must be stopped. On the other hand, this could be a wonderful tool to feed much of the world far more efficiently than ever before. About half of the world depends on rice for a significant portion of their food needs. It takes them a lot of time and effort to grow it. Making it more abundant, easier to grow, and more tolerant of adverse conditions would be the makings of a Nobel Prize."

"Paul, let's stay focused here," said Franco. "We have a job to do and saving the world isn't it. We need to confirm who did this and figure out where they took these plants. After that, the problem is the State Department's or the USDA's or however they want to handle it."

The waitress returned with the check. Franco read it and left a few bills on the table.

"Mike, of course I know it's wrong that American technology was stolen," Sloan persisted. "But think of the good this could do."

"Paul, you're a caring man. I don't want to think about food anymore tonight. We can talk again at breakfast. Let's go."

CHAPTER 12

Rorke, Sloan, and Franco met in the hotel lobby after breakfast. Sloan had arranged the logistics of the meeting at the hotel with Buddy's scientists.

"Buddy insisted that we meet his people," Rorke explained to Franco. "We're still operating on the strategy that whatever Buddy wants, Buddy gets, so he'll keep his lawyers out of this as much as possible. We'll meet his technical people and tell them what we've done with their rice. Most of it is true. Paul already knows these people, and Paul and I have agreed on the script for what we'll say to them. You just keep your mouth shut and listen, Franco. Do you think you can you manage that?"

Franco answered coldly, "Yeah, I think I can manage that."

"The academic community is smaller than you might think," Sloan said, changing the subject, trying to soften the mood. "We all pretty much know everyone after a while."

They took an elevator to the third floor and made their way down the hall.

Two men were in the small conference room when they arrived. One was about forty and the other man was in his early thirties.

Both men treated Sloan like an old friend. After greeting Sloan, the older and larger of the two men—and he was very large, at least six feet five and three hundred pounds—extended an enormous hand to Rorke as she approached him.

"John Cooper," said the man in a southern accent, and Rorke responded, introducing herself and shaking his hand. Rorke and Cooper exchanged business cards.

Franco followed, and also took one of Cooper's business cards. John Cooper was a Vice-President and the Technical Director of BE Jerome, Inc.

"I thought Buddy's middle name was Winston," said Franco.

"It is," said Cooper. "'BE' stands for biological enhancement. We could call ourselves 'genetic modifiers of food' in most parts of Texas outside of Austin, but it probably wouldn't fly too well much beyond the state line. That's why it's 'BE' rather than 'GM'."

"Okay, that's helpful," said Franco.

The smaller man waited for Cooper to finish speaking before introducing himself as Andy Tien.

Rorke took a chair after the introductions were over and the men followed her lead.

When everyone was seated, Sloan explained to his colleagues, "John was a post-doc in my laboratory a few years ago, and Andy worked in my laboratory on a student research project when he was an undergraduate. It's a small world in the Ivory Tower."

Rorke said politely, "Thank you for taking the time to meet with us. Buddy said it would be a good idea for us to brief you on our progress with your quarantined plants. He thinks that you and our department will be working on the rice project for some time to come and that we needed to speak to you. Buddy also said that you offered to give us an overview of the rice project from your perspective." She paused for a moment. "Let me tell you what we are doing. I'll give you the top line information. Paul can elaborate on this later if you have any questions."

She directed her comments to Cooper. "We have your plants growing in our greenhouse, away from the other plants. We have gradually introduced other species near them to assess their invasiveness. We are simultaneously exposing them to a battery of indigenous insects to assess if there is any effect on them. We will also alter conditions for rainfall to determine what will happen to the plant mix in semi-drought conditions. When we are satisfied with the safety of these laboratory observations, we will re-introduce the plants to the outdoors and make similar observations in USDA test plots."

She paused again and looked at the two men and then at Sloan. "Did I cover everything, Paul?" she asked.

"Yes," said Sloan. "Those are the broad strokes anyway. I can fill in the details with John and Andy later."

"Buddy wanted us to ask you how long this is going to take," said Cooper. "He's becoming a little impatient, and you know Buddy."

"Yes, I do know Buddy," said Rorke, her tone was suddenly brittle and intimidating. "Let me remind you that Buddy broke the law and you're operating under a consent decree. We'll keep the plants for as long as we think it's necessary, to preserve public safety. We think we might be done with the testing in three or four months or possibly a little longer. The bottom line is that we are processing this as quickly as we can, and it will take the time it takes. Now, do you have any further questions for me?"

Cooper looked at his junior colleague and back to Rorke. "No, I think we're good here. No more questions. Godspeed to you. I'll tell Buddy." Cooper added, "I think Buddy knew that it would take you more time since he's already reassigned us to a new project with corn."

"If you have any other questions, address them later with Paul," said Rorke.

Cooper spoke again. "Thank you. Now we'll review for you how we became involved with this project. Andy was the project leader for our rice protein expression group before we suspended our research on the project. I'll let him tell you what we were trying to do."

Sloan spoke up. "Andy, I've told them the big picture of what you and John were trying to do, and you can move over that quickly. Try to keep it as non-technical as you can since Sam and Mike are administrators and not scientists. I think if you can concentrate on the reason for the protein and what you had hoped to achieve with this technology, that would be most helpful."

"Sure," Andy began, "I'll tell you what we were trying to do, and a little bit of how we did it. If you have any additional questions or you want me to go into the details of any of these topics, I'd be more than happy to."

Tien turned on a projector and images appeared on the screen illustrating his points.

"About two years ago, Buddy came by the laboratory and asked us if we could genetically engineer rice to make it express a specific protein. We looked up the protein's structure in the published patents and went at it. Buddy told us he knew the CEO of the pharmaceutical company that was developing it and that we might have a partnership opportunity. The problem was to express the protein in rice so it could be manufactured cheaply. The alternative manufacturing approach was to make it in insect or mammalian cells, which would be much more expensive.

"The molecule is a small protein that is used by the body to turn on many processes that make new cells. The new cells are like a tumor only they're well controlled. The protein does this by going into cells and once it's in the target cells, it's broken down to an active fragment and it turns on numerous cell genes that make the cells divide. The cells divide, differentiate, and heal the problem—whether it's an ulcer in the stomach, or a wound on the skin.

"What makes this protein special is that when you swallow it, it retains its activity. Most proteins are rendered inactive in the stomach. That's why, for example, a diabetic can't just swallow insulin. It must be injected because it's inactivated by the stomach acid and the intestines if you swallow it. Our protein resists being broken down in the normal stomach. In the ulcerated stomach or intestine, it's cleaved inside the cells of the ulcer. These wound-healing cells absorb it, and it can accelerate the healing process there. Also, this protein can be applied topically and, again, it will be cleaved when it enters the cells of the healing wound—you just need to give it in a greater concentration. So, you can eat it or apply it topically, and heal any kind of ulcer or wound in hours, rather than in days to weeks.

"Buddy wanted us to make the rice produce this protein. In rice, we could make kilos of it for pennies, and be the sole supplier to the pharmaceutical company that owns the rights to the drug. Any questions?"

Tien paused for a moment and then started again. "Okay, that's why we did it. Now this is what we did," he said, and turned his attention back to the screen where he advanced the slide. "Rice is probably the most heavily studied plant on earth. It feeds about half the world, and this food supply is coming under more stress every day. The issues throughout Asia, and most acutely, in China, are a combination of more cities, less arable land, fewer people to work the land, and pollution in both the air and the water. Consequently, Chinese scientists have been creating hybrid rice for many decades to increase the production yields and the fitness of their crops. They have multiple state institutes focused on rice science and improving rice production. In short, science knows a lot about rice.

"What we did was to start our work with a typical short grain white rice strain. It's one of the rice clones that plant scientists routinely work with. I'll describe now on a single slide what it took ten of my staff six months to accomplish."

Tien focused on the screen and highlighted each step on the image with a laser pointer. "In the old days, hybrids were made by crossing the female aspects of the plant with desired male variety and seeing what came out. Comparing the old techniques to what we do now is a little like comparing a Piper Cub to the Space Shuttle. We have much more powerful and faster approaches. We now use several types of methods to introduce the desired genetic characteristics. In this plant, we used a technique based on 'agrobacterium.' This bacterial method allows us to transfer programmed genetic material into plants. The organism infects the plant cells and leaves a little of its genetic material behind. It's been used to create many GMOs including corn, cotton, soybean, wheat, and, yes, rice.

"We were not interested in the usual parameters of the food scientists who select strains primarily for their yield and hardiness. We just wanted to see if we could make this protein for Buddy. Frankly, we didn't know how this new strain would do in the field. What we did know is that we succeeded in making this rice strain a real protein factory. The other feature we learned about the protein was that it would be great from a processing standpoint. After several days of sitting in water to soften the grains, the protein was unaltered. We could even boil the rice, like you would to cook it, and the protein's structure was still unchanged. By all indications, it was going to be very easy to work with on an industrial scale. That was an unexpected bonus.

"Our initial testing did show that, in greenhouse conditions, the plant strain was robust and it grew quickly. The gene transfer improved growth as well as protein production. The amount of protein it produced continued to exceed our expectations. It was all very exciting and I guess we transmitted a little too much of our enthusiasm to Buddy. He pushed us to grow the rice in Hawaii to assess its production value in the field. That's where you came in, and that's about the end of the story from our end. Any questions?"

Sloan spoke. "Andy and John, every time I hear that story, I'm more impressed. What you've done is very special and I don't know if Mike and Sam appreciate just how amazing this is. Although you directed your work at harvesting a single product, the aggregate of what you've done could be hugely important in feeding a hungry planet. This genetic modification not only increased the protein production, it also improved the fitness of the plant. It enhanced virtually every growth and cultivation characteristic.

"Certainly, increasing the protein supply of developing nations is a major challenge and I know I speak for the Department of Agriculture when I say that when we're able to release this strain into production, it's going to be a huge benefit to mankind."

"Thanks, Paul," John Cooper said. "Andy and his team have done an amazing job, and I can tell you that we are just as excited to make this available to the world as you are. Since the plants were taken by the USDA, we've been working on other projects." Cooper let his eyes linger on Rorke as he made the point. "We are very hopeful that you will finish your work quickly so we can go back to learning what the rice could do." Rorke's blank expression told him nothing, and Cooper continued. "Sam and Mike, do you have any further questions that we can help answer?"

Franco and Rorke both shook their heads.

"Okay," said Cooper. "I'll let Buddy know that you are still working on the plants and that you hope to be done in about four months."

"Good, you tell him that," said Rorke. "He heard it from me a few days ago. Maybe he'll understand you better."

Cooper smiled. "Yeah, Buddy's got this nervous habit of asking a question over and over until he hears the answer he likes. When I say 'nervous,' I mean he makes us nervous. I'll pass on that information."

Rorke stood and said, "Thanks for your time." She shook hands with Cooper and Tien and Franco followed her lead and stood. Rorke began to walk out the door with Franco.

"Sam, I'll catch up with you later," Sloan told her, "I want to ask John and Andy a few technical questions."

She nodded and continued walking out of the room without speaking.

Rorke walked quickly and Franco followed her down the hall toward the elevator.

Midway down the hall, she turned abruptly and asked. "Did you learn anything, Franco?"

"Biology was never my strong suit. I thought it was interesting enough."

"I wasn't talking about the rice lecture."

"Well, what are you talking about?"

"I was talking about Sloan."

"What about him?"

"I'm not delighted with the way he's behaving. He's far too rah-rah about the benefits of the stolen rice."

"What did you expect? That's his life. That's what he's been trained to do."

"You need to control him."

"'Control him'? Control him how? From what?"

They passed an open meeting room and she grabbed his sleeve and pulled him into the room. She stood very close and locked eyes with him.

"Let me be perfectly clear. I'm not happy having Sloan on this operation and by extension, I'm not happy having you here either. Unfortunately, we need Sloan to identify the plants and confirm the extent of the theft. That's half the mission. I don't like it, but it can't be helped. Your role is to keep Sloan in line. You've got one job. Can you understand that?"

"Yeah, I can understand that. How has he been out of line?"

"Just watch him," she snapped back at him. "No one can know these plants came from the U.S. I don't want him talking to his academic friends, and I don't want him having these great thoughts about American rice saving the world."

"I still don't understand why you're so jumpy about this. He hasn't done anything."

She stared at him in a way that made him uncomfortable. When she spoke, there was anger in her voice. "Look—Sloan is a boy scout. He doesn't have the personality for this operation. Unfortunately, he's the only one with the right expertise, and we don't have the time to train another person. We also need to keep this a small circle and Sloan already knows everything. Nevertheless, his halo is too damned bright for my liking."

Franco bristled in response to her tone. "What's the real story here? Why are you so worked up about a few seeds stolen from the Department of Agriculture? We aren't talking about these Chinese brothers stealing the plans of a new super computer or a new fighter jet. We're talking about seeds! What is wrong with you?"

She narrowed her eyes at him and said, "Just do your one job, Franco, and we'll all be fine." She began to walk away.

"Hey," he called to her. "What's the other part of the mission?"

"Just do your job, Franco! Don't get distracted with anything else."

She turned her back on him and stormed off.

CHAPTER 13

The mid-day traffic over the Oakland Bay Bridge was minimal, and the trip from downtown San Francisco to the Oakland airport was an easy drive. Their taxi drove to the airport's general aviation area. Chen paid the fare as Rorke walked into the building.

In the small terminal, several flight crews sat on the couches or at the surrounding desks, while a few of their well-heeled passengers floated in and out between business meetings and their private jets on the tarmac. Rorke received more than a second glance from virtually every man in the place as she entered. A large man in a business suit sitting in a side chair looked up from reading and saw her, giving a small wave. She walked over to him and the man stood and walked to the security gate at the end of the building. Rorke followed him. Chen caught up with her and the three of them walked past the security guard to a car parked on the edge of the tarmac next to the building.

The three said nothing as they entered the large sedan. Rorke and Chen sat in the back and the other man sat in the front passenger seat. The driver drove them past the line of business jets and down to the end of the long taxiway where a large, white jet was parked. The three exited the car in front of the air stairs. Rorke and Chen then climbed the jet's stairs while the third man stood on the ground at the foot of the steps.

As they stepped inside the jet, Pauling looked up from the papers in front of him.

"Good morning, Admiral," said Rorke.

"Hello Sam, hello Hal. Sit down. Do either of you want coffee?"

"No, thank you," said Rorke.

"Nothing for me, sir," said Chen.

Pauling gestured for them to sit on the divan opposite his desk in the cabin.

"Okay, to business," said the old man brusquely. "How are we doing?"

Rorke smoothed her skirt before speaking. "Well, sir, this San Francisco jaunt has taken a few days out of the schedule. Other than that, we're doing all right."

"We still need to play ball with Jerome," said the Admiral. "As long as he thinks we're working to free his plants, he'll keep cooperating. He's the one thing we can't control, and I don't want him and his high priced legal team demanding all his plants back."

"We could still encourage the DOJ to prosecute him and his company, or arrange for a violation of the consent decree," said Rorke.

"No, I don't want his lawyers climbing all over the USDA records or what we've left of them. That would create a publicity storm we can't afford. Remember, the rice is just a play toy for Jerome to impress his golfing friend. He has no clue about the bigger picture. We have to keep it that way—at least for now."

Pauling took a drink from the coffee cup on the desk and made eye contact with Rorke. "What about Sloan?"

"Nothing new," she said. "He thinks Buddy's rice may save the world. He loves the science, and for now, he's still able to keep his mouth shut about the theft to China."

"Good. Is Franco behaving?" asked the old man.

"More or less. Buddy seems to enjoy his company."

"That takes a little pressure off you, doesn't it?" asked the old man.

"It does. I suppose it's nice that Buddy has found a new male friend," she said. "You know, Admiral, with Buddy Jerome, it's hard being a girl."

"I'll take your word for it, Rorke, although everything considered, you seem to pull it off pretty well."

"Is that a compliment or harassment?"

"Take it any way you like," said the Admiral. "Other than playing with Jerome, what else is Franco doing?"

"He's just a part of the team. Nothing special. He seems to be able to keep his mouth shut on the project. I don't worry about that."

"Franco understands security," said the Admiral. "I have no concerns there either. I still think Franco's our best bet as a chaperone for Sloan if we need one. The good professor has contacts all over the world from his academic life, and we know about his pals in Hong Kong. I don't want him going native when the big news comes out. Sloan will listen to Franco, or at least I hope he will."

"Maybe it won't come to that," said Rorke.

"No," said the Admiral. "I'm quite sure it will." Pauling looked from Rorke to Chen. "Hal, how well are you prepared on the ground?"

Chen inched forward on the divan. "My network is in place both in Hong Kong and on the mainland. We can move when we need to."

"Do we know anything more about the brothers Liu?"

"They haven't changed their patterns as far as my people can determine," said Chen.

"Sam, when do you see Jun again?" asked the Admiral.

"Thursday," she said.

"How is his portfolio doing?"

"He's up 18 percent this year. That's after being up 20 percent if you annualize last year," she said proudly.

"What is it without Company support?" asked the Admiral.

"The numbers are still about 12 percent for each year without the Company buyouts of the private equity plays. You know, sir, I'm pretty damned good at my day job."

"Jun still loves you?"

"Yes. He now wants me to manage the money of a few of his friends. That's one of the stated topics of conversation on Thursday."

"What are you going to tell him?"

"It depends on who the friends are," she said, smiling at the Admiral. "I may need a real job after this operation."

Pauling turned back to Chen. "As far as you know, the Liu boys have kept their own counsel as to where they stole these seeds?'

"Yes, sir. The brothers are very discreet. That's how they stay in business. We know they've contacted the Ministry of Agriculture and have arranged that their seeds will be planted on one of the government farms in Hunan Province. The farm workers told my contacts that these were new seeds from Thailand. I guess that's what the brothers are telling the government."

"Does the government know the seeds were stolen?"

"Yes and no," said Chen. "I suspect they know the seeds were stolen. They won't try to prove it. Plausible deniability on their part is very important."

"No one except the brothers knows the seeds are from the U.S.?" asked the Admiral.

"The brothers, and likely the uncle," said Chen.

"Oh yes, the uncle," said Pauling. "Too bad about that."

"It would make sense for them to bring the seeds to his little farm on Lantau before going anywhere else with them. However, we have not confirmed that," added Chen.

"Okay, that goes on your 'to do' list as well," said the Admiral.

"Yes, sir," said Chen. "The brothers would never tell the MOA that the rice was from the U.S. New technology in rice from the U.S. would not be popular with the Chinese government."

"Are you sure these are our seeds that your men in Hunan were hearing about?"

"No sir. Not yet absolutely certain, although the timing was right."

"Okay," said the Admiral. "We want Sloan to see the plants from that government farm and the Lantau farm. Do you think we can examine those specimens without raising any attention?"

"Yes, my guys are ready to pull the samples and let Sloan have a good look. They can certainly spot the plants that are spreading like weeds. Sloan can confirm that they're ours," said Chen.

"Do we think the plants are well established over there?" asked the Admiral.

"We have nothing confirmed now, but my men suspect the rice is being grown in three sites, all on a small scale." answered Chen.

"Okay," said Pauling, "Once you have been able to prove that the plants are well established in multiple locations, we'll clean things up."

"I understand," said Rorke.

"Okay, that's it," he said. "Confirm that our rice is in those fields and we'll go from there."

"Yes, Admiral," said Rorke.

"Give me frequent updates of your progress. Call on the message line. When you're ready to finish the job, call me on a safe line to brief me on the particulars."

"Yes, sir," said Rorke.

"Lastly, try to keep Buddy Jerome in check. I know he's a pain in the ass and he's a serious loose cannon. It will work out eventually. Until it does, we have to keep him happy."

"'Happy'? How do you want me to keep him 'happy'?" asked Rorke.

"Well, Sam," said the Admiral, "As you said, it's hard being a girl, but I'm sure you'll figure it out."

CHAPTER 14

They flew to Hong Kong under separate bookings and on different flights to avoid any unnecessary suspicion at customs. Franco and Chen left that day. Rorke and Sloan would travel the next day. Their covers were all largely true. Franco and Sloan were tourists, Chen was doing business on a work visa, and Rorke was an investment advisor with clients in Hong Kong.

Franco was still uncomfortable with the situation and his unfinished conversation with Rorke. He didn't know exactly how he was supposed to control Sloan, or even what that meant.

Franco was still troubled as to why a few rice seeds commanded this level of attention. Still thinking over his last conversation with Rorke, he wanted to call Admiral Pauling to better understand what was going on. Unfortunately, he had been told that all communications had to go through Rorke unless there was an emergency. None of this felt right to him, and he wondered if he had made the right choice in accepting Pauling's offer and leaving Stewart Island. He hoped he would feel better about it when he met with the team.

After landing and clearing his bag through customs, Franco found his way to the Airport Express train and after only a short wait was able to board the train to Hong Kong station. Following the half-hour trip, he briefly wandered around the train station until finding the shuttle bus to his hotel. Franco went to his room, dropped onto his bed, and resolved to fix his jet lag before meeting the others in two days.

* * *

They were to rendezvous at his hotel for drinks. Its popular upper floor bar was often packed with westerners because it offered great views of Victoria Harbor. It was normal for Americans to be there. At 4:15, the bar was nearly empty, quiet before it hit its happy hour stride.

Franco was the first to arrive. A few couples were scattered about in the lounge area. They all looked like tourists to him. Franco sat at the bar and ordered a beer. He was the only one sitting there. He was a few minutes early, and anxious to move forward with the job. As he understood it, he would be available for counseling the professor until Sloan identified the stolen plants, to confirm the theft. After that, Franco would load Sloan on a plane back to the U.S. What Rorke, or Pauling, would do with the information wasn't anything he was supposed to worry about.

About three quarters through his beer, Sloan came into the room and walked up to him, smiling.

"How was your trip?" he asked.

Franco shrugged. "Like any trans-pacific flight in economy— cramped and long. How was yours?"

"Rorke flew me first class. It wasn't bad at all."

Franco shook his head and lowered his voice to Sloan, "First class? That woman has it out for me. I know it."

"I'm sure it's nothing personal," Sloan whispered back to him. "My cover as a successful consultant demands that I fly in the pointy end of the plane."

"I don't think that's all there is to it."

"You shouldn't make too much of it."

"Right. Did she tell you what our strategy is to find this elusive rice seed? Finding a few seeds of a special rice in China sounds like a fool's errand if ever there was one. Are we supposed to go door to door?"

"Don't sweat it, Rorke will have a plan. She'll figure it out," said Sloan.

"I don't share your faith in that woman."

"Mike, take it easy. It'll be fine. She knows what she's doing."

"I'm just not an optimist when it comes to dealing with a prima donna," said Franco, and he took another sip of his beer.

Sloan spoke as Franco was drinking. "This whole rice thing has me pretty excited. Think about it. Buddy Jerome might save the developing world from hunger with a fast producing, high yielding strain of rice. The funny thing about it is, he has no idea of what he's done."

"Well, the rice has been stolen, so however you make money on seeds, it's going to be hard to do."

"Buddy's lawyers filed all the intellectual property disclosures on the rice technology and when they find that the seed was stolen, they can demand royalties and damages from the thieves or maybe the Chinese government. Of course, Buddy doesn't care about the money aspect as much as he does about the bragging rights he'll have over his biotech friend, Shelly."

"Wouldn't it be easier for Buddy to sue the U.S. government for allowing his seeds to be stolen in the first place?"

"I don't know. The government may be off the hook as part of the consent decree since Buddy broke the law."

"I guess it's not our problem," said Franco.

"No, it's not our problem. Still, you have to admit that introducing a new technology to help feed the world is an amazing and wonderful advance."

"Let's focus on the small issues, like seeing how far these thieves went with their ill-gotten goods, no matter what their potential."

Sloan was quiet.

"Are you really going to be able to identify this super rice?" Franco asked him.

"I'd say that I'm about 90 percent accurate. Differences in the leaf morphology from usual rice can be very subtle."

"I guess that 90 percent will be okay with Rorke. You'd better be right. I get the impression you really don't want to be on her shit list. You'll be flying economy class with me." Franco finished his beer.

"Yeah, I agree that isn't where I'd want to be."

"Where are you staying?" Franco asked, as he put down his glass.

"I'm in this hotel. How about you?"

Franco shook his head. "I'm here, on twelve."

"I'm on twelve, too," said Sloan. "How's your view? I look out over the Harbor."

"Not great," said Franco. "I look at another building, and I listen to an ice machine all night long. I tried to change rooms; there were none available. I think Rorke arranged it like that."

"You worry too much," said Sloan.

"What are you drinking?" Franco asked, as the bartender approached.

"Club soda," he said.

"And I'll have another beer," said Franco.

The barman nodded and left them alone again.

"Where are Rorke and Chen staying?" Franco asked.

"I have no idea," said Sloan. "You can ask her in about ten seconds."

Franco looked up to see Rorke walking across the lounge floor.

She wore four-inch pumps, a tight blue dress with a deep neckline, and was made up for a night on the town.

"Hi," said Franco as she approached. He looked her up and down and asked sarcastically, "Are we seeing Buddy again tonight?"

She did not respond to his question. "Franco, I need a very dry martini with three olives. Meet me at the table. Come with me, Paul."

She did not wait for Franco to respond, or for Sloan to move, before turning and walking back into the lounge.

Franco considered telling her where she could shove her three olives. Instead, he ordered the drink as he was told and thought about the check he'd receive when Rorke said his job was over. When the barman returned with their drinks, he carried them to the table.

She took the martini without saying "thank you" and continued her conversation with Sloan. Franco sat in an open chair.

"Paul, can you identify the plants if they've been out of the ground for 24 hours?"

"Yes, although the more they dry, the harder it is to be certain of the striation pattern on the leaves. Rice normally has parallel leaf veins that go straight up in sort of a north-south pattern. Our rice has a leaf vein pattern that varies a little, more north-east-south-west, and occasionally is almost netted. The pattern is more obvious in mature plants, but can still be subtle."

"Aren't we kind of missing the elephant in the room?" Franco asked Rorke. "How are we going to find out where these plants are to begin with?"

"Be quiet, Franco," she snapped, without taking her eyes off Sloan. "Now, Paul, how long will this drying take? Can we stick the plants in a plastic bag with a little water to slow the decomposition?"

"Not too much water," said Sloan. "If they're sloshing around, the plants become macerated and the leaves are the first to decompose."

"Do you think you can identify them if we bring them to you within 24 hours?"

"Yes, I'm pretty sure that will work."

"Okay, that's helpful. "

She turned to Franco for the first time. "Now, Mike, you thought you could make a useful contribution?"

Franco worked to collect himself and to remove his strong temptation to douse her with his beer. "What I was saying," he began slowly, "is that I have not yet heard how we are going to find the plants over here at all. Do we have a magic rice plant GPS we are going to use?"

Rorke gazed at him with her beautiful face and those disarming green eyes and said softly as she placed her hand over his on the table, "Yes, Mike, in a manner of speaking, we do."

"Sam, would you mind explaining that?" asked Franco, very pleasantly aware of her hand.

She looked at her watch and said, "No, soon it will be clear. I'm meeting a friend here in a few minutes who might be able to help us out. When he comes, please remember your cover story and try not to say anything too stupid. Let me do the talking for all of us."

"Sure thing," said Franco, gritting his teeth. "By the way, where's Hal?"

She shook her head and Franco was worried she was going to change out of her sweet mood again. Instead she quietly said, "Hal is doing a few errands now. He's just fine."

She looked up as a tall, well dressed, and exceedingly handsome Chinese man entered the room and walked toward their table. She smiled warmly at the man as he came over to them.

She stood and said a few phases in Chinese.

The man looked at her and said in perfect English, "I'm impressed, Sam. Your Cantonese is now almost as good as your Mandarin."

She gave him a kiss on the cheek.

"I've been practicing for you," she said, and turning to Sloan and Franco said in English. "These are two friends of mine from the States, Mike Franks and Paul Silver. I learned they were here when I bumped into Mike at a Starbucks this morning. They were just leaving. I've told them all about you, so they have you at a disadvantage."

They managed to keep the surprise out of their expressions.

"It's nice to meet you both," he said. "Any friend of Samantha's is a friend of mine. Welcome to my city. I hope you are enjoying your stay," said Jun.

Rorke interjected, "They only arrived yesterday from the U.S."

"How long are you staying?" asked Jun.

"We'll be here a week," said Sloan, after catching Rorke's eye.

"Barely scratching the surface of this wonderful place," said Jun. "Are you traveling to other places beyond Hong Kong?"

"No, just here and back to the States in a week," said Sloan.

"You too?" Jun asked Franco.

"Yes," said Franco.

"Where is home?" asked Jun.

"Chicago," said Sloan.

"Me too," said Franco.

Jun spoke, "Sam may have mentioned that I spent a few years studying in Chicago. I love the city. It's been years since I was back. I was expecting Al Capone, gangsters, and all sorts of mayhem when I went. I was a little disappointed not to see any of that, to be honest. It's still very colorful and the architecture is beautiful."

"Al Capone is gone and yet we still have plenty of gangsters, although most of them are in elected office," said Sloan. "Shall we sit, and can we buy you a drink?"

Jun looked at Rorke, who kept her eyes on his as she spoke to her colleagues, "I'm sorry, guys, we a have an early dinner reservation and we can't stay. We have to be going."

Jun watched her as she picked up her purse, then turned to the two men.

"Very nice meeting you both. Please have a wonderful time in Hong Kong. There is no better place on earth." Jun shook their hands once again and walked with Rorke out of the lounge.

Franco and Sloan stayed standing until they left the room.

"Did you know that was coming?" asked Franco. "Who was that?"

"I have no idea," said Sloan. "If he's our guide to the stolen rice, he might be one of the thieves?"

"That would be rather convenient," said Franco.

"He seemed like a nice guy."

"For a thief; if that's who he was."

"I'm telling you, this rice and these brothers might just help feed the world and save a lot of hungry people," said Sloan. "Are you ready for dinner?"

"Sure, let's eat," said Franco, adding, "You know, if Pauling has these brothers in his sights, they may want to try to save themselves first."

CHAPTER 15

The three men moved with precision and purpose, none speaking, as they walked quickly up the darkened dirt road. The night was humid, and the heavy air swallowed any small noise they made as they traveled. They walked in single file, about ten meters apart, well off to the side and almost in the brush. There was no moon. They were dressed all in black. They were invisible.

The road bled into a small lane and they turned onto it. About sixty meters down the road was a small shack of a house fronted by a covered porch. The three gathered around the house and peered in. All was silent within, only a small yellow entrance light giving shape to the porch. A half-empty bottle of whisky sat on a small wooden table on the side.

At the top of the lane, two of them headed for the rice paddies that lay beyond the home. The third stayed, watching for any movement or stirring within. The man at the house occasionally saw a glow from a red flashlight close to the ground. One of the men then left the paddy and walked the dike to the small hillside beyond. The soft glow of his red light was visible for just moments at a time. In a few minutes, the two men rejoined their colleague and they left as they had arrived. It started to rain, as was hoped, to further wash away any sign of their presence.

* * *

Rorke and Hal knocked on his door just before dawn. Despite their earlier call alerting him to their arrival at the hotel, it took Sloan a minute or two to open his door and let them in.

"What's going on?" he mumbled, sleep still heavy in his voice.

Rorke ignored the question as she walked into the room, and said to him, "Paul, I want you to look at these plants. Tell me if they are from our seeds."

Hal pulled out seven small plastic bags of leaves from a larger sack. Each bag was labeled. He laid them out on the desk in Sloan's room.

Sloan went to his nightstand and removed a magnifying glass. He opened each bag in order and removed the plant fragments within. When he finished with each specimen, he placed it in one of two groups. After examining all seven, he spoke to them.

"These are very fresh. I assume they're local."

Hal and Rorke said nothing, waiting for Sloan to speak again.

Sloan noted their stony silence and said, "Specimens A, C, D, E, and F are definitely from Buddy's seeds. Specimens B and G are probable—actually, highly likely. I can't be completely certain. If I were betting, I'd say they were too."

Rorke looked at Sloan. "Thanks, Paul," she said. "Today is a free day for you. Tomorrow, I may have more specimens for you to examine."

Hal retrieved the bags and placed them in his larger satchel. "I'll call you later," said Rorke, and she and Hal left the room.

She walked with him down the hallway to the elevator. Neither spoke until the lift brought them down to the lobby. Once in the lobby, she led him to the coffee shop that was just opening for the day. They took a table as far away from any new patrons as possible.

"Okay, Hal," she said. "Tell me what he identified."

"It was pretty interesting. Three of the five definite samples were from the hillsides off the sides of the paddy. The rest were from the paddy."

"It's spreading."

"Yeah, I think if we went back there in the daylight, we'd see it all over the place."

"Jun and Chao will be thrilled."

"Yup. I bet the Ministry will be pleased as well. They'll probably plant more of it."

"It's going to be hard to pinpoint any theft. Especially if it grows in other paddies."

"Nearly impossible," agreed Hal. "And I don't think there's any doubt about it moving into other rice paddies."

The waitress came by and they stopped talking until she took their order and left.

Rorke changed the subject. "What did you learn about the old man?"

"Nothing new. Liu Quan is just a quiet old man who likes to tend his small patch of land. He farms three mus of land—or about a half-acre. He grows his rice, and a few vegetables. He never graduated beyond the Cultural Revolution thing in the 60's. He seems to like whiskey; I did learn that about him. Otherwise, there wasn't much we didn't already know."

"Who takes care of him?"

"As far as my people can determine, Jun and Chao are his only living relatives. They arrange for delivery of groceries to him on Tuesday and Friday mornings. He has two men who help him in the field on Tuesday and Thursday mornings."

"How often do the brothers visit him?"

"I don't think very often, maybe once a month."

"What else does he do?"

"Not too much from what I can see. He lives off the land, occasionally listens to music, and probably thinks deep thoughts all day long. From what my guys say, he doesn't own a TV or even a cell phone."

Rorke thought about what Hal reported and then said, "The longest window is from Friday afternoon until Tuesday morning."

"Yes, although it may be even longer because the delivery man typically just puts the grocery bags on the porch early Friday mornings and then leaves."

"We should do it on Friday," said Rorke.

"I think that will be the easiest," said Hal.

"Let's plan on that," she said. "I'm going to have Jun take me to Guangdong and I'll take pictures to help confirm the rice is there. Will you be able to have your people bring those plants over for Sloan to inspect?"

"That shouldn't be too much of a problem, although it may take a day," said Hal.

"When will the specimens come in from Hunan?"

"I think we'll have them the day after tomorrow, if all goes according to plan."

"We'll make sure Sloan is available then. What about Chao?"

"I'm going to look for a little nightlife tonight down on D'Aguilar Street and Lan Kwai Fong. He should be there, if he stays true to his habits. I'll have my people out looking. We'll find him if he shows up."

"Good. I have a business meeting today with big brother and I'll confirm that I'm on for the visit to Guangdong."

"Will Franco be briefed on this?"

"No. Franco doesn't need to know any of this. What he doesn't know won't hurt anyone, particularly him."

* * *

After Chen left, Rorke pulled out a disposable phone. She called a local number and after a few rings, a woman's voice said in Cantonese that the recipient was not available and that a message could be left.

Rorke was not expecting a person to answer and was prepared to leave the message. "Confirmed at one site," was all that she said at the tone. She switched off the phone, knowing she would dispose of it later that day.

CHAPTER 16

Franco was asleep in his hotel room when his cell phone woke him. It was Sloan.

"Mike, I'm sorry for calling so early, but I wanted to catch you before you started your day."

"No problem," muttered Franco through the sleep still foggy on his voice. He tried to focus on the clock in front of him. "I'm up. What's going on?"

"I just wanted to tell you what I was doing today, since Rorke has nothing scheduled for us. I wondered if you had any interest in joining me?"

"Sure. What are you doing?"

"I'm going to be a tourist today. I want to see the City Museum and then meet an old academic colleague for lunch. Do you want to join me?"

"Okay, what time?"

"I'd like to catch a Kowloon ferry at around 9:30 and walk up to the museum."

"Sounds great. Should we meet in the lobby?"

"No, I want to take a walk first. I'll meet you at the Star Ferry Pier, the Central Terminal about 9:15."

Franco wondered whether he should join him for the walk, then decided that Sloan was safe on his own. "I'll see you at the ferry," he said.

The Star Ferry Pier was not far from their hotel and Franco arrived early. He bought himself a cup of coffee, and ferry tickets for both of them.

He sat off to one side of the waiting area and watched the commuter crowd start to build for the boat. All the people seemed consumed with themselves and their day-to-day lives. Most of them had distracted or detached looks about them.

Sloan arrived a few minutes before the ferry departure and waved to Franco before joining him in the waiting area.

Franco returned the gesture as Sloan approached.

"I bought the tickets," said Franco, anticipating Sloan's question.

"Thanks," said Sloan. "I was running a little late." He was slightly out of breath as he spoke. "Nigel, the guy we're meeting for lunch, called and I stopped walking to speak with him. He kept me on the phone a little longer than I planned. It's been a few years since we last spoke, and he wanted to start catching up before lunch. We were post-docs at Cornell and were nearly inseparable in those days. It was before Peg and I met. Unfortunately, Nigel and I fell out of touch after I left academics."

Franco glanced at his watch. "No worries."

Franco looked past Sloan, scanning the pier. It was out of habit, rather than searching for anything specific. He did see a man whose appearance merited a closer look, however. The man appeared to be trying too hard to be interested only in his newspaper. Ever suspicious from years of training, Franco honed in on the man and continued to monitor him.

After the ferry docked and the arriving passengers disembarked, Franco kept the man in sight while they boarded. He sat on the upper deck along with Franco and Sloan, although he was well toward the stern and out of their sightline. The harbor was calm now, with rain in the forecast. Clouds completely hid the mountains behind the Kowloon skyscrapers. The top floors of the buildings were barely visible as they made the fifteen-minute passage across the harbor from Hong Kong Island.

At the Tsim Sha Tsui ferry terminal, Franco continued to maintain his vigilance. As his fellow passengers left the upper deck, Franco spoke to Sloan.

"Paul, do you mind if we let the crowd thin a little before leaving?"

"Sure," Sloan answered, as he stood at the rail and watched the people leave. "We're in no hurry."

Franco looked to the pier and saw the man he noticed disappear into the crush of late commuters on the street.

"Okay, now I'm ready," Franco announced. "Too many people."

They walked the mile to the museum changing course frequently through the narrow streets of the district. Franco chose the route that would have several opportunities for side streets and the ability to look back easily.

The uneven sidewalks were narrow and crowded. The shop owners took up a large share of the walkways with their storefront stands, which funneled the crowds more tightly. Franco continued to keep a lookout, but saw no more of the man. After a block or two, he began to relax and engage Sloan in conversation.

"Tell me about your colleague," said Franco, remembering Rorke's mandate to keep Sloan under control.

Sloan maneuvered around his fellow pedestrians. Unlike the U.S., where people mirrored driving habits and walked on the right, the sidewalk throngs seemed to walk randomly, and it took more concentration to avoid running into other people.

After a few steps in the crowd, Sloan said, "His name is Nigel Fong and he's a Brit or at least he was born and lived in England for most of his life. He was at Cambridge before I met him at Cornell. After his post-doc, he went back to the U.K. and took a faculty position at Cambridge. I had thought he was a lifer there. About three years ago, he fell in love with one of his post-docs. She's Chinese and they decided they could both live in Hong Kong. He says they're both very happy here. He is at the University of Hong Kong now. His lab is well funded, and he said he made the transition from England to China a lot more quickly than he thought he would."

"Good for Nigel," said Franco, not terribly interested unless Nigel was part of a smuggling ring.

Franco continued to maneuver them in and out of side streets, lengthening the trip while satisfying himself they were not being shadowed.

When they arrived at the museum, Franco took a final, long look around again before they entered. There was no sign of trouble outside, and there were no overly interested observers in the museum.

After almost two hours in the museum, Franco was more than ready to leave. He looked around to see if they could exit by a different door without tripping an alarm. Since that turned out to be impossible, they backtracked. Once outside, Franco again looked carefully at the street and saw nothing suspicious.

All during the museum tour, Sloan provided additional facts about the city of Hong Kong, supplementing what was presented in the museum itself. Franco barely listened, preoccupied and wondering why someone, most likely Rorke, would have them followed. The seeds were already stolen, and there would be little he or Sloan could do to worsen the situation. Did they suspect Sloan was in on the theft?

As they started to walk back toward the ferry terminal, Franco had another thought. He stopped Sloan and said, "Paul, I got a blister from these shoes. I wonder if we could catch a cab?"

"Of course," said Sloan.

"I have another favor," added Franco apologetically.

"What's that?"

"Would you call Nigel on your cell phone and confirm the restaurant and the time?"

"I just e-mailed him yesterday with that information."

"I'm sorry," Franco persisted. "I'm just a little compulsive about these things. Would you mind calling?"

"Okay," said Sloan, reluctantly.

Franco listened while Sloan made the call and knew that if Sloan's phone were tapped, a surveillance crew would be at or near the restaurant to listen in on their lunch conversation.

"Thanks," he said, when Sloan was done. "I feel better now."

Franco hailed a cab. When they were situated in the back seat, Franco turned to Sloan. "I wonder if I could bother you for one more thing. We have time before we're supposed to meet Nigel and I'm kind of interested in what they've done to the old Kai Tak airport site. I flew in and out of there when I came to Hong Kong before they built the new airport. It was a great airport, very convenient, if you made it in alive—scary, short, lots of obstructions, frequently marginal weather. The Cathay Pacific pilots earned every dollar working out of there. It's only a few minutes from here."

"Okay," said Sloan. "Since we're tourists today. Although, seeing an airport re-development project is not exactly on everyone's bucket list, we have the time."

"I appreciate your patience, Paul."

When the cab pulled out from the museum, Franco looked behind to see if they were being followed.

"Are you expecting someone?" asked Sloan.

"No," said Franco. "Just an old habit."

"I wish you'd stop looking around. You're making me nervous."

"Funny, it has the opposite effect on me," said Franco, as he took another look behind them.

They drove to the old airport site before going back to the center of Kowloon. The streets were packed with the lunch rush, and they left the taxi a few blocks before the restaurant. They were ten minutes late when they arrived and their guest was already seated.

Nigel was charming and interesting. Inevitably, the conversation steered to botany, as Franco knew it would. He surprised himself by being interested in what they were discussing. He enjoyed the lunch up until Sloan said he had heard rumors about a new strain of fast growing, drought-resistant rice that could make triple cropping possible. Nigel pressed him on it. Fortunately, Sloan didn't divulge any more information.

When they had entered the restaurant, Franco had a suspicion about two men seated one table over. Franco let his eyes travel to them during the exchanges between Nigel and Sloan. After a few minutes of listening to the plant discussions, he was not just suspicious of the two men; he was sure they were listening and probably recording every word. More disturbing for Franco was that they had been expecting them at the restaurant.

What the hell was going on? They either had access to Sloan's e-mail, or could monitor his cell phone, or both. They probably had a tracking device on Sloan as well, possibly on him too, Franco thought.

On the way home in the cab, Sloan started to talk about his friend Nigel Fong. Franco interrupted him.

"Paul, you have to know that we are being watched over here."

"Mike, I think you're a little paranoid. This is not North Korea or Iran."

"No, I mean our people are watching us. You have to understand that."

"I think you're exaggerating."

"Listen, I'm not exaggerating, and I need you to promise me something."

"Maybe."

"No, this is way more than 'maybe.' I want you to promise me that you won't talk about this project or anything remotely related to this project with any of your pals over here. I know all the science is very interesting, but you just can't discuss it. If you have a strong need to share anything with your colleagues, please run it by me first."

"Mike, censorship is very ugly, particularly for an academic."

"Yeah, lots of things are very ugly. You have to do this."

Sloan hesitated before saying, "Okay, I will."

"Good," said Franco.

This was starting to feel much bigger than stealing rice seeds. Franco needed to have a conversation with Rorke, and soon.

* * *

Jun felt good about the day even before the call came. He had been looking forward to his investment meeting with Samantha Rorke for weeks. After all, what was there not to like about the meeting? The hours spent with this beautiful, intelligent woman who continued to make him wealthier always made this one of the better days on his calendar.

He was cleaning dishes from the small lunch he had prepared when the telephone rang.

He answered, and heard a voice he did not immediately recognize.

"Jun," said the caller excitedly, "I have wonderful news."

Jun, now interested, was still not sure whose voice this was.

"Yes?" he said, cautiously.

"Jun, this is Zhang Wei and I just received news from the Minister about the Thailand rice."

"Oh, yes?" said Jun, now fully engaged.

"Yes, the Minister is so impressed with the test crops that he has ordered the remaining seeds to be planted on our government farms. These are the large farms in Jiangxi, Sichuan, and Anhui provinces. Your rice will be the most exciting development the Yangtze valley has seen in a long time. The Minister is extremely pleased with the way the Thailand rice grows."

"I am delighted to hear that. Thank you very much for calling."

"I am also pleased to tell you that we have begun to process your fee for finding this important rice for us."

"I am very grateful," said Jun.

"Jun, I guarantee that you will not be disappointed. We have reviewed your earlier payments for helping the Government acquire the new microchip technology last year and because this is much more important to China, we have doubled your fee."

"I am speechless. Thank you."

"China is in your debt, Jun. Thank you."

Zhang Wei disconnected the line. Jun stood there holding the telephone and smiling for a long time.

CHAPTER 17

Rorke was late to Jun's 3:00 pm meeting by design. Even though he was her client, her tardiness was her small gesture of control. With the performance of his investment portfolio under her control, there was no danger of her being fired. She arrived at 3:20, exactly as she had planned.

The meeting was in his apartment, not his office. They had been meeting like this about every two months for the last year and a half. Early on, during their second meeting, Jun had made a clumsy effort to steer her toward his bedroom after their investment meeting. She had been pleasant, yet firm, in her refusal. Jun, who had earned his M.B.A. from Kellogg, had spent enough time in the U.S. to understand her fully when she told him that she didn't screw her clients, in any meaning of the word. He laughed at her line. She thought about that day and his gentle acceptance of her rebuke. It hadn't stopped him from buying her a five-star meal after the meeting. He was a perfect gentleman.

She had carefully planned what she would wear to their meeting, remembering what had earned his compliments in the past. She chose a straight tight skirt with a matching jacket over a plain white buttoned blouse. The jacket would come off as soon as she sat with him and she made sure that a few buttons at the top of the blouse were free before putting on the jacket. She wore her favorite perfume, the brand that Buddy liked. She checked her appearance in the mirror before she left. She looked at her front, her profile, and her rear. She stood again in profile. With what she saw, coupled with Jun's twenty percent year over year returns, she knew she could pretty much have anything she wanted from him.

Rorke took a taxi to Jun's building and greeted the sleepy doorman when she arrived. He seemed to remember her and bowed as she entered the building. She knew the combination to the punch lock, and when the security partition unlocked, she pushed through the door, walked to the elevator and pressed the button for the Jun's floor. Jun's building was a little older than most in that neighborhood. His apartment on the sixteenth floor had a large terrace overlooking the zoo and botanical gardens. Although he lived alone, the apartment was large with three bedrooms, one of which Jun used as his office. Rorke loved the apartment and its view, and she knew it made Jun happy when she commented on it.

The lift arrived at the sixteenth floor and she walked toward his apartment door. She looked at the hallway carefully on both sides after she left the elevator and saw no security cameras. She made three raps with the knocker below the peephole. The door opened almost before she finished the third knock.

Jun greeted her warmly. "Samantha, you always look so lovely," he said and he kissed her cheek. "Please come in. I've been thinking about some good news I received earlier today. It was about one of my new businesses so it is most appropriate that I am seeing you now. Today has been a day of very good fortune."

"I'm sorry to be late, Jun," she said. "I ran into a Chinese bureaucrat and he slowed up everything."

Jun raised a finger and said, "Today, we do not make fun of the system. At this moment, I'm in love with government bureaucrats. Today is a beautiful day for the planned economy."

She laughed at him. "You're in quite a good mood. What is this news? I have to hear all about it."

"And you will. Please come to the terrace with me."

He led her out to the terrace where the table was covered with a lace tablecloth, a wine bucket with an open bottle of champagne, and two champagne flutes.

He poured a glass for her. "I toast the beautiful Sam Rorke; I toast the wonders of modern technology; and I toast my excellent friends in the Ministry of Agriculture. Gan Bei!" He emptied his flute.

"Gan Bei," she echoed, draining her own glass.

"Shall we do another?" he asked.

"Of course, let's sit and talk while we enjoy this wonderful champagne."

After he re-filled the glasses, he gestured to the chairs further down the terrace. She led the way while he carried their glasses. "Shall we speak in English or Chinese?" she asked, as he gave her the glass.

"English," he said. "It's more direct and better for business. And after a few glasses of this," he said raising his glass, "we can see where the conversation leads us."

"Fine. Now, why are you in such a great mood?" she asked.

"It has to do with an investment I made."

WILLIAM CLAYPOOL

"Without me?" she pouted, feigning disappointment.

"Yes, sadly," said Jun.

"What kind of investment?"

"Agriculture."

"Really, where?"

"China."

"You're kidding. How do you make money on a Chinese agriculture investment?"

"I sell seed stocks. Like Monsanto does in the States," said Jun happily.

"There's no way their business model works in China," she said.

"No, our model is more efficient. The government is our only customer."

"And you grow seeds?"

"I do."

"Where? Hong Kong?"

"Close. Lantau. In addition to a small plot on Lantau, Chao and I have a modest farm in Guangdong Province, just north of Shenzhen," said Jun.

"I never knew this side of you. You are a real man of the soil. Uncle Mao would be happy," she said in a mocking tone.

"Since the handover, I've been trying to be a much better proletariat. This deal is proof of my re-education."

She stood and looked over the terrace rail to the busy street below and the botanical gardens beyond it. "Yes, Jun," she said, gesturing to the elegant apartment around her, "I think your re-education is complete. You are an outstanding example of how all Chinese peasants should live."

She drained her glass, and he did as well.

She went to the table and poured them both another. "Now, tell me how you came to be a farmer," she said, settling in her chair again.

Jun took a sip from his glass. "It will not come as a complete shock to you to hear that I don't do much of the farming."

"No, but for a moment I had this delightful image of you wearing a coolie hat and holding a hoe in your hand."

"Before you give up on that picture, I will tell you that I really do have a new agricultural royalty business. When Chao and I were in Bangkok a few years ago, a colleague took us to a farm to meet a man who has been crossing rice hybrids for decades."

"Really?" she said, with genuine interest in his story.

"Yes, and his findings were amazing. He discovered a strain of rice that grows faster and is far hardier than our usual Chinese rice. We licensed the rice seeds from this farmer and found that all the amazing things he claimed about his plant strain were true. It is quite remarkable."

"I'm impressed, Jun," she said.

"Yes, I must say, Chao and I did well with this one. Occasionally, we take a chance, and it pays off."

He allowed her a few seconds to respond. When she stayed quiet, he continued, "A few months ago, we showed these plants to the Ministry of Agriculture and they were tremendously excited about it. They tried it in their test plots in Hunan and expanded it from there. Today, I received a call from the Ministry to tell me they were planting the rice all along the Yangtze basin on large government farms. They wanted to see how it grows in our most productive soils." He took a long drink. "That is the good news."

"Congratulations," she said sincerely, and added, "It is a great day for you."

"Yes. Thank you. And now, because of this, my investment strategy can shift to more speculative and hopefully higher return investments. The rice royalties will be coming in large chunks and I am feeling very comfortable about my cash flow for the foreseeable future. We'll have to talk about re-modeling my entire portfolio to adjust to my new situation."

"I'm happy to do that. Since we're on the topic of farms, I've never seen a farm in China, even though I grew up in Hong Kong. Would it be possible for me to see your farm in Guangdong?"

"Sam, of course. I am happy to organize that. I would love to show it to you. It cannot be tomorrow because I must arrange the paperwork. I can guarantee that we can do it the day after tomorrow if you'd like. We'll have a short visit to my modest little plot, and I'll plan an elegant lunch. Will that be acceptable?"

"Wonderful. I would not have it any other way."

"Good. I'll call you tomorrow with the final arrangements."

"Thank you," she said, as she took another sip of champagne. "Jun, with your exciting news, I wonder if we should do an exercise here that I do with all of my long-term clients."

"Of course," he said. "What is that?"

"I ask my clients to write out—not type out—their long-term investment goals, their lifestyle needs, their charities, and heirs, and how they would see these financial needs evolving over a five, ten, and twenty-year time period."

"Why not type it out?"

"I think people spend more time thinking about what they express when they write it by hand," she explained.

"I suppose I can do that," said Jun. "If we're talking about giving money away, it will all be to charities. I'll have to think that through. I don't have any other relatives besides Chao and Uncle Quan.

"However, if we're talking about spending money, I have lots of ideas." He smiled at her. "You are the closest thing I have to a girlfriend, and since you aren't working too hard at the girlfriend role, I don't have to spend much money on you."

"Except for my management fee," she corrected.

"Yes, except for your management fee. As you know, I have quite a number of interests and places where I'd like to spend money, and we can plan for that."

"Jun, that's exactly the idea. Write down whatever you want. Be as frivolous or as frugal as you wish. Just make it what you would honestly want to do."

"It may take time, for self-examination, and then to write it all out."

"Well, start it now and if it takes too long, you can finish it another time. Otherwise, if you don't mind me drinking champagne here on your lovely terrace while you write, take all the time you need." She kicked off her shoes, curled her knees over the cushion, and sat back in the large chair. "Would you bring me a magazine and re-fill my glass before you start writing?" she asked with a seductive smile.

"You're a lot of work, your Ladyship."

"Yes, well this is my system and it's how I'll keep generating your 20 percent returns."

"Of course," he said, as he walked back into the apartment, quickly returning with a fresh bottle of champagne and a magazine. "Now I'll do my homework. I'll write it in English for you."

"No," she said. "If you don't mind, would you write it in Chinese? It helps me to practice my comprehension of hand-written Chinese."

"Okay, smart lady. Now, would you like to read it in simplified or traditional characters?"

"Whatever you usually use."

"I only use simplified characters these days. Life is too short."

"I agree, Jun. Life is too short. But take all the time you need to tell me about your future."

"If I do my homework diligently, can we have dinner together?"

"Yes, I think I can agree to that, if it's an early dinner."

"Oh, do you have plans for later?"

"Maybe, but more importantly, I missed lunch."

"Okay, an early dinner. I'll get to work," he said.

He sat at his desk just inside the terrace sliding door. Rorke watched carefully, noting both the pen he used, and the drawer of his desk where his stationary was kept. She turned to her magazine and her fresh glass of champagne. Before reading, she gazed beyond the rail to the botanical gardens and the zoo and thought about the wonderful view from the sixteenth floor.

CHAPTER 18

Rorke left the restaurant a little before 7:00 pm, and after saying good-bye to Jun on the sidewalk, took a taxi to her hotel. She spoke with Hal shortly after she arrived. They met in her hotel room.

"Are you going to the Guangdong farm tomorrow?" he asked.

"No, the day after. Can you have your men there?"

"They'll be there. They're already working on the farm."

"When did you arrange that?"

"A month ago. Experienced farm workers are becoming harder to find."

"Do they think we have the right rice?"

"Yes. They call it 'Thailand rice' and whatever this 'Thailand rice' is, they think it's amazing."

"Can they bring it to us?"

"Just point out the specimen you want and they'll make sure I have it for Sloan."

"They'll probably have a better idea of the specimens of interest than I will."

"Probably. Your photos of plants outside of the paddy can confirm how invasive this strain becomes. Why don't you want to take Sloan?"

"He's traveling on his own passport and he'd need to show it to Jun for papers to go over the border. After that our smuggling brothers would do a little research on him. We don't want to risk that."

"How about Franco?"

"We keep him in the dark."

"Okay," said Hal.

"Are you seeing Chao tonight?" Rorke asked.

"I'm going to try. He's a regular at the bar I'll visit, and we'll see if he shows. My guys say he goes there three or four days a week to have a few quick drinks before going to dinner."

"Do you have it all worked out?"

"Yeah, pretty much. I'm bringing Alissa Low over tomorrow."

"From Singapore?"

"No, she's still in Malaysia. You're confused because her go-to routine is that Singapore shtick."

"Singapore Sling?"

"For her, sweet drinks can be very useful."

"I suppose," Rorke said quietly. "Okay. That'll work. Alissa is very effective." She hesitated, "Are you going to burn her when you're done?"

"Yes. She'll have to go back to Langley for a year or more. She's fine with it."

"Good. Are you sure of the background information for Chao?"

"Yes, of course," said Hal. "My alter-ego is an orphan with no local family. He's a software engineer in Boston. He looked a lot like me when I was his age."

"You're going to do the old prep school geography method?"

"Yeah, it works every time—the fancier the prep school, the easier the conversation, and Chao's school is one of Hong Kong's most exclusive. Their yearbook is amazingly descriptive. If he does any research on me, there I am. We'll be old friends in five minutes," said Hal.

"How are you going to cement the relationship after the old boy introduction?"

"I updated our Cambridge software company's website a few weeks ago. It's right up his alley. I'm sure we'll have a great conversation about how much money he can make for me."

"Well, happy hunting tonight. If I don't speak with you again, your men in Guangdong will recognize me, won't they?"

"Yes, Sam. You'll be the only redhead in the province."

A half-hour later, under a neon sign at the busy corner on D'Aguilar Street, Hal stood, expecting news. The sidewalk was jammed with people going to the many restaurants, nightclubs, and bars in the neighborhood. From out of the crowd, a man came up to Hal and pulled him aside.

"He's in there," said the man, gesturing to the bar across the street. "He just arrived, and he's alone." The man dissolved into the stream of walkers.

Hal walked over to the bar the man had pointed to. The bar was the front room of a pricey restaurant, and everything in the place spoke of extravagance. The long polished mahogany bar and shelving were accented with a brass foot rail and brass bar rails cordoned the wait-staff station. The lighting was soft, and seductively adequate. The bar stools were leather and elegantly comfortable. Chao perched on the last seat of the bar, exchanging friendly banter with the barman, and gesturing to the television.

Chao appeared larger than his profile. He had gained weight, although it looked to be more muscle than fat. The impression was that he was large, strong, and fit. He was dressed in slacks, an open-collared shirt, and a sports coat. They looked expensive. He wore a Rolex watch and a large ring with a stone Hal could not identify from where he sat.

Chao's interaction with the bartender was like that of an old friend. They were both laughing at something the other had said. They paid attention to each other and to the television in the corner of the bar above Chao's seat.

Hal took a stool in the middle of the bar. He waved at the bartender who came to take his order, filled it, and walked back to resume his conversation with Chao. Hal enjoyed his drink and watched the television. After a short while, Chao casually glanced over to him and back to the barman. Hal casually looked at him before turning his attention back to the television.

A minute or two later, Hal left his stool, walked down the bar to Chao and asked tentatively, "Excuse me, did you go to Pelham College?"

"Yes," Chao said, "Why do you ask?"

"I think we were there at the same time. You're 'Chao' right? You were two years ahead of me. I remember you played on the football team. You were the goal keeper."

Chao smiled and said, "That's right. What's your name?"

"Yuen Chu, but I'm used to being called 'Carl.' I live in Boston now and I've gotten used to my Anglo name. It's easier for them."

He gestured to the barman for a refill. "I only went to Pelham for three years after we moved from Shanghai."

"You didn't play football at Pelham, did you?"

"No. I played handball."

"That's a good game; you can keep up with it all your life without needing a team," said Chao, taking a sip of his drink.

"I prefer to play squash now—same idea."

"What do you do in Boston?"

"I own a software company I started after college."

"You went to college in the States?" asked Chao.

"Yes. I did the dutiful Chinese son route. I worked hard at PC and left to study with the barbarians in the U.S. After graduation, I had opportunities there, and took them."

"Are you back here visiting family?"

"No. My parents died a few years ago and my only relative is a cousin who lives in Singapore. I just came back to visit the city. I try to make it back about every three years. The place changes so quickly."

"That's for sure," said Chao, sipping his drink.

Then Hal asked, "What did you do after Pelham?"

"I stayed local and went to university here for a year. It wasn't for me. I left, and joined my brother's company."

"What do you do?"

"Well, we scout out and broker technology from the originators to companies we think would be good customers in China. We do mostly computer hardware components. We've also done several big software deals."

Hal listened closely and looked very interested.

"Tell me about your company," Chao said.

"Are you actually interested in it? Most people find it kind of boring."

"No. Really I am," said Chao. "Tell me about it."

"Okay," said Hal. "Well, we deploy a mechanical engineering approach to software or a software approach to mechanical engineering, depending on how you want to look at it. Basically, we design computer holographic quality assurance into assembly lines or packaging lines. We image items as they roll down the line and infer the production quality from the images we see. Depending on the product, the tolerances obviously vary widely. We can measure down as far as we need to, with the right optics."

"Who do you sell to?" asked Chao.

"We've installed our systems in lots of diverse industries," explained Hal. "We have lines that image low-tech molded plastic items, like kid's toys. We also have lines in both a microprocessor factory and a finished electronics factory. We've learned that if the image of the product looks all right to our computer algorithms, and if they had good QA of their materials, their electronics work right 100 percent of the time. We've shown the value of our systems in a wide group of industries."

Chao asked, "Have you set up any systems in China for U.S. companies who manufacture over here?"

"Not yet," said Hal. "All of our assembly line systems are in the States."

"Are you going to expand into China?"

"We're growing like crazy in the U.S. We've talked about working in China—certainly for U.S. companies manufacturing here, although we haven't done anything about it yet."

"That all sounds great," said Chao. "If you don't mind me asking, what kind of revenues do you have?"

"We did 40 million U.S. last year," said Hal, "and we look to grow it to 60 million next year, if all our orders come through."

"Impressive!. You know, if you are interested in expanding in China, I may be able to help you out," said Chao. "My brother and I have a lot of the right kinds of connections, and we could make it much easier for you to start your operations here."

"Thanks," said Hal. "Like I said, I've certainly thought about it. We could export a lot of what we design. There is definitely a fit for us with many companies in China." Hal reached into his pocket. "This is my business card."

Chao examined it carefully. "I might be able to place your technology in China. I have clients who I think would be very interested in what you do."

"That's great. I'd like to hear about them."

"Let's talk about it. What are you doing for dinner tonight?"

"I don't have any plans," said Hal.

Chao looked pleased. "I was going to meet a few friends at a restaurant. I'll call them and cancel. It's not every day I can enjoy dinner with a fellow Pelham man, who lives among the barbarians."

Hal smiled and started to sing, "Pelham men will stand courageous, true and strong forever."

Chao responded, also singing, "Love for school and classmates guiding, duty beyond measure."

They both laughed.

"Let's eat here," said Chao. "I'll call to cancel with my other friends. You grab a table for us. We can talk import and export."

"Great. I'll see you at the table," said Hal, as his new friend walked off to make his call.

CHAPTER 19

hao was impressed that his new friend's company did 40 million U.S. dollars in revenue after being in business for only three years. Chao told "Carl" that he felt very positive about his interest in expanding to China. "Carl" said he was willing to hire a staff of ten Chinese nationals to start, and they discussed the optimal placement of their office. They agreed that the office placement should not be decided until they had their first Chinese customers, and that it would take further analysis.

After dinner, Chao suggested they have a nightcap.

"Count me in for that," said Hal. "I'll buy. What do you want?"

Chao appeared to think carefully about his words before he spoke again.

"I was thinking of maybe going to a club I know over in Kowloon. It's kind of a wild place if you're interested."

Hal said to him, "Sure. I'm game for anything. Will we see any other PC alums?"

Chao shook his head slightly. "I don't think we will. It's not a Pelham College kind of a club."

"All the better," laughed Hal. "Let's go."

From the background investigation, Hal knew where they were going. He was very curious to see if the reports about the place were accurate.

They waited at the valet stand until the parking attendants pulled Chao's car around. The car was a late model Porsche 911 Carrera.

"Business must be good," said Hal enthusiastically, seeing the car.

"Yes. We're doing okay," said Chao, as he sat in the car.

Hal bent over the seats as Chao was fixing his seat belt. "I've always wondered about the back seats in these models," he said, as he stuck his head behind the passenger seat. "Have you ever had anyone back here?"

Chao laughed, and said "No." He didn't see his new friend slip a small, tightly rolled, plastic bag with powder into the pocket behind the passenger seat. He also didn't see that Hal did it with a small dark eyeglass cleaning rag in his hand. Had Chao cared, he might have seen Hal use the rag to grasp and wipe down both the inside and exterior door handles.

Chao waited for Hal to buckle up, which he did while he again palmed the black rag in the darkened car. After he was satisfied that Hal was secure, Chao let the car spring to life and they headed directly to the East Tunnel crossing under the harbor to the Kowloon side.

The tunnel was clear and there were no delays. On the Kowloon side, they trekked a little west to a neighborhood of midrise buildings and nondescript storefronts. They drove down a side street and entered a dimly lit alley. Several other high-end cars were parked in the alley. They all seemed to be watched by a large, burly man standing by a black steel door in the center of the block.

Chao parked the car in the alley and they walked toward the bear of a man who greeted Chao by name. The man stood aside, allowing them to enter.

The entrance room to the club was small and dark, and another bouncer guarded the front of an inner metal door. The room was vibrating with the techno music coming from within. Chao patted the inside guard on the back who returned the gesture as he opened the door for them.

Inside the club, the loud music required shouting to communicate. The room was surprisingly large and Hal saw that two exits led off the main room. One door led to a long hallway and the other to a set of stairs. The women at the bar were young, beautiful and wore stylish, revealing dresses. Several other women were dancing with one another. The men were older; most wore suits, and most were older than Chao. The women outnumbered the men by two to one. The circulating barmaids wore short black skirts and were topless. They all wore a large red feather in their hair.

Chao looked at his guest, "Carl, do you see anyone from Pelham?"

Hal laughed and shook his head.

"Stay here a minute. I have to see a friend at the bar."

Hal watched closely. Chao walked to the dark end of the bar where a man in a suit sat alone on a stool. Chao greeted him and they looked like old friends as they talked. The man left the stool and they walked further into the shadows. He exchanged something with Chao. The man turned his back and Hal was screened from the transaction. He did not see what was traded, but had a pretty good idea of what it was, knowing Chao's tastes and interests.

While Hal watched Chao, he saw two couples, both middle-aged men and beautiful women in their twenties, come down the stairs. Hal also had a pretty good idea of what was going on upstairs.

When Chao returned, he gestured for Hal to come with him. Chao walked to the bar and tapped two of the young women on the shoulder and gestured for them to join him. The trio walked down the hallway beyond the bar and Hal followed. Many of the doors to the rooms were left ajar and Hal saw people dancing in a few of the rooms. Some of the people, both male and female, were naked.

Chao led Hal and the two girls to an unoccupied room with a couch in each corner. The furnishings were expensive and after they entered, Chao closed the door. Although the base vibrations continued, the rest of the music nearly vanished.

Hal and Chao sat on separate couches, each joined by one of the girls.

"Who are our new friends?" asked Hal.

"We don't usually use names," said Chao. He turned to the girl sitting with him, "Do you want to use names?"

She giggled and said, "Just call me number one."

"That's funny," said the other girl, "That's my name, too,"

"See?" said Chao, "No names."

Chao was being a conscientious host, and gestured to each of the young women while asking Hal, "Which one would you like, Carl? Any one you want. Would you like 'Number one?" he gestured to the first girl, "Or perhaps 'Number one?'" he said, gesturing to the other young woman.

Hal looked at the women saying nothing.

"Perhaps you'd like a little fog," Chao continued pulling out a small bag with rolling papers and cut leaves, "or maybe a little snow?" He pulled out another bag with white powder.

"How about just a little bourbon on ice for now?" asked Hal.

"No problem," said Chao and he pressed a button on the end table. In about five seconds, one of the barmaids entered the room. She took drink orders from all of them and left.

"Tell me about this place," said Hal.

"Well, it's pretty much what you see. For a monthly fee, the members can come here, relax, and have whatever they want... absolutely anything they want. The only rules are no needles, no drugs or booze for the girls, and no female guests. The security guards at the door are off duty cops. The girls are checked weekly for, let's call it, microbial hygiene. The rooms upstairs are very nicely furnished and cleaned after every club member is done. It's a first-class operation."

"I imagine the monthly fee is hardly worth mentioning," said Hal.

"Well, you get what you pay for," said Chao, pulling out the bag of white powder and taking a small glass coaster off the end table.

He laid out a line of the powder.

"You want to try?" he offered to Hal.

Hal said, "No thanks. A few years ago, I 'tried' almost every night for too long, and I nearly went broke. Three months in rehab convinced me that I shouldn't 'try' anymore. I can't handle that stuff, but don't let me stop you."

"I won't," said Chao, laughing as he rolled a bill and snorted the line. "I've been able to handle it just fine."

Hal looked up as the barmaid returned with their drinks.

"Great service here," commented Hal.

"You have no idea," laughed Chao again.

"Do you come here a lot?"

"Depending on my travel schedule, about twice a week. It helps me unwind."

Chao took a sip from his drink. "What do you think? Do you like the club?" he asked Hal.

"I imagine it's an easy taste to acquire," said Hal. "Is there a long waiting list?"

"Since you are neither a barbarian nor Japanese, I imagine I could move you right into membership if you'd be interested."

"Do you think this club is a good argument to headquarter my China operation in Hong Kong?" asked Hal.

"It would convince me," said Chao enthusiastically. "We're still a little more free-wheeling here than on the mainland."

"What would Mao say?" asked Hal.

"I think it would be wise not to discuss it with him, or with other members of the party," said Chao.

Hal took a sip from his bourbon. "Your secret is safe with me."

The two Number Ones stood and started to disrobe. Chao cheered them on as they began to dance.

Hal cheered them, too, then said to his host, "I'm sorry to be a kill joy. I think I'll just have this one drink and go. I was up very late last night and I don't have the energy to keep up with you."

"No problem," said Chao. "The girls won't be offended. I'll run you back to the island."

"No, you stay," said Hal. "I wonder if we could meet again on Saturday night? I'd like to discuss your business ideas more and, perhaps we can see where the evening goes. I'll be more rested."

"I'd love that," said Chao. "Where should we meet?"

"Let's start with drinks at the same place as tonight, and I'll pick a spot for dinner. Will 7:00 o'clock be convenient?"

"That's great. Can I call you a cab?"asked Chao.

"I'm sure I can find one on the street. See you Saturday."

"I'm looking forward to it. We'll have a great time."

"We will," said Hal. "Goodbye Number Ones."

CHAPTER 20

Franco rose at 5:00 am, but did not call her until 7:00. When he did, there was no answer and he left her a message to call him. By 8:00 am, she had not called back and he phoned again. The message he left this time was not as friendly as the first.

After the second call, he contacted Sloan who, by this time, was expecting a morning call from Franco. Sloan wanted to do more sightseeing that day, and was interested in riding the tram to Victoria Peak. He asked Franco if he wanted to join him on this glorious day. Franco declined. He was in no mood to deal with the crowds on the scenic tram. Sloan didn't mention anything about rice, patriots, or smugglers saving the world, and Franco felt he would do just fine on his own for the day. They did agree to meet for dinner.

Rorke still had not called back. At 9:00 am, his third message was even less friendly, now bordering on rude. Just before 10:00 am, his cell phone rang. It was Rorke.

"Sam, we need to talk," he said gruffly.

"Uh, sure Mike. Is something wrong? You sound upset."

"Yes, I am."

"Gee, I'm sorry. What's the matter?"

"Not over the phone."

"Okay, let's meet."

"Where are you staying?"

"I'm at the Hyatt Hotel on Harbor Road."

"I'll see you in the lobby there at 10:30," he said and switched off the phone.

He reflected on Rorke's mood, expecting her to take a hard line. He was confused by her friendly tone and still angry at her having him followed without telling him.

He quickly put on his shoes and started walking to her hotel. He chose not to take a cab. The walk would take only about fifteen minutes, and he felt it would help him relax before he confronted her.

The weather was unseasonably warm and delightful. As he walked, the cloudless sky gathered blue and hung over the green, un-shrouded mountains behind Kowloon. Even the busy harbor waters hinted of an azure hue. Although the streets were crowded, he already felt calmer.

He took a detour and made it to the hotel at 10:25. She was sitting in a chair in the lobby when he arrived. "Good morning, Mike," she said happily. "It's a lovely day, isn't it? I had a great run out there this morning."

"Yeah, it's nice out."

Rorke continued with her cheery tone. "It's hard to find any city more beautiful than Hong Kong when the weather's cooperating."

"Is there a coffee shop here? We need to sit down and talk," he said.

"Do you want to come up to my room?"

"Let's see how crowded the café is first."

"Sure, it's this way," she said, and started down the lobby hallway.

She was wearing a light cardigan sweater over a tee shirt and wore a very short skirt that might have been a little young for her—except she looked great in it. Her perfect legs were lightly tanned, and she wore a pair of casual flats to finish the look. Damn, he thought to himself, it was hard to stay mad at this woman. Franco was already thinking that if there was an argument between them, it wasn't going to be a win for him.

The cafe in the hotel was quiet, running between the breakfast and lunch crowds. They were led to a window table that had an expansive harbor view. He thought to himself that she wasn't particularly worried about being seen on surveillance cameras or she wouldn't have chosen this hotel. With her red hair and green eyes, the only place where she wouldn't stand out might be Dublin.

He looked around the elegant café with its extensive view. "You know, my hotel room doesn't look at anything except another building."

"That's too bad, Mike."

"I also have an ice machine outside my door that makes a racket all night long."

"Oh, I'm sorry about that. Is that what you wanted to talk about?"

"No, that is not what I called you about."

Franco watched the waitress come up to their table. They both ordered coffee and after the waitress left, he scanned the room again and said to Rorke in a gruff voice, "I wasn't happy about yesterday."

"What part of yesterday bothered you?"

"You had at least two different surveillance teams keeping an eye on us. Why?"

"Surveillance teams? Are you sure?"

"Stop it!" he said, annoyed

"How do you know it was me?" she asked coyly.

"Give me a break. Why did you do it?" he asked, starting to be less charmed by her again. "Do you think Sloan is connected with the thieves and you haven't told me?"

She smiled, looked back out the window and then turned to him. "Mike, first I want to thank you again for agreeing to work with us. I know Sloan is in good hands and that I can trust you to manage him."

"Sam, you're not thanking me 'again.' This is the first and only time you've thanked me."

"Well, I'm sorry for that. It's way overdue," she said, smiling as she turned to look at the harbor again. After a moment, she continued, "No, we don't think Paul Sloan is one of the thieves. Is he still talking like the thieves are wonderful patriots fighting to save the world and stop all hunger?"

"Well, without the patriot angle, yes he is."

"You know he's a terrible security risk with his alcohol problem."

"Former alcohol problem."

"No, 'recovering' alcohol problem," she countered. "Alcoholics use that term. They're the ones who know how hard it is to stay dry and keep functional."

Her comment hung in the air as the waitress came with their coffees. She continued when the waitress left them.

"Based on Sloan's past and how far he sank when he was drinking, he couldn't hold even the lowest security clearance today."

She lowered her voice, "And we're not talking about a low level of clearance on this operation. This is one of the highest profile industrial thefts we've ever had. This isn't hacking into IBM and walking off with their candy, as bad as that is. This is a physical theft of U.S. government property that we were holding in trust for one of our most powerful citizens. We don't want that news leaking out. We'd have a serous problem."

Franco nodded. "I know that. That's why I'm here, to help prevent Sloan from feeling he needs to discuss this rice project."

"Yes, Mike. That's why you're here. You're not here to be a one-man surveillance team. You're here to be Sloan's friend, if he needs one. It's why I have a back-up plan if for any reason something happens to you."

"'Happens to me?' Like what?"

"Like Sloan wanting to give you the slip and go off on a bender with one of his old academic pals without telling us. You know, to re-live the good old days."

"Nigel Fong didn't strike me as much of a party animal."

"No, but Sloan has two other old close friends in Hong Kong who are not as temperate as Dr. Fong." Looking at her watch she added, "As a matter of fact, he's riding up the tram with one of them right now. Did you know that?"

"Yes, I knew he was taking the tram ride."

"You didn't know it was with an old drinking buddy from his faculty days."

"No, I didn't know that."

"Did you know that this drinking buddy is a divorcee that Sloan was very friendly with even when they both had good steady marriages?"

"No."

"Did you know that Sloan's other pal has been away at a conference in Europe, although he's tried to reach him a few times?"

"No."

"Do you have any other questions for me about the surveillance on Sloan?"

"Why didn't you tell me?" he said, taking a drink of the coffee.

"There was no need. You have enough on your mind ensuring Sloan's continued cooperation and discretion. Your job is preventing bad behavior rather than monitoring for it." She turned to look out at the busy harbor.

"How well do you have him wired?" he asked.

She turned back to him. "What do you think?"

"I would guess you went all in with cell phone intercepts, and GPS, and audio transmitters in clothes linings and shoes and wherever else you can hide one of your toys."

She looked back to the harbor and said very casually, "Yeah, we put an electronic device in pretty much every place we could. We covered it all."

Franco thought about this. "What about me?"

She turned and studied him closely with those incredible green eyes and asked softly and slowly, "Yes, what about you, Mike?"

Franco felt extremely vulnerable when she used that seductive voice. "Am I wired, too?" he asked.

"Should you be?"

"No."

"Well," she said, "Given the fact that Pauling seems to love you like a son, and your history of service speaks to being able to keep big secrets, we gave it a lot of discussion."

"And?"

"Oh, we still talk about it."

"What about the fact that I don't know anyone over here, that I don't know anything about rice, and that I don't know where the brothers have taken it? Hell, I don't even know who they are."

"We talk about that too, Mike," she said. "You wouldn't have much of a story to tell, even if you managed to find an audience, would you?"

Franco drank from his coffee. "I'm also pissed off that you ignored my calls."

"Oh, please," she said with mock offense, "I didn't ignore them. I just didn't answer them yet."

"Why not?"

"I'm sorry, I was busy."

"Taking one for the team with one of the brothers?"

She looked amused. "Maybe. Would that be a problem for you?"

"No, not at all," he said, "How long have you been setting these guys up?"

She leaned forward to speak to him, lowering her voice. "Franco, I want you to understand that we've been onto these thieves since before they got started with this rice theft. We spent a lot of time watching them rip off technology assets. I've been the older brother's financial advisor for the last eighteen months. It started small; he liked my results and now I run most of his portfolio. Just know that we've spent a lot of time on this. We're almost at the end, and I can't risk Sloan or you screwing it up now. If I seem a little upset or impatient with you, you must know we have a huge investment in this operation. If I don't answer your calls right away, I'm sorry. Please don't be offended."

"What if there had been an emergency and I was trying to reach you?"

She looked steadily at Franco and smiled before resting her hand on his wrist. "Mike, if there were an emergency, I'd know. Trust me, I'd know all about it."

Franco spoke again. "I've been thinking a lot about this business. This is a big deal for you. There's something very important here. It's more than just seeds being stolen from an USDA outpost."

Her tone became a little harder when she answered him. "Mike, I didn't hear a question in there—and that's a good thing, because you know how I feel about you asking a lot of questions." She paused, and then continued in the same firm tone. "Whatever you don't know, you don't need to know and, believe me, you don't want to know."

"The stakes are bigger than a few seeds being stolen."

"Truthfully, Mike. They're not. It's all about the seeds."

"I don't believe you."

"That's your problem. It doesn't matter what you believe, as long as you do your job, and help to make sure Sloan stays on the rails—at least until he goes back home."

"Okay," said Franco, "And how much longer is this job going to be?"

"It will be over sooner than you think. We have additional plant specimens coming in for the Professor's inspection tomorrow and we'll go from there."

"Where are these plants from?"

"Mikey, what did I tell you about asking too many questions? I'm going to give you a 'time-out' if you can't behave."

"When do you need to have Sloan available?" he said, ignoring her tone.

"Make sure he's in his room tomorrow at 1500 hours. This may be the last we need of Sloan and that means your job will be done, too. You can punch out from the factory floor as soon as Sloan boards a plane back to the States."

"Should I book his flight?"

"Let's see how it goes tomorrow. If he can identify Buddy's rice in these next specimens, you can both leave."

"Okay, that soon. Great."

"One thing though, after we're done. I do want Sloan back in the States. I don't want him wandering around here without supervision. We'll likely be pulling our people from his surveillance detail here after he identifies the specimens. It's critical he returns to Hawaii when his job is done."

"I understand."

"Franco, one other thing. I don't want you all upset if you can't reach me tomorrow. As you put it, I'm 'taking one for team.' I'm going to see our thieves' rice paddies on the mainland to see our stolen goods in the wild. Don't bother me. I'll be strolling about in the rice and mud."

"I don't hear a lot of excitement in your voice. You're not really a country girl, are you?"

"Bugs, oxen, manure—they are not my favorite things. This trip will be an example of extreme loyalty and duty for me. I want you to be impressed."

"Will you come back with dirt under your fingernails?"

"Shit, I hope not. I'll see you and Sloan at 1500 tomorrow."

CHAPTER 21

A t 7:00 am, when the phone rang, Jun was sitting on his terrace drinking tea. It was a lovely day and, at that moment just before the ring, he wondered to himself how life could possibly be any better for him. The sun had not yet risen higher than the surrounding skyscrapers and the sky above was flawlessly blue. It was going to be a perfect day. Although the crowds in the streets were starting to build, it was peaceful and beautiful sixteen floors up. He had not brought a phone out to the terrace and it took him several rings to track one down. The only person who called him this early was his brother and that was usually at the end of the night rather than the beginning of the day. When Jun found the receiver on the stand, he did not recognize the flashing number of the caller. He answered anyway.

"Hello," he said, a little annoyed at being disturbed.

"Jun, this is Zhang Wei. I know it's early. I'm calling because I have an important invitation for you."

"Yes?" said Jun, now very interested and no longer annoyed.

"I would like to apologize for the late invitation. I only heard last night that the Minister of Agriculture might be able to meet you and your brother today. His secretary just phoned me to tell me of his availability this afternoon. The Minister will be at a luncheon today in Kowloon, and he would like to visit with you and your brother afterward for a short meeting. He is excited to meet the men who found this Thailand rice and who know how important it will be for the Chinese people."

After catching his breath, Jun managed to stammer, "I am very honored the Minister wishes to see us."

"Yes, and to thank you personally. It is a great honor for you."

"We will certainly accept the invitation."

"Excellent. You and your brother should be in the reception lobby of the Ritz-Carlton Hotel at 1:30. I am at the airport in Changsha now and I should arrive in Hong Kong by about 10:00. I will be joining the Minister in Kowloon for the luncheon. The Minister is having a high-level meeting at the Tin Lung Heen restaurant and will visit with you afterward. I will meet you and your brother and take you to a meeting room to see the Minister.

"1:30 at the Ritz-Carlton Hotel. We'll be there. Thank you."

"Very good. I'll see you then. Goodbye."

After switching off the phone with Zhang Wei, Jun immediately called his brother's number. There was no answer. Jun cursed and called again with the same result. He placed the phone down and left to prepare himself for the day.

After showering and dressing in his best suit for the Minister, he called his brother's line again and there was still no answer. Frustrated, Jun left his apartment and started out for his brother's flat. Chao's building was just three blocks away. Jun managed to call three times from his cell phone while he walked the short distance. The result was the same.

His brother's building was far more modern than his own. Jun was known to the doorman there, and he had his own security card to allow him to direct the lift to the twentieth floor. When he reached the apartment door, he leaned on the buzzer for a long time. Jun waited for a full minute and there was no answer. He pushed the buzzer again, this time giving it an even longer burst. About half a minute later, he heard noises from within and the door bolt snapped open. The door cracked wide enough to for a face to bend around the door. It was a young woman.

"Chao is still asleep," she said in a hushed voice.

"I'm his brother," said Jun, angry now. He pushed the door in and the woman stepped back. She was completely naked and ran to the bedroom as Jun entered.

Jun stood in the room hearing the young woman speak to his brother. He looked around the living room and saw clothes strewn on the furniture and carpet. Without needing much imagination, Jun could determine that she had come to the apartment wearing a dark blue skirt, a white blouse, pink panties, and black strappy sandals. Chao appeared to have been wearing his favorite sports jacket, an open collared shirt, and dark slacks.

Jun heard stirring in the bedroom and moments later his brother walked out in his shorts. "Hey, good morning. Pleasant surprise to see older brother here. What's going on?"

Ignoring Chao's question, Jun said, "Had a pretty good night last night, it seems."

Chao replied. "Oh, well, Daiyu and I are good friends. I saw her at the club last night and it was like old times. More importantly, and I know you will enjoy this; I met this guy who lives in Boston who attended Pelham when I was there. He owns a company there that does some type of fancy holographic, 3D, or whatever, way of imaging products and parts in real time on assembly lines. This company does manufacturing quality assurance for a whole lot of products in the U.S. Their website suggests their technology might be just perfect for exporting to China. I looked this guy up on the Pelham old boy site and he was one smart kid in school. He could be a great client for us."

"Was he part of this?" Jun gestured around the room as he sat on Chao's sofa.

Chao laughed. "No, he left the club early to go to bed. It didn't seem that clubbing was his thing last night."

"But you carried on?"

"'All work and no play makes Chao a dull boy,' right?"

"I'm not worried that you'll ever be accused of 'all work.'"

Jun noticed a half-smoked joint and small plastic bag of white powder on the soft table. "I thought you swore off those bad behaviors," he said.

"Daiyu brought them last night."

"And you did not partake?"

"Now that would have been rude, wouldn't it?"

With that, Daiyu walked into the room wrapped in a towel, and started collecting her clothes. They watched as she walked around the room. She gathered most of them before coming up to Jun. "You're sitting on my bra," she said.

Jun stood and she pulled it from the chair and went silently back to Chao's bedroom.

After she retreated, Jun spoke. "It sounds like this Boston company is a good find. But now, we have a more pressing matter to talk about."

"Right, what's so important that you wake me from my beauty sleep at the crack of dawn?"

"It's 8:30."

"I work a different shift. What's your emergency?"

"You have a lunch date today."

"Yes, I know. Daiyu has to leave town today and I'm taking her to lunch at that Italian restaurant you took me to last week."

"No, that's not what you're doing. We're meeting the Minister of Agriculture for lunch—or, rather, after his lunch. He wants to thank us personally for the Thailand rice."

"Are you serious?"

"Yes, Zhang Wei called me earlier this morning to arrange it."

"Wow. I guess I won't be able to see Daiyu later."

"No, we have to be in Kowloon at 1:30 to meet the Minister."

"1:30, hmm," Chao said, and turned to his bedroom, calling out, "Daiyu, don't dress yet. Change of plans." He turned back to Jun. "When do you want to go to Kowloon?"

"I'll pick you up with a car here at 11:00 to be safe."

Chao again looked back toward his bedroom, "Make it 11:30; we have lots of time."

* * *

The trip through the Western Harbor tunnel to Kowloon was not crowded at mid-day. Jun was feeling prosperous and he hired a car for the day rather than take a taxi. The car dropped them off in the courtyard of the International Commerce Centre and they walked to the lifts to take them to the hotel on the upper floors. They went to the initial check-in desk on the ninth floor and then boarded the upper lift to the reception lobby on the 103rd floor.

When they arrived, the lobby was not crowded and they had about an hour to kill.

"I told you we had time," said Chao. "I could have spent another half-hour with my dear friend."

"Didn't you surrender enough of your 'essence' to her already?" asked Jun.

"It's sad. You are only a few years older than me and your horizon of expectations is drastically different from mine."

"I think you flatter yourself."

"In truth, it's Daiyu who flatters me, but I doubt you want to hear about that."

"No, not a word," Jun said. "Let's go into the café for tea."

"No," said Chao. "I need a Bloody Mary. We have an hour. Let's go to the bar."

They went down one level to the bar and Chao ordered a Bloody Mary while his brother drank tea. Jun told his brother again what he knew from Zhang Wei and asked about the Boston software company.

"I think this will be a terrific deal for us," Chao said. "We have plenty of contacts that could use the technology. He's Chinese and he would like to develop a market for his company over here. Most importantly, this could be an evergreen deal since most of our new high tech manufacturing companies could use it. We could make a ton of money brokering this and..." Chao lowered his voice to a whisper. "It would all be perfectly legal."

"It's a happy day all around," said Jun. "When do you see him again?"

"He's going up to Shanghai for a few days, then we're having dinner again on Saturday. I'd invite you along except that he said we should go out clubbing afterwards since this time he'll be rested and not have to leave early."

"Then why don't you invite him to come by the office? We can talk business terms at that meeting."

"That's exactly how I saw it, big brother."

"Good, you're learning. Now let's go to the lobby and look for Zhang Wei."

In the lobby, they were almost alone, sitting in a central place so they would not be missed.

At 1:40, Zhang came off the lift and greeted them warmly. "I am delighted you were both able to come. I am sorry we are running late. The Minister is looking forward to meeting you. Let us go."

He led them to the lift. When they reached the conference room, the Minister was standing with another ministry staffer on the far side next to the window with a magnificent view. Beyond the Minister, the panoramic view of the Kowloon skyline, with the mountains behind and the east bay in the foreground, was spectacular. On this crystalline day, the shipping movement in Victoria Harbor was almost more interesting than the high government official in front of them.

The Minister noticed them as they walked in, while continuing to listen to his colleague finish speaking before he turned to them. "Liu Jun and Liu Chao, I presume?"

"Yes, Minister," said Jun.

"Thank you so much for meeting me here on such short notice," said the Minister. "I am grateful to our friend Zhang Wei for arranging it" He looked at Zhang who seemed more than pleased. "Let us sit. Would you like any tea or water before we start?"

"No, thank you, Minister," said Jun.

He and Chao were directed to seats opposite the Minister around the long table. When they were all seated, the Minister cleared his throat. "I first want to share with you all a bit of irony. Over the last hour and a half, I have been sitting with my Ministry of Agriculture counterparts from Thailand, Vietnam, and Myanmar. We have been discussing rice production and specifically, their countries' projections of surpluses for export and our country's projection of deficits for import. As you know, sadly, we have had to buy a large amount of rice from these countries over the last several years."

The Minister spoke directly to the two brothers.

"Now because of your Thailand rice, we believe we may dramatically reduce our imports from Thailand and the other countries as well. We will still need to import, but we project steady reductions of this need over the next several years. This is a most hopeful projection and it is directly related to your understanding of the domestic food needs of Chinese people. Your importation of this new special rice will help our country at this very critical time in our agricultural modernization."

Jun began to speak, but was interrupted as the Minister turned to Zhang and said, "Please show them the images that I shared with you earlier today."

"Yes, Minister," said Zhang, and he walked over to the table projector and computer in front of Jun and Chao while he explained. "These are pictures of the Thailand rice now growing in the Yangtze valley. Our inspectors tell us the rice is growing rapidly in three provinces. The plants are thriving there. The farmers responsible for these crops estimate that a thirty percent greater yield in rice will be produced from this strain. The inspectors also said that the Thailand strain will require fewer farmers to plant and fertilize it. They expect that because of the speed of growth of this rice, they may be able to generate an additional crop this year in certain growing areas. This would be amazing."

Jun stood and addressed the Minister. "We are humbled by this display of thanks and we have been honored to serve our country in this small way. We are most excited that the Ministry has taken it upon itself to plant this rice on its most productive farms. We could not be happier knowing that we might have played a small part in helping to secure food for the future of China."

The Minister said to them. "You have done a great thing. I would like to invite you both to Beijing in two weeks when the Prime Minister and other high Party members can thank you personally. We will arrange all the transportation for you. It will be a great privilege for me to be able to show you this honor."

Jun looked at Chao briefly and exclaimed, "Minister, we are overwhelmed. Thank you very much."

"No Mr. Liu, thank you."

The Minister motioned to the door and waiters came in with full champagne flutes and distributed them around the table. When everyone had a charged glass, the Minister stood. "I propose a toast to Jun, Chao, and the People of China; may they never see hunger again."

"To China," they all said. The Minister added, "She will never be hungry again."

CHAPTER 22

The large sedan arrived exactly at the agreed time. Rorke was standing in the hotel lobby and promptly walked to the portico to meet the car when it pulled in. The hotel doorman opened the car door and she slid into the back seat with Jun. She placed the large bag she carried on the floor in front of her. It was just she and Jun with the driver.

"It's a welcome change of character for you to be punctual," he said as she entered the car.

"It's the least I can do for you for showing me a part of China I have wondered about for a long time."

"And for taking you to a wonderful lunch in Guangdong as well."

"Yes, of course, and for the wonderful lunch you have planned," she said. "Remember, I have to be back by 3:00 pm for a conference call."

"Where's the call to?"

"Perth. It's another client—big money in mining and shipping."

"I'm jealous," said Jun, only half in jest.

"Don't be. He's got a wife he loves, six kids, and he's kind of a bore."

With that the car drove off into Hong Kong traffic and toward the tunnels. They were quiet and watched the city pass by the windows for a while until Jun asked, "What did you bring in the bag? You don't need a snack. I'm taking you to lunch."

"I didn't forget about lunch. Let me show you what I have," she said. "I was excited to find these. I bought them yesterday, specifically for your farm." With that she opened the bag and pulled out a new pair of flower patterned rubber boots.

She turned to him. "Aren't they lovely?"

"Yes, Sam, they're lovely. It's nice to see you embracing the spirit of the day. My employees at the farm will be very impressed."

"What do you wear when you inspect your farm?"

"Oh, that's easy. This is what I wear," he gestured to himself and his dark suit. "I inspect the farm from the back of the car. I can see all I need to see from back here."

"Well, that's no fun. If I'm going to a farm, I want to see the farm."

"I appreciate that you are as diligent in investigating my farm as you are in studying all your investments."

"From what you say, the farm business is an investment, and a good one right now."

"Yes, and it continues to improve."

"Oh? How is that?"

"Can I tell you over lunch?"

"If you'd like, certainly."

"Yes, it's news best shared in a lovely restaurant over a bottle of fine wine."

"Well, you've piqued my curiosity, but I can wait if that's what you'd prefer."

While they drove, Jun told her about his purchase of the farm, with government connections, and that it was specifically bought to test the Thailand rice after he and Chao closed the deal in Bangkok.

"I've never driven to the mainland," said Sam. "I've flown to Beijing, and to Shanghai many times, but I've never driven over."

"Then I'm delighted to be able to share this new experience with you," said Jun. "We have a special permit, again with good government connections, and we can drive in a private car rather than take a bus. You'll see how convenient it is when we go over the long bridge to the border crossing."

When they left the Hong Kong Special Administrative Region for the Shenzhen Bay Bridge, theirs was the only car, although there was heavy bus traffic. On the mainland side, the driver met the border police with the documents Jun had obtained from his government connection the day earlier. After a brief look by the boundary policeman, they exited their right drive island car and moved to the left drive car waiting for them.

"Did you see how smoothly that went?" asked Jun, proudly.

"Yes, very impressive," said Rorke.

"That's the beauty of having solid government connections."

"You continue to be a superb example of a man of the people."

"Government works for the people as well as the other way around. You just want to ensure the right balance," said Jun.

They avoided the bulk of the traffic of metropolitan Shenzhen, and drove along the countryside, passing through smaller villages for most of the time.

"This is beautiful," said Sam, as the scenery they passed was dominated by lowland farms in the foreground and camel-backed, rocky cliffs creeping out from the emerald green fields beyond.

They drove for about fifteen minutes when the car pulled off to a side path—no more than an ox path—and slowly moved on the path for a few hundred meters. Cultivated rice paddies lined both sides of the path, and farmers worked in the fields on the rice crop. Without an obvious landmark, the car stopped abruptly in the path.

"Welcome to my farm," said Jun.

Sam looked around from the back seat. Three men stood in front of their car. They were surrounded by rice paddies.

"Jun," she asked, smiling, "Where is the manor house? Where are your stables?"

"We can talk about that over lunch," he said.

"Well, that should be interesting. Now are we going to inspect the farm?"

"This is where we part company for a while. You are going to hear about the Thailand rice and I am going to have a cigarette—possibly two, right here, depending on your interest in my crop."

"Okay, I will carry on without you." She dropped her heels and slipped into her floral rubber Wellingtons. "I'll miss you."

"I'm sure you will," he said, as he removed a pack of cigarettes. "Mr. Wu will answer all of your questions. Let him speak to you in English. He's been practicing, and he doesn't know you are fluent in both Mandarin and, if I may say, Cantonese as well."

"Fine, I will be happy to be a simple Anglo. Be a love and please open the window before I come back," she pointed to his cigarette.

She exited the car and walked to the three men, bowing slightly to them before speaking in English, "Mr. Wu, I am Samantha Rorke."

The oldest of the three men bowed back and said, "We are happy to show you Mr. Liu's farm." He waved his hand toward her boots. "I see you are prepared. Please follow me."

Wu led her away from the car to a path leading onto the paddy. The rice plants were tall and full and blanketed the fields on all sides. After walking to the rim of the paddy, Mr. Wu stopped.

"Ms. Rorke," he said, in heavily accented English, "Mr. Liu owns all of this property on this side of the road. The boundaries of his land are the road behind us, the road you can see off to your right, a stream that you can't see ahead of us, and the line running from the stream to the shed."

He looked to see that she understood and continued speaking. "We have rice growing on most of the land. The rice on that side of the road," he pointed with his hand, "belongs to another farmer. That is our usual Chinese rice."

The he turned slightly. "The taller rice on this side is Mr. Liu's Thailand rice. It was planted at the same time as our neighbor's rice. You can see that compared to our usual rice, the Thailand rice grows much more quickly."

Rorke caught the eye of one of the other two men and exchanged a knowing nod.

"May I take a picture of the two rice fields?" she asked.

"Yes, of course," said Mr. Wu.

She took out her cell phone and captured several images, including pictures of the three men.

"Other than how quickly it grows, is the Thailand rice any different?"

"Oh yes, very different," said Wu. "The Thailand rice does not seem to need as much water to start, and its roots go deeper. It also produces more rice than normal plants."

"Can you tell the difference between the two rice strains just by looking at them?"

"Yes, and no," said Wu. "You see, when we have two fields side by side, the difference now is obvious and we know they are different because each field was planted at almost the same time. One field grows much faster. After the plants mature, the Thailand rice is a little taller but it is not that different. We think the Thailand rice mixes in with the normal rice and makes the comparisons difficult. Also, the rice yield is higher with the Thailand rice. You can't appreciate that by just seeing the plants in the field."

"Is anything else different about them?"

"The rice does seem to plant itself, or at least spreads on its own."

"Can you show me what you mean when you say the 'rice plants itself?'" asked Rorke.

"Come, I'll show you," Wu said, and led her back to the road. Sam caught the eye of the other workers and discreetly pointed to the field of the Thailand rice. She followed Wu up to the road and beyond the car. Liu was talking on his cell phone and smoking a cigarette in the car. He waved to her as they walked by.

"See the small plants growing just outside of the paddy across the road?" gestured Wu. "Those are Mr. Liu's rice plants that planted themselves on our neighbor's land. I'm sure our neighbor will be happy that we are growing rice for him. I think it will be hard for Mr. Liu to keep his Thailand rice on his own land if he is trying to sell it."

"That is very interesting, Mr. Wu. Is there anything else you would like to show me?"

"I think that is the end of the show," said Wu. "Unless you want to see our fertilizer and tool shed."

"I think I can miss the tool shed," she said. "Thank you for the tour."

She followed Wu back to the car. Before leaving, she gestured with her head to the other two men in the direction of the rogue rice plants.

A light rain began to fall as they walked back to the car.

"Perfect timing, Mr. Wu. Thank you again for the tour."

The driver left his seat and walked back to open the door for Rorke. She entered the car and sat next to Jun.

Liu put up his finger as he was still on the phone, and she heard him beg off the call to whomever he was speaking with. He switched off the phone and asked, "How did you enjoy the tour of my estate?"

"It was interesting—modest, of course, but interesting."

"We do what we can do. Unless you have additional questions for Mr. Wu, let's go to lunch and we can talk about additional farms in my future."

"Mr. Wu was quite helpful. Please tell him he gave me a wonderful tour and that his English was more than acceptable."

"Thank you. He'll be pleased when he hears that." The car backed down the small path and merged onto the dirt road. There were few automobiles on the lightly traveled country roads and they reached the restaurant in about fifteen minutes.

Jun left the car before the driver could open his door and he walked around to open Sam's door. He said to the driver, "Just bring in the wine, please."

They walked to the door of the small inn and Jun allowed Sam to enter first. The entrance room was dark, which did little to hide the very welcoming expression of the innkeeper who greeted Jun in Cantonese when he arrived.

Even though there were few other patrons in the dining area, the innkeeper showed them to a private room with a small round table and two chairs that had obviously been arranged for them. The driver walked in with four bottles of wine.

The Innkeeper hustled into the room with a wine bucket for the two bottles of white, while the driver placed the two bottles of red wine on the table.

"Are you hoping to get me drunk?" she asked.

Jun smiled, and was quiet until the innkeeper left the room. After he left, Jun spoke to her quietly. "I'm not trying to get you drunk. His food is wonderful. However, his wine list is a little lacking for my taste. I selected two wines that are excellent complements to his meals, depending on what you order. This Spanish Chardonnay is not very oaky and will not fight most of the flavors in Chinese cooking. The other is a French Grenache, a little sweet, but Rhone wines go well with any number of Chinese sauces. I think you'll find a combination you like."

"Thank you. You're the perfect host and, again, a model proletariat for the Peoples Republic."

"I try to do my part."

A waiter was sent in and he uncorked and poured the wine and took their lunch orders.

When he left, Jun spoke. "You know we still have about a third of our workforce in China working in agriculture. In the 1900s, about 40 percent of American workers were involved with agriculture and now it's less than two percent. It was all due to mechanized farming. With the number of our young people going to the cities and the number of factories being built, we need to be more efficient with our agriculture. Even the Japanese have a better approach to implementing farm machines to help with the work. That is why the Thailand rice is such a benefit. Our farmers will be able to be more productive with our current methods, and we can gradually change over to more modern farming practices."

"Can the Japanese help you?"

Jun laughed. "That's worse than having the Americans help us." He added, "How do you like the wine?"

"I like the Rhone. I don't usually like sweeter wines, but this is very pleasant."

"I thought you would enjoy it. Now let me tell you about the meeting I had yesterday that I was teasing you with—although you probably already forgot you were being teased."

"No, I hadn't forgotten. I was simply being polite, waiting for you to bring it up."

"Of course you were," Jun said. "Well, I said that my agriculture business was improving. I don't think it can be any better than it is now. Chao and I met the Minister of Agriculture yesterday. We were called to meet him in Kowloon and he was most enthusiastic about the seeds we imported."

"That's very exciting. Congratulations."

"Yes, and I want to show you a digital souvenir from that meeting, a wonderful gift as it were. Zhang Wei, our contact at the Ministry, sent these images to me on my cell phone."

Jun reached across the table and showed her each image of the rice fields. "Those are lovely, aren't they?"

"Lovely. What exactly am I looking at?" she asked.

"You are seeing our rice growing on government farms in three provinces along the Yangtze. These are our most productive farms, and they will now be supercharged with the Thailand rice. The Minister was most excited."

"Can you send me those images?" she asked. "I'd like to print them and add them to your investment file."

"Yes, I would be happy to share them with you."

"You must be proud of your success," she said. "Congratulations again. Here's a toast to you," she said, lifting her glass to him.

"Yes, a toast to me," he laughed.

"Now that your agriculture business is going so well, I suppose you want me to convert all of your investments into bonds and cash. You can just clip coupons and never have a loss."

"No. The more the cash flows in, the more comfortable I am taking risks."

"You wouldn't need me at all if you converted all your portfolio to fixed income. It will be easy, and you wouldn't have a financial worry in the world."

"That would be no fun at all."

"That depends on what you consider 'fun.'"

"Please, Sam, you know me. You know I'm a player."

"Yes, Jun. I know that well. You are a player. We'll have lots of fun."

He smiled at her. She smiled back, thinking of something else.

CHAPTER 23

Franco sat with Sloan in his hotel room when the knock hit the door. Franco walked to the door and let Hal in. Hal carried a large satchel over one shoulder and seemed to be in a good mood.

"The specimens from both provinces are here," he said to Paul. "Both of my guys came through with these today." He slipped the bag off his shoulder. "Sam called. She'll be a little late. Let's start."

Hal began laying out the contents of the satchel on the bed. The contents were again leaves in plastic bags. One group of bags was numbered one to six in a black pen. Another group was marked A through E in a blue pen.

"Tell me if you see our rice plants," he said to Sloan.

Sloan became excited seeing the leaves. He put on his glasses and started to examine the specimens on the bed. "These are older plants," he said almost to himself.

"Is that a problem?" asked Franco.

"It's good and bad," replied Sloan. "It's good because the veins in the leaves are easier to see and they don't deteriorate as quickly. It's bad because they are more variable in their orientation."

"Are you going to have enough specimens to identify Buddy's plants?" asked Hal.

"We'll see," said Sloan, as he removed the first specimen and examined it with a hand magnifier, holding it up to the light.

Hal and Franco watched Sloan go through each of the bags, carefully examining each of the leaves before replacing them in their bag.

He separated them into four piles as he finished with them—two piles for each group.

When Sloan finished, he looked at Hal and Franco and pointed to the larger piles, "These are Buddy's rice for sure."

Sloan pointed at the smaller piles, "These are almost certainly Buddy's rice, too. There is just a little too much variability of the leaf direction to be completely certain. Anyway, Buddy's rice is definitely growing in both these places."

"Very good, Paul," said Hal. "Thank you for..."

Hal was interrupted by another knock on the door. Franco opened it, and Rorke came in.

"What did I miss?" she asked.

Hal spoke. "Paul confirms that Buddy's rice is in both groups."

"Are you 100 percent on this, Paul?" she said.

"Yes, 100 percent," he confirmed.

"Okay, good," she said. "Paul, we'll see you later. I think we've done what we needed to do here today. I'll give you a call tomorrow to let you know what the schedule is."

"That's fine," said Sloan. "I'll be expecting your call."

"Goodbye." She turned and said brusquely, "Franco, come with me."

Franco smiled at Sloan as they walked out the door.

In the hall, Rorke led the way to the elevators and pressed the lobby button. No one spoke on the trip down. In the lobby in front of the elevators, Rorke turned close to Hal and spoke to him in a whisper. Franco did not hear what she said. Hal nodded and turned.

Rorke added, "I'll speak with you later when I know a little more. Franco, come with me."

Hal gave a small wave as he left them, and Franco followed her to a corner of the lobby.

She turned to Franco and said, "I was having a pretty good day until about twenty minutes ago," she said.

"I assume you want to talk about it."

"Yeah, I do, because it involves you."

Franco said nothing.

"I received both a text and an e-mail earlier in the day that I just got around to reading. I was tromping around in the rice fields and entertaining our thief for most of the day and, to be honest, it was kind of fun. Unfortunately, your drinking pal, Buddy, sent me the text and spoiled the whole day."

"How did he do that?"

"Buddy says he needs to see me in Honolulu as soon as possible. He has urgent news that he must share."

"Do you know what's going on?"

"Probably. He also says he needs you to come. He says he trusts you. I'm not sure why. You need to come with me to keep Buddy happy. We all have to keep Buddy happy."

She moved closer to Franco. "To be honest, I'm more than a little pissed off he's demanding that you come along. Unfortunately, he was very clear about that. I don't like it but it will be less painful for me to bring you along than to deal with Buddy if I don't."

"I guess I'm flattered. What's the big emergency? You said you thought you knew."

"Franco, damn it, I try to teach you one little lesson, and you just won't learn. Now, how do I feel about your constant annoying questions?"

He said nothing.

"You'll know what you need to know when you need to know it. Now what you need to do is to pack a travel bag for two days, max. I think we'll be leaving within the hour, and I'll call you when I know."

"Okay."

"I imagine you have more than one passport with you. Knowing you, I'm sure you didn't surrender all of them when you retired from Naval Intelligence."

"Well, yeah, I do."

"What countries?"

"Canada, Italy, and Spain."

"Good, use the Spanish one for this trip. Bring your U.S. passport, too. You may need it when we come back to the States. Stay in your room. I'll call you when I confirm the plan."

* * *

Rorke took a cab to her hotel and packed a bag for the trip ahead. She took another cab to a property a few blocks from the Hong

Kong Macau Ferry Terminal at Sheung Wan. She had been to this building several times before.

The building was a tired and decaying three story mixed-use structure set in the middle of a block and flanked with similar buildings on both sides. She circled the block once before stopping at the front door, cautiously looking around her. Satisfied that no one was giving her any special attention, she stepped up to the landing and pushed the buzzer at the door. Although no surveillance equipment was visible from the doorstep, Rorke knew the person or persons manning the equipment in the building were watching her.

The door lock snapped open and she entered. She walked down the small hallway to the metal door on the left. She saw no one else. She had not expected to. The metal door was secured with a mechanical combination door lock that she opened with the correct nine number code. She pushed the door open to the plain room that contained a metal desk, two unpadded metal chairs, and a telephone on the table. She closed the door behind her and punched in the number. A few minutes later, an old man's voice came over the line.

"Yes?" Sleep was in his voice, as she expected.

"Sorry for the early hour, sir, but you wanted to know."

"Go ahead."

"We have confirmation, solid confirmation, at three sites and soft data for several more."

"That's enough to move on."

"I have a problem, though. My rich friend is summoning me for an urgent meeting."

The Admiral hesitated.

"Where?"

"Hawaii."

"You know what he wants to talk about. He just had his golf game two days ago."

"Yes, sir, I do. He wants your old friend from New Zealand to come with me."

"I suppose that's okay. You'll have a chaperone. My old friend from New Zealand may help you save your virginity."

"That's a funny joke from you for this time of day."

"Thank you," said the old man.

"You know, sir, I should sue your ass for harassment."

"You keep threatening that. Of course, you should. Go ahead. I'm sure I deserve it."

"Maybe later. Right now, sir, I need transportation to Hawaii."

After a short pause, he said, "I have a ride sitting in Taipei. I can arrange for it to take you there, and I'll have another one ready to take you back."

"Where do you want me to meet it? Macau?"

"Yes, you know the drill. Our contact in Macau is still good. The bird can be there in a little over two hours."

"I'll head there right away. Depending on the ferry times, it may take me closer to three."

"That's fine. They can use any extra time for fueling and food." He hesitated and asked, "When is cleaning day?"

"Scheduled for this weekend."

"You should make it back easily if you don't spend too much time with your rich friend."

"I don't plan on doing that." She changed the subject, "What do you want me to do about the professor? His job is done."

"How ready are you for him in Hawaii?"

"His electronics are fine. I don't have 'eyes' there yet. That will take a day or two."

"Do you have 'eyes' where you are?"

"Yes."

"Well, I suggest you keep him over with you until you're comfortable with your preparations in Hawaii."

"That was my plan."

"Good, one other thing," said the old man.

"Yes?"

"You better put the fear of God into your randy Texan. We have to start getting control of him."

"Yes sir. I will."

"Have a good flight, and make sure everyone on your team goes to smoke after this is over. Everyone leaves the country, no exceptions. Keep them away with no contact for at least three or four months, depending on how it goes."

"Yes, sir," she said.

"Anything else?"

"No, sir."

"Call me when it's all done." With that, the Admiral switched off the call.

CHAPTER 24

Franco sat in his room. He was packed and ready to leave when she called.

"Meet me at the Macau Ferry Terminal at Sheung Wan. Get there right away. The ferry leaves in forty minutes."

"Understood," was all he said, and she disconnected the phone.

He caught a cab right away from the hotel cab stand and felt lucky to get it since rush hour was already in full swing. Although it was a short distance to the terminal, it still took his taxi fifteen minutes to navigate the packed streets. When he approached, he saw Rorke on the sidewalk.

As he exited the cab, she walked up to him.

"Do you have the Spanish passport?" she asked quietly.

"Si."

"What's your name?""

"Miguel Fernandez," he said. "Como te llamas?"

"Bridget Donohue."

"Not very original, yet certainly appropriate," he said, speaking English with a Spanish accent.

"Do you think you can remember it?" she asked.

"Si, probably. Are you Irish?"

"No, Canadian. I don't fake accents well. Here's your ticket." She handed him the ticket. "If you're asked, you work for a casino in Spain and you're checking out the gambling on Macau."

"That's easy. I lived near Marbella for a year. I loved that casino there. I can do that one."

"Good. For purposes of this trip, I'm your girlfriend."

"Hmm, that won't be as easy. I may not be able to pull that off."

She leaned up to his ear and kissed it. "Miguel, if you want to keep your nuts where they are, you'd better figure out how to play that role fast. Let's go."

She took his arm, and they walked to the ferry. It was the jet ferry and the travel time for the forty-mile ride to Macau was just about an hour. The crossing was smooth and there were no delays. They cleared border control without a problem, particularly as Rorke, or Bridget Donohue, had a Hong Kong permanent identity card, and charmed the border control man in Cantonese.

Once inside the arrivals terminal, Franco asked, "Where to?"

Rorke shook her head and spoke under her breath, "Dipshit. Just one thing I ask you to remember…"

Franco said nothing, and followed her to the cabstand.

She spoke to the driver in Chinese, and Franco understood the words "Venetian Hotel."

In the dying daylight, they drove across Macau and down the Cotai Strip. As all the casino lights came to life, the "Las Vegas of Asia" label was appropriate in every way. One had to work hard to see any of the old Portuguese influence left on the strip.

The Vegas feel continued into the hotel lobby, which seemed strangely familiar and western. They checked into the room with their new identities and she continued to hold his arm like a newlywed.

When the door closed to their room, her sweetness evaporated immediately and she was all business.

"Franco, here's what we're going to do. I'm leaving in about two minutes to go to the general aviation terminal at the Macau airport. It's called the Macau Business Aviation Center Terminal. You'll follow me there in ten minutes. Don't go through the lobby—go out one of the side doors near the little shopping mall they have here. You'll be able to catch a cab on the street. It's about a five-minute ride from here. When you arrive, if you don't see me, ask for Mr. Yang at the main desk. Tell them you are Senor Fernandez. Tell them you are flying to Las Vegas tonight and you want to know if your plane is here. Now, if you have any questions about what I just told you, you may feel free to ask a question."

"Yeah, why Las Vegas if we're going to Hawaii?"

"Because casino executives go back and forth from Macau to Vegas every day. No one will think twice about the itinerary."

"So I shouldn't mention Hawaii?"

"No, Franco. You shouldn't mention Hawaii. Any other questions? This is your chance."

Franco shook his head.

"Good," she said, taking the "Do Not Disturb" hangtag from the inside door handle and moving it to the outside door handle. "I'll see you there."

"No goodbye kiss?" asked Franco.

"Sorry," she said. "We broke up." She turned and left with her overnight bag in hand.

Franco left ten minutes later and found his way to the street via the glitzy shopping area. He hailed a cab and arrived at the terminal a few minutes later.

The modern and large general aviation terminal was easy to find and it was adjacent to the commercial terminal. The runways were beyond, isolated on their own separate landfill island and connected by two land bridges to the terminal.

After leaving the cab, Franco walked into the terminal and stopped at the main desk. A young woman sitting behind the desk looked up at him.

"Do you speak English or, maybe Spanish?" he asked her in his Spanish accent.

"English," she said with an equally heavy Chinese accent.

"Yes, my name is Miguel Fernandez. I am looking for Mr. Yang."

She said, "One moment, please." She picked up the telephone, pressed a number, and spoke in Chinese, although he heard the name Fernandez mentioned.

After the call, she turned to him and announced, "Mr. Yang will be right here."

Franco waited there briefly until he saw a man open a door down the hallway and walk toward him.

"Senor Fernandez," said Yang in perfect English, "I am Mr. Yang. Please follow me. Your colleague was asking about you."

Yang led him back through the door he had just come through, down a hallway that coursed through a lounge area, and to a separate conference room at the end of the hallway. Rorke was sitting in a chair across from a man dressed in the usual general aviation pilot's uniform of a white shirt with epaulets and dark slacks.

At the doorway, Yang looked to Franco and asked, "Senor Fernandez, may I have your passport please. I will clear you through the customs process."

Franco glanced at Rorke, who had overheard Yang and she nodded to him as he handed Yang the passport.

"Thank you," said Yang, and left the room.

After he left, Rorke spoke to Franco.

"This is Bob Talbot who will be flying us to Vegas tonight," she said.

The pilot extended his hand. "Nice to meet you, Mr. Fernandez. I expect that you and Ms. Donohue will have a comfortable flight. We'll have great tailwinds and it should be a relatively short trip."

"When do we leave?" asked Franco.

"We topped off our tanks when we arrived and we'll leave as soon as Mr. Yang finishes your passport and customs clearance. I'm going back to the plane. I'll see you there." He stood and walked out of the room.

Franco and Rorke said nothing while waiting for Yang, who returned in a few minutes.

"May I take you to your plane?" Yang asked, returning the passport to Franco.

Without waiting for an answer, he led them back out and down another hallway to an exterior door. A guard sat behind a desk in front of the door. He nodded to Yang and his visitors and they walked past him, out the door, and onto the tarmac where the large business jet was parked.

At the foot of the air stairs, Yang said his goodbye and turned to walk back to the terminal. A large man was stationed at the foot of the stairs. "Welcome," was all he said, as Rorke and Franco climbed the stairs. The man followed them up into the plane and closed the aircraft door behind them. He sat in one of the forward chairs as the engines started.

Rorke pulled a magazine off the rack, took a chair, and kicked off her shoes. Franco walked to the cockpit to introduce himself to the co-pilot and look over the flight deck before coming back to sit across from Rorke.

He said nothing to her, nor she to him, until they had taken off and reached their cruising altitude.

Franco broke the ice and asked her, "Can we talk?"

She half looked up, put down her magazine, and said, "Sure."

"Am I still Miguel Fernandez?" he asked in a quiet voice.

"No. You're back to Franco. This is a 'Company' plane and Talbot and the crew work for the 'Company,' just like me."

"Oh, good," said Franco, looking around the cabin. "Now, you said you think you know what Buddy wants."

"Yes, I did."

"Do I 'need to know?'"

"I've been giving that serious thought. I'm not sure if I want you to be naturally surprised, or for you to be briefed ahead of time to ensure that you don't say anything stupid."

"Have you made a decision yet?"

"I have." She focused her stare at him. "I want it all, or at least parts of both of them. Does that surprise you?"

He laughed. "No. Not a bit."

Rorke stood and said, "Let me bring you a drink and we'll discuss Buddy. What would you like?"

"Lots of scotch on a little bit of ice," he said.

"Coming right up," she said, walking to the galley. She found the ice and the scotch bottle, poured his drink and came back with his drink and a glass of wine for herself.

"Thank you," said Franco, when she handed him his glass.

She curled her knees under her in the large chair and took a sip of her wine. "What you're going to hear from Buddy is that the biotech product, this special protein his friend, Shelly, was working on has been cancelled. Buddy will have just learned it last week when they had their annual golf game."

"You seem pretty sure of that," he said.

"Yes, 100 percent."

"How?"

"Not your problem," she said dismissively.

"Okay, so how does that affect us?" asked Franco, changing the question.

"You'll have to hear that from Buddy. That's the 'naturally surprised' part."

"I'm a pretty good actor. You can tell me now."

"I don't think so. What I need from you is to be sympathetic rather than anything else. Above all, Buddy must not hear about the theft of his rice. That part is the absolute requirement. As far as we all know, his rice is happy, safe, and secure with the USDA on Molokai. Is that all perfectly clear?"

"Sure," he said.

"Franco, is it perfectly clear to you that Buddy cannot know that his rice was stolen?"

"Yeah, like I just said, perfectly clear. What's going on?"

"Franco, repeat after me, 'The rice is safe on Molokai.'"

"I got it."

"Say it!"

"'The rice is safe on Molokai,'" he repeated, rolling his eyes.

"Well done. That's the story when we see Buddy." Her eyes darted back to her magazine.

There was a tense silence.

"Okay, let me change the subject. Why have you spent all this effort setting these guys up? You've given them a lot of time."

She had a distant look in her eyes before she answered him. "It's very personal with me, and it is for Hal, too, for that matter. My family had been doing well in Hong Kong until my father was ruined by a crony business deal the Communist Party bastards set up. Dad's business tanked and my family went broke. We had to move back to the states. My poor father never recovered from it."

Franco watched her.

"For Hal, it's even worse. Four party goons beat up his father over a trumped-up offense and threw him in jail. His father died there a few years later. As you might guess, Hal is still very angry at the PRC and the Communist party."

"So that's what moves you?"

"Yup, revenge and hate—not very attractive, although highly motivating. Generally speaking, I don't like thieves. I have nothing personal against our thieves. In fact, I think the older brother is quite charming. However, their activities are greatly damaging to American interests, and they have to be stopped."

"I guess that helps me understand," he said.

"Good. No more questions," she said, looking down at the magazine.

"Not quite," he said, holding up a hand. "What's the schedule? When do we see Buddy?"

"We're due at his place at 1330 tomorrow. We should arrive in Honolulu about 2300 local tonight. We'll have plenty of time for beauty sleep before we see Buddy. You're off duty until 1315 when I'll expect to see you in the lobby of our hotel. You can have another drink or two now if you like. You have free time all morning."

"Gee, thanks," he said.

"It's an easy job for you, Franco." She turned a page on her magazine as she said it.

"I do have one more question," he said cautiously.

She sighed loudly and looked up. "Okay..."

"What's going on with Sloan?" he asked.

"What do you mean?"

"Is he being watched?"

"What do you think?"

"Never mind. It was a stupid question," said Franco.

"Mikey, remember I've told you to watch out for asking idiotic questions. Now, if you don't want me to be angry with you, would you be a dear and do the honors for the next round?" She held up her glass. "After that, I'm going to the couch on the port side of the plane and I'm going to sleep. I'll leave you alone with your imagination."

CHAPTER 25

When he came down to the hotel lobby the next afternoon, Rorke was standing there, texting on her phone. She said nothing when he walked over to her, and just turned abruptly and walked to the doorman to tell him she needed a cab. The doorman whistled and the first cab in line came through the portico. Franco followed her to the curb and into the car.

Without a "hello," she launched in. "We have a departure slot at 1600. We have no more than 90 minutes to give Buddy, if we need to stay that long."

"What time do we arrive back in Hong Kong?" he asked.

"We should land in Macau about 1900 local on Friday and after that it depends on when we catch the ferry back to Hong Kong."

"Do we go back to the Venetian?"

"No, we'll be checked out."

"That seems a shame."

"Yeah, a real shame," she said absently. She pulled her cell phone from her purse and began scanning it for texts and e-mails. Franco correctly assumed the conversation was over.

Without another word, they drove across Honolulu, down Ala Moana Boulevard past the boat harbor and into Buddy's neighborhood. The friendly doorman at Buddy's building welcomed them and addressed Rorke by name. Paku was standing with the doorman and, after a quick greeting, he walked them to the private elevator. Paku placed both thumbs on the security reader and on seeing the green light, pressed the floor number to Buddy's apartment. The ride up was silent.

When the elevator discharged them in Buddy's entrance hall, Paku activated another security pad on the wall and, when the lock snapped open, led them to one of the interior rooms on the floor.

"Mr. Jerome is on a call that will be ending soon. Would you like a drink while you wait?" he said.

They declined and Paku left them, closing the wood and smoked glass door behind him.

The room was a classic study with high full bookshelves made of cherry, stained dark. There was no desk, and the rest of the furniture was a mix of leather couches and chairs arranged around a large circular coffee table with the same finish as the bookshelves. Franco began to seat himself in one of the chairs while he admired the room.

As he was sitting, Rorke said, "Don't sit there, Franco. Buddy will want that chair. Sit on the couch."

Franco did as he was told without comment.

She sat in one of the other chairs and again pulled out her phone, reading messages.

"How did you sleep?" he asked.

She didn't respond, just continued to read the cell phone. "Did you have lunch at the hotel?"

She didn't look up or answer the question.

Franco gave up and started walking around the room inspecting the library. He wondered how many of the leather-bound books Buddy had actually read. He decided the answer would probably surprise him either way.

About ten minutes later, the door opened and Buddy's round, smiling face beamed in. Buddy wore an open collar Hawaiian shirt, blue jeans, and cowboy boots, and he charged into the room. Franco walked over to greet him, although Rorke stayed sitting.

"Mike, good to see you again," he said, shaking Franco's hand. "Sam, you look beautiful as usual. You must still be working out."

Rorke just said, "Hello, Buddy."

Buddy leaned over to kiss her cheek and remarked, "You smell good. Same perfume?"

"Yes, same perfume."

Buddy sat in his chair. "You're probably wondering why I asked you to come here on such short notice."

Rorke looked at him and replied evenly, "Yes, we are."

"Sam, before I tell you, I have to ask you something."

"Sure, what can I tell you?"

"Tell me what's the dollar limit on gifts federal employees can accept?"

Rorke waited briefly before answering. "For gifts, since we are the agency regulating you, the answer is 'zero.' We can't accept anything. We're also not supposed to be enjoying any of those wonderful dinners that Paku has prepared for us in the past. Strictly forbidden. That goes for your fifty-year-old scotch, too."

"That's no fun," said Buddy. "What if you weren't regulating me?"

"It goes all the way up to $50 in value in a year."

"Hell, Sam, I can't pour you a good glass of wine for $50."

"I know, Buddy. We public servants need to make serious sacrifices, or at least that's what's in the rulebook. I don't want an inspector from the Office of Government Ethics to spoil our fun. Sadly, that's how it is."

"You don't seem to fret much about that," commented Buddy.

"No, not much," she said coyly. "It never seems to help."

Buddy thought for a second and his expression brightened. He asked, "What if I just loaned something to you?"

"I still don't think it will cut it with the OGE. Why don't you tell me what you're talking about?"

Buddy opened the drawer on the lamp table next to his chair and took out a small velvet case. He walked to her chair and opened the case for her inspection. In the case lay a diamond necklace, lots of diamonds, large diamonds.

"It's exquisite, Buddy, and it looks as if it might be valued at a little more than $50."

"Yeah, like maybe a hundred and fifty grand. Do me a favor and show me how it looks on you."

She looked at the catch and said to him, "Would you help me put it on?"

She turned her back to him on her chair and pulled her hair aside. Buddy gently draped the jewelry around her neck, and fastened the catch.

When he returned to his seat, she turned toward him and asked, "How do you like it?"

"I love it. It's just like I imagined it would look. Just fantastic. It helps draw attention to your lovely chest, not that you need much help there. It looks like it was made for you—and literally, it was."

"Buddy, thank you for the necklace. It was very sweet of you. I'm not sure I'm going to keep it, though. It might land me in a lot of trouble." She swept her hands over the diamonds before asking, "Would you give me a job if the OGE found out about this and fired me?"

Buddy looked very pleased with himself as he chuckled, "Honey, you know the answer to that."

"That's comforting. Now, what's the reason for the gift?"

"First, I don't know that I need to have any special excuse to help you look even more lovely than usual. To your point, you saved me several millions of dollars over the last year. This is payback for that."

"What do you mean?" asked Rorke.

"Well," said Buddy slowly, "I saw my friend, Shelly, last week for our annual golf game. As you know, I launched this rice project because of Shelly's pharmaceutical interest in this protein he's been working on." Buddy paused and looked at Franco and Rorke to see that they were following him.

"Well, it's been two years since I saw Shelly, and it's been over a year since you USDA types took my rice. Had I asked Shelly about his project a year ago, I would have been surprised to learn they shelved the project. They closed it right up, tight as a drum, about 18 months ago."

"That's too bad, Buddy. All that work for nothing," said Rorke.

Franco wondered why Rorke hadn't immediately asked why they shut down the project.

"Why did Shelly abandon the project?" asked Franco. He noticed that Rorke gave him a sharp look.

"That's an interesting story, Mike. It turns out that Shelly's protein failed their safety testing—specifically their tests to see if it caused cancer in mice and rats. And boy, oh boy, did it ever! Shelly said his toxicology guys said they never saw anything like it before. In both species, all animals came down with lung tumors, malignant lung tumors, cancer, and they all died of them. It happened at about the seven-month exposure time. The animals looked good until boom, lung cancer everywhere.

"Shelly said it was a fragment of his protein that got activated in the liver or kidney or something like that. It was this activation that made it cause cancer. I guess this is a little like the gluten story only not with wheat protein and celiac disease. With Shelly's protein, it's lung cancer. Shelly said it was a pro-onco something or other and some de-repressor type of thing that hit the lung. Anyway, bingo, bad news for rats. Professor Sloan would probably know about how these things work. He'd be interested. Maybe I should have invited him here?"

"He's on assignment," said Rorke quickly. "He couldn't have come anyway."

"Let him know," said Buddy. "I'm sure he'll find it fascinating."

"I'm sure he will. We'll take care of that," said Rorke.

"Do they think cancer could happen in people who might be exposed to this protein?" Franco blurted out.

Buddy said excitedly, "Yeah, the FDA sure does. Shelly said the toxicology boys in his company have over two hundred years of combined experience in looking at these sorts of studies, and they have never seen anything like this. They said that if you smoke, it would likely even be worse."

"That's very interesting, Buddy, and that's too bad," said Rorke, before Franco could speak again.

Buddy continued, "Now if y'all hadn't come along and busted me for jumping the gun on this, I'd have spent millions more on growing and processing this protein out of rice and after all that money was spent, that damned Shelly would have the last laugh when he told me they scrubbed the project. Well, you saved me a lot of serious cash by taking my plants out of circulation. The only good news in all this—besides meeting you, Sam—was that I didn't have to tell Shelly what we were doing. I didn't have to give that sorry New York bastard the last laugh."

"You didn't say anything to Shelly?" asked Rorke.

"Certainly not. Not a word. It would have been too damned embarrassing. The joke was on me, again," said Buddy. "Anyway, you take all the plants. We don't want them now. My lawyers will be giving you full permission to dispose of them however you want to do it. I'm officially going to forget the whole thing. I'll figure out another way to get to Shelly."

Franco tried to process what he had just heard. Buddy grinned at Rorke. "Honey, that's why I want you to have this little necklace. Just me, Mike, and you know about it, and I'm damned sure none of us will tell anyone. Right, Mike?"

Franco said nothing.

"This is all for saving you a little money?" Rorke asked.

"No, Sam, it's all for saving me a lot of money." He had a silly grin on his face as he watched her play with the necklace. "Nice, huh?"

"Yes, very nice, Buddy. However, we have another issue," said Rorke firmly.

"What's that?"

"If your rice protein is so powerfully carcinogenic, we may need site inspectors to interview and evaluate our employees' practices with the plants and possibly we'll have to do testing on them. I don't know. You might be endangering USDA staff."

"Let's be clear, Sam. I didn't exactly force this rice on you. You took it."

"Sorry, Buddy. You do have a role in this."

"Okay. Well, the ball's in your court, and you can damn sure keep the ball. You do what you have to do. I don't want that rice back. I don't even want to think about it."

"It may not be that easy. I want to check around to see if there are any workman's comp claims coming or, I hate to say it, to determine the potential for lawsuits in the future."

Buddy looked at her closely. "Lawsuits for what?"

"I don't know. There may be process violations that I don't know about. Possibly, there's negligence for putting federal employees at risk. I don't know. Things can turn ugly when the Inspector General's reports are picked up by the plaintiff's bar. You know that. You have deep pockets. That attracts the sharks."

"I'll have my legal boys take a look at it."

"No. Before you do that, let me investigate this a little myself. I think there's probably a very good chance of making this just go away, and burying this material the way we do with most of the quarantined items," she said.

"Okay, I'll keep quiet until I hear from you."

"Good, and it's critical that you don't tell anyone about this. And I mean no one. I don't want employees lawyering up, or going to the press, or getting anxious over nothing. I don't want your legal staff putting any of this on paper anywhere That means don't tell them anything for now. Do you agree?"

"I do. I won't tell anyone."

"Who knows about Shelly's cancer-causing protein and your rice?"

"If you mean who knows about both, the way they're connected? It's just the folks in this room."

"We need to keep it that way," said Rorke.

"I promise," said Buddy. "I feel pretty dumb about this whole thing and I sure don't want it coming out, and particularly, I do not want it to ever reach Shelly's ears. You'll never hear another word of this from me."

"I hope not," said Rorke, as she fondled her new necklace.

Franco just watched them. He was aware that his breathing had changed and that his breaths were shallow, coming more frequently. He said nothing. He had no words to form his questions or to express his feelings.

CHAPTER 26

The three men watched the old car creep down the dirt driveway of Happy Stream Farm and return to the main road. The car had arrived about five minutes earlier and the driver only had time to make his delivery and to say a quick hello to the farm's elderly resident. At the end of the driveway, the driver stopped, left the car running, and pulled the gate closed behind him before proceeding onto the road. The three men were stooped low in the foliage, and no one saw them watching the car on this secluded portion of Lantau Island.

As the car disappeared around the curve in the road, the first of the men left their hiding place and started walking up the edge of the driveway, well into the shadowed cover from the early morning sun. He didn't look back, and the other two followed in his steps without direction. They walked quickly, just below a jog, choosing their foot placements carefully. They covered the distance rapidly. The lead man paused near the top of the drive in the marginal scrub. When the other two joined him, they moved forward as one body.

The only anomaly in their profile was that one of the men carried a large dark bag that looked like a laundry bag. The bag was black and although it was not empty, it was neither full nor obviously bulging. The bag was made of Kevlar and its interior was lined with a fine woven chain mail. The man with the bag moved fluidly, like his colleagues, and maneuvered the sack with its ten-pound weight as if it were nothing at all.

The old farmer was making it easy for them. The men could see him through the modest wooden columns of the covered porch. The bag of groceries still rested on the porch floor near the front door. The old man tended his vegetable garden planted near the flowerbeds on the side of his house. He was kneeling and his back was to them as they approached. He wore a straw hat to battle the rising sun that would come later in the morning. He also wore his usual thick rubber boots for his daily trip to the rice paddy beyond the house. The man sang to himself, meticulously collecting and stacking the weeds he carefully removed from between his prized vegetable plants. The farm beyond matched his mood. It was serene, uncluttered, and undisturbed, nestled in a flat hollow, flanked between sets of rolling hills on all sides. The small farm was totally quiet except for the old man's muffled singing and the chirping birds singing in the woods beyond. Uncle Quan seemed utterly at peace.

When they pounced, the three men were on him in an instant. After turning him slightly, to spare the plants, one pushed him forward from his knees to prone and pulled back his arms. The first attacker also pinned the old man's legs by sitting on them. Another pulled the old man's head to one side and covered his mouth with the rag in his gloved hand. The third readied the bag, its contents now wriggling. The old man could not see the bag, but still he tried to cry out. It was impossible with the gag in place.

The man carrying the bag wore a fine chain mail glove with a Kevlar covering, similar in composition to the bag. His dexterity was slightly reduced. It didn't matter since this was a crude job he could do easily, even with the hand protection. He worked the end of the wriggling contents up to the surface and grasped it just below the apex. With his free hand, he loosened the drawstring of the bag and peeled back the opening. The cobra's head was now exposed and the rest of its body thrashed below in a vain attempt to be freed.

The animal was not yet fully grown and, as such, was more nervous than a full adult would have been, not that it mattered, given the circumstances. However, the cobra was old enough to produce sufficient venom to achieve the end result the men were there to accomplish. The snake handler shook the head of the viper to make the animal even more nervous and aggressive. The snake's body flailed wildly in the bag. Beneath the gloved hand, she worked to flare her triangular hood, and the lighter, greyish markings of the hood stood out more starkly on the snake's black skin as she struggled.

The bagman turned the snake's head toward the helpless old man. The attacker holding Quan's arms used one hand to pull down the old man's simple peasant shirt, exposing his neck.

The man holding back the old man's shirt looked at the snake handler and said quietly, "It's time."

He looked down at the terrified old man and said in English, "Sorry, Uncle Quan. This is not fair—however, it is necessary."

The handler dropped the snake's head to the old peasant's neck. It struck immediately and, when the handler shook the snake, it struck again. Its fangs entered the old man near the large vessels in his neck. The old man tried to scream. He could not.

The serpent was given a small rest until its handler again brought her close to the old man and allowed her to strike. The snake did not hesitate. She struck when pushed close to the exposed neck. The snake handler pulled her away, shook her again, and held her against the old man's flesh. The snake obliged.

Small dots of bleeding marked the bites and faint red halos were already growing around the first of the puncture marks. Uncle Quan's breathing became fast and shallow, and he began to struggle less. The three men continued to hold him. The old man continued to breathe, but it was progressively more labored until the fight was fully gone from his frail, fettered arms and legs.

"I'll move his arm now," one of the men said to the snake handler. He adjusted his position to allow one of Uncle Quan's arms out.

"Let her do it again," said the attacker.

The snake handler allowed the serpent to strike again through the light fabric of the old man's sleeve. The dying man did not seem to feel it at all. The assassins repeated this on the other arm, both on the forearm and the upper arm.

They continued to restrain him for several more minutes until the venom had its full effect. The old man was gasping for air. His arms were flaccid and he offered no resistance at all. His end was close at hand. One of the men felt for a pulse. It was thready, fast, barely palpable.

The snake handler pulled his lethal charge fully back into her bag. The other two men hoisted the nearly dead old man and carried him down a small path into the underbrush off his rice paddy. The snake tender placed his bag down and carefully brushed the dirt to hide any sign of them. He scattered the small pile of weeds into the brush as well. He joined the other two men who arranged the brush to make it appear that the old man had stumbled and fallen, and had been an unwelcome visitor to the dangerous viper lying there. The effect was that the peasant fought with the serpent when he fell and lost both the battle and the war. As they laid him out, the necrotic margins of the snakebites were visible on his neck, and in a few days, when the body was found, they would be even more pronounced and open because of the usual insect scavengers in the brush.

Quan was flaccid and had stopped breathing. There was no pulse. One of the attackers dropped his ear to the old man's chest and listened. He heard no heart sounds. They were satisfied with the result. Before leaving the site, they surveyed their work and the appearance of how they left the victim and the brush.

The snake handler asked in Cantonese, "Hal, what shall we do with Delilah?"

Hal looked down at the dead peasant and back to the handler. "I think she's earned her freedom. Let her go."

The handler shook out the bag over the old man. Upon landing on his chest, the snake's hood flared again as she stared at the downed farmer, looking long into his face. When the cobra sensed there was no threat, she relaxed, turned away from the dead man and gazed into the scrub. After a quick acclimation, the cobra slithered into the undergrowth while the men retreated, double-checking to be sure there was no trace of them as they left.

CHAPTER 27

Franco said nothing to her after they left Buddy's. He was quiet all the way to the airport. In part, he was deep in thought. In part, he was in shock. He wanted to call Pauling, but not with Rorke around.

The large business jet had a different crew, and it was a different plane than their arrival ship. With a few nods to the crew, Franco and Rorke each took a seat and almost immediately the big plane's cabin was sealed, and it started to roll toward the taxiway. In a few minutes, they were on the active runway, then airborne and headed west to Asia.

In the climb, Franco was still tormented and tangled in the swirling thoughts in his head. Consciously inflicting a potent carcinogen on a billion and a half people was such a monstrous idea, he could not believe his government could do it. But it had.

At cruising altitude, Rorke looked to him. "Can I bring you something from the galley, a snack or a drink?" she asked.

"No," said Franco.

"Suit, yourself," she said, and walked to the galley bar and poured herself a glass of wine.

When she returned, she sat on the chair closest to his. "Are you giving me the silent treatment for the whole flight?" she asked.

He looked at her and quietly said, "How could you do it?"

She waited before answering, "We didn't do anything, Mike. We just watched what happened after bad people stole something they should not have taken."

"You made it easy for them to steal it," said Franco.

"No, not particularly. This wasn't entrapment. This was no purse sitting on a park bench with a fifty creeping out. These are professional thieves who previously had stolen billions of dollars' worth of U.S. technology and sold it to our, let's call them, 'competitors.'"

"You knew exactly what was going on, didn't you?"

"You know I don't like too many questions," she said.

"Okay, I won't ask questions. I'll tell you a story. I don't have any questions about this part of the story. First, you've been setting up the older brother for a year and a half as his financial advisor, which is, oh, just about the time Buddy's pal, Shelly, found out he was dealing with a potent cancer-causing chemical. That's an interesting coincidence. As I remember it, it was just about that time that the HDOA and the USDA quarantined Buddy's rice. You found out what Buddy was trying to accomplish with his invention, only he didn't know anything about Shelly's safety study results at the time, yet, you did. Of course, had Buddy seen him, he would have pumped his friend Shelly about the special protein and he would have learned about the failed safety study of the protein. He would have shut down the rice project a year ago and washed his hands of it. That would have been inconvenient, since the government would then be responsible for any further activity with the rice. It was cleaner all the way around to still have Buddy involved, even though the rice was in government custody. The Chinese government would be far more likely to start a war with the U.S. if they felt the CIA was behind this rather than believing the problem started with their own people stealing from an American company."

Franco looked at Rorke intently and continued. "Now, unfortunately, Buddy's pal, Shelly, couldn't make their annual golf match last year—before the theft—because he had a broken leg after someone crashed into his car just a few days before their annual golf game. I don't know why I think this, but I'd bet it was a hit and run accident and the driver abandoned the car at the scene. I'd bet the car was recently stolen and that the case was never solved. This is wild speculation on my part, that's just how my mind works. Anyway, the fact that Shelly was out of commission and had to keep his story quiet for a year was another remarkable co-incidence. This allowed everyone at the USDA to consider the quarantine as business as usual, perhaps proceeding a little slower, probably a lot slower, than most quarantines, although still within reasonable limits."

Franco paused again to examine her face, although Rorke showed no emotion.

"All anyone might remember officially at the USDA was that they had this super rice that could be a remarkable food source. I imagine there is no record of this anywhere and that all the people who had been associated with this project were either transferred or furloughed. I wouldn't be surprised if it's been decided to shut down the facility completely after you confirm the rice is growing in China. If it hasn't been done already, it probably will be soon.

Also, when the rice was in quarantine, it was kept behind cream puff security that any middle school kid with half a brain could figure a way around. Therefore, all that was left to do was to tell the thieves that this super rice was theirs for the taking."

Franco stopped talking and stood. "That's my story. I'm going to have that drink now; can I refill yours?"

Rorke lifted her glass to him, and he walked to the galley and returned with two drinks. Franco returned the now full glass to her. "Now I have a few questions."

She took her drink from him. "Okay."

"Are you going to answer?"

"Maybe, ... or maybe not."

Franco was not expecting much more than that. "How did you find out that Shelly's protein caused cancer?"

"That one I can answer. I work for the 'Company.' Remember, all that drug safety information goes to the FDA. Obviously, we're both part of the same U.S. government 'Corporation.' Even though the FDA doesn't know it, we've always kept an eye on these safety issues for defense reasons. We don't want anyone coming over our fences and throwing nasty stuff around in the homeland."

"You mean the way we did to the Chinese?"

"No, they did it to themselves."

"When did we learn the rice could cause cancer—before or after we let them steal it?"

"Again, we didn't let them do anything. As far as the cancer part, I'm surprised you'd even think we'd consider doing that."

Franco persisted, "Did you know it caused cancer when they stole the seeds?"

"Next question, Franco."

Franco hesitated, controlling his temper. "All right, how did you set it up with the brothers?"

"It wasn't so hard. The younger brother is very enterprising."

"How?"

"To plant the seed, so to speak, an unknown stranger came up to the younger brother at a tech convention in Seoul about eighteen months ago, give or take, where the brother was assessing the tech landscape to see what else he should steal. They were at a bar and this stranger—let's call him a Malaysian Chinese—started to engage our thief on what he did for a living. The brother told him, almost truthfully, that he was a technology importer for China in a company based in Hong Kong. The Malaysian steered the subject to China's biggest problem, that is, having to import food. He started to educate the brother on the magnitude and the economics of the food import problem. These numbers piqued his interest in agriculture. The Malaysian let our greedy smuggler know that a U.S. company had developed a strain of super rice that could revolutionize world food production. This rice was being evaluated in Hawaii, and with the right contacts, he might be able to license it for the Chinese market. According to the Malaysian man, the USDA was running additional tests before the rice technology was to be put up for sale. The first mover on this would make more money than could be imagined.

"The younger brother and his new friend parted at the bar. Then a few months later, we tracked our boy coming to Hawaii on a B-2 visa to see the U.S.A. as a serious tourist. As it turned out, the younger brother had just set up shop in Molokai and, in time, encountered our late USDA employee. They became friends and, well, you can use that imagination of yours to figure out how the rest of the story goes."

She took a sip of her wine as Franco asked, "Was this the USDA employee who drowned before anyone could question him about the missing seeds?"

Rorke replied, "Yes, that's right."

"Another interesting coincidence," said Franco.

"I suppose it is," said Rorke, absently.

"And now you're going to poison everyone in China?"

"Franco, first, we didn't plant it. They stole it. And what happens is not my call. I do what I'm told to do, just like you."

"Were you told to set up a sting that would poison their entire population?"

"I'm not answering that."

"Why?"

"Because you don't need to know. All you should worry about is that Sloan returns to the U.S. before he tells his Chinese colleagues or anyone else that their super rice came from Texas. Right now, how we got here shouldn't matter to you."

"I think it matters. I'd like to think we didn't know it caused cancer when you set all this up and that you were just trying to smoke out the guys you suspected of industrial theft."

Rorke looked at him hard. "Well, if that's what you'd like to think, go right ahead and think it. It may be true; it may not be true. It doesn't matter."

Franco shook his head. "I'm still at a loss for words to understand this. When do we let the NSC and the White House know all this has gone on?"

She did not respond.

"We are going to let them know, aren't we?"

Rorke spoke to him in an even tone. "You know as well as I do what Pauling will want to do. You can predict how the National

Security Council, the senior congressional leadership, and the White House will want to react. I don't know how or when we'll let the Chinese know. It's my guess that we will."

"Only a guess?"

"Call it an informed hunch."

She drained her second glass of wine and walked over to the bar to pour herself a third.

"What about Buddy?" asked Franco, when she returned. "Are you going to tell him what happened to his rice? Are you going to let him know it was stolen by the Chinese?"

Rorke shrugged her shoulders. "Yeah, I think we'll probably have to tell him, otherwise he'll eventually tell someone about his clever idea to screw with Shelly. He'll make a big deal about dodging a bullet, blah, blah, blah and the PRC will eventually hear about it. They'll easily connect the dots and it will come back to us. We might have a chance of keeping it quiet if Buddy is uncharacteristically discreet."

"You mean you're going to have to scare the shit out of him if he opens his mouth."

"Exactly, and it won't be just an empty threat." Then she said, "Let's come back to Sloan. I want him out of the country tomorrow. I want you to babysit him in person until we load him on his flight. We booked him on a 10:00 am United flight to Honolulu via Narita. We'll have people watching him in Tokyo and he'll be well observed when he returns to Hawaii. I still think he's a serious security risk. We'll keep eyes and ears on him in Hawaii until I'm comfortable he'll stay quiet about this, and until I'm sure he understands that Pauling has to handle it. Your job is done when that plane takes off from Hong Kong with Sloan on board."

"What do you want me to do after he leaves?"

"When Sloan's gone, I just want you to go. I don't care where you go or what you do. Just leave Hong Kong. Trust me, we'll find you and settle up with whatever money Pauling promised you."

"Okay," said Franco. "I have just one other question."

"Good. Last question."

He paused before asking, "How do you sleep at night?"

"I usually have a glass of white wine before bed. If it makes you feel any better, Franco, since I've been working on this rice project, I often need two."

CHAPTER 28

Rorke slept for most of the flight; Franco did not sleep at all. He woke her during the final approach. She was still rubbing the sleep from her eyes and combing out her hair when the plane came to a stop at the general aviation terminal on Macau.

The Gulfstream's air stairs dropped onto the tarmac outside the terminal and Mr. Yang and a customs agent came aboard to check passports. With everything in order, Ms. Donohue and Senor Fernandez were welcomed back to Macau. They left the plane and took a taxi directly to the ferry terminal. Rorke again charmed her way through the border crossing with her boyfriend and the trip back to Hong Kong was uneventful.

It was about 10:00 pm when they arrived back in Hong Kong. The cab dropped Franco off first. Before he left the cab, Rorke held his sleeve and said, "Make sure you call me when he leaves Hong Kong."

"Okay. Do you want to know when I leave too?'

"No. You just go."

"I guess this is goodbye," he said, not sure how to leave it with her.

"Yeah. Bye, Franco," she said quickly, and pulled the cab door closed before he could think any more about it.

Franco watched the cab drive away. He thought about these last days and still could not believe what was happening. He thought about what he'd do after he put Sloan on the plane and realized he didn't have any clear plan. All he knew was that Rorke was right about a few things. What he didn't need to know, he didn't want to know. Now there were more than a few things he wished he didn't know.

Franco went into the lobby and made a call. Aware that his cell phone was not secure, he still punched in the number Pauling gave him to call in an emergency. After a few rings, a recorded female voice came on the line and asked the caller to leave a message. Franco thought about it, and didn't know how to frame his questions. He settled for, "This is me. Please call. It's urgent."

He hoped Pauling would understand the message and call him back to direct him to a secure line for a longer conversation.

He then called Sloan. There was no answer. He called Sloan again, and again there was no answer.

A few minutes later, he rang Sloan's room on the hotel's house phone. There was still no answer. He tried a few more times with the same result. Franco went to the lift and punched the number to their floor. He walked off the elevator, down the hall, and knocked on Sloan's door. Initially, there was no answer. Franco knocked again. He heard movement within followed by the release of the lock mechanism before the door opened. Sloan pulled open the unlocked door and Franco pushed in, closing the door behind him.

The first thing Franco saw was a pint bottle of vodka on the floor. It was empty. Another pint bottle was on the nightstand by the bed, and it was half empty.

"Paul, are you okay?" asked Franco.

"What do you think?" said Sloan, slurring the words.

"What's wrong?"

"Buddy called me today."

"Yeah?"

"The rice causes cancer."

"What did he tell you?"

"He said Shelly's protein causes cancer, that he told you and Rorke and that I should know, too."

"What did you tell him?"

"I didn't tell him anything about the rice being over here. I didn't tell him it was stolen. I was too shocked. I didn't process it for a little while but... my God, how could this happen? We have to tell the Chinese authorities. What a tragic mistake. How awful this is."

"Paul, I'm sure that Rorke is delivering the news to Pauling. They'll handle it."

"It's got to be done right away! That stuff spreads like wildfire. They can't tell the difference from regular rice."

"I know. They're going to deal with it."

"No. I can deal with it faster. I have friends who have a direct access to the top of the Agriculture Ministry. One of them is a good friend of the Minister. I should give her a call."

"No, Paul. You can't. This would be devastating for the USDA and for Buddy, and it could undermine our relationship with China in a way that can't be predicted. This has to be handled gently through the appropriate channels."

"We don't have time for appropriate channels!"

"We do. It's only been a couple of days since we learned where the plants are. They're all still in test plots. Isn't that right?"

"We don't know where they are."

While he spoke, Sloan stumbled around the room and finally sat down on his bed. Franco sat next to him and tried to calm him.

"Okay, wherever the rice is planted, it has to be a very small problem now."

"I don't know," said Sloan. "We can't be sure of that."

"Right," said Franco. "We can't be sure. We need to let the process go through government channels. It will be done more efficiently that way."

"I'm not comfortable with that." Sloan raised his voice, saying, "This stinks. It's awful, just awful."

"Look," said Franco, taking Sloan by the shoulders, "I saved your life once and you owe me for all I've done for you. I want you to sleep off the vodka tonight and sober up tomorrow. I'll take you out to the airport tomorrow morning. Rorke booked you on a 10:00 am flight back to Honolulu. I'm sure Rorke will give you a full debrief of all this when you return to Hawaii."

Sloan had a vacant stare in his bloodshot eyes, although he seemed to slowly process what Franco said.

"Okay, Mike. I am tired. Will you call me in the morning to make sure I'm awake?"

"I'll sleep here on your couch tonight," said Franco. "I want to make sure you catch your flight tomorrow."

"Good," said Sloan. He reached over to his nightstand and took a long drink out of the open bottle and dropped back on his bed. He was snoring in a few seconds.

Franco pulled out his cell phone and entered in the number for Pauling again. Still there was no answer. This time he did not leave a message.

Franco poured the rest of the vodka down the bathroom sink and turned out the light on Sloan's nightstand before lying on Sloan's couch. He hadn't slept in over 24 hours. He set an alarm on his watch. He was asleep in a few minutes as well.

* * *

When the alarm sounded, Franco needed a few moments to re-orient himself to the room. As he fumbled to turn off the alarm, he noticed with a start that Sloan was not in the bed. He looked over and saw that he wasn't in the bathroom either. He had not heard him leave.

Franco jumped out of bed and walked around the room as if expecting to see Sloan emerge from a closet or from under a bed. He was gone. Franco cursed himself and Sloan. He hated to do what he had to do. He pulled out his cell phone and dialed. Rorke answered immediately. Instead of saying "Hello," she simply said, "We have him here. Collect all his things and meet us curbside at Terminal One, United Airlines, at 0830."

She disconnected. He hadn't said a word.

Franco checked his watch and saw that he didn't have much time. He found Sloan's case and dumped in his clothes, toiletries, and identification documents, including his passport. Sloan traveled light and it took no time to scour the place clean of all his possessions. The old, soft leather case he always carried around was not in the room and Franco assumed he had it with him. Franco was out the door with Sloan's clothing five minutes after the call.

A taxi was at the cabstand and within a few seconds, he was away and headed for the airport. Traffic was heavy leaving Hong Kong, but thinned out as they came closer to the airport on Lantau Island. He would make the trip in about an hour, which was very good for that time of day. Franco did not want to face Rorke, and particularly did not want to keep her waiting.

When his cab pulled up at the terminal, four of them were standing outside. Rorke stood with three other men. The two men each held one of Sloan's arms. Franco recognized the two as part of the surveillance team he'd identified earlier. Sloan looked disheveled and had a large red welt on his cheek. He was distracted, perhaps drunk, and didn't immediately recognize Franco.

"Where was he?" asked Franco.

"Going to see his lady friend for an early morning shooter and a serious conversation, I'm guessing," said Rorke. "He's drunk and he didn't want to come, so we had to resort to some persuasive, and maybe a little bit coercive, methods to help him along."

"You punched him in the face?"

"No, more of a slap," said Rorke. "It was ugly, nonetheless. We had to call his colleague and explain why he couldn't meet her, but I think we smoothed that over. We listened to his call with her. He didn't tell her anything."

She looked at Sloan and Franco and then back to Sloan. "It's time to go home now, Paul. You did a great job, and we'll be in touch. Don't screw up."

She turned to Franco and said quietly, "He's all yours. Usher him to the security line and my guys on the other side will watch him from there. I listened to your talk with him last night. It was a good talk. I thought it would have stopped him, but he seemed to want to go about it differently."

Rorke turned and walked to the large sedan parked at the curb. The other two men joined her, leaving Franco alone with Sloan.

Sloan looked weak and confused, standing there clutching his leather case. He seemed to look to Franco for guidance.

"Let's get you home, Paul," said Franco putting his arm around the drunken scientist. "Let's get you home."

If there had been any fight in the man earlier, there was none remaining. Sloan walked with Franco to the check in, received his ticket, and sent his bag through. He kept clutching the briefcase, clearly not wanting to let it go. On the way to passport control and the security gates, Franco asked Sloan to sit with him.

They found a quiet bench and sat. Franco looked him in the eye, and put his arm around Sloan's shoulder. "Paul, do not do anything stupid with this plant information. Do you understand?"

Sloan said weakly, "Yes, I understand."

"You haven't told anyone about this, have you?"

"No. I wanted to discuss it with my friend before I went any further with it." Sloan was slurring his words badly.

"Don't' even think about going any further with it. The NSA and Pauling's other groups can hear anything they want and see anything they want. They'll know what you say almost before you even think it. For this operation, they will look and listen to everything. How this information is conveyed to the Chinese government is highly sensitive and very delicate. You must understand that."

"I know it is."

"You have to leave it up to them to do it."

"I know."

"You can't say anything to anyone about this."

"I understand."

"If you say anything, they'll know."

Sloan nodded.

"Are you going to be okay?"

"I guess," he said.

"You have to get sober again."

"Yeah, I know. I will."

"When you get back to Hawaii, keep your mouth shut and never ever speak to anyone about this. They will always be listening."

Sloan's sad eyes seemed to understand. Franco felt sorry for this man who had been such a brilliant academic. He wanted to sit there until a little of the character of the person he had known in the past returned. Unfortunately, there was no time for that. Instead, Franco walked him to passport control, hugged him, and watched him leave.

After Sloan disappeared, Franco walked to the side of the waiting area and called Rorke.

"He's in passport control. I just said 'goodbye' to him. He'll be coming to security soon."

"We've got him."

"Sorry about him getting loose on me."

"You did all you could last night. We'll make sure he leaves the country without further mishap. Count it as a success. I hope he takes your counsel when he gets home."

"Me, too."

"It was good working with you, Franco."

"Yeah, you too, Sam," he said without conviction.

After a pause, she said, "Leave town."

"I'm going."

"Okay, have a good life," she said, and the phone was switched off.

Franco thought about what he should do. His assignment was completed. He had time on his hands and his only obligation was to eventually pick up his things on Stewart. He didn't want to dwell on the last 48 hours.

He thought he had an idea of what he might do. Franco walked down to the arrivals area and saw what he was looking for. It was a travel agent's office. He entered and made a few inquiries. He sat with the travel agent and made the arrangements. The timing was perfect. The cruise ship would sail at 5:00 pm that evening out of Kowloon and he could hop off the ship in Singapore in seven days and, from there, return to New Zealand. He booked the most expensive cabin available, airfare from Singapore to Stewart, and looked ahead to the coming week, wishing he could forget the last one.

CHAPTER 29

While every night was a good night on Lan Kwai Fong, Saturday night was special. The restaurants and bars were always full on Saturdays. It was an area where everyone was generally in a good mood, at least at the beginning of the evening before the ugly drunks came out.

Chao greatly anticipated seeing his new friend, "Carl," at the same bar where they had met before for drinks. Chao was excited both for the diversions the night portended as well as for the business possibilities that it might spawn. He was looking forward to drinks, an elegant dinner, and a long night of interesting entertainment at his club. The club was especially fantastic on Saturdays since they booked extra talent from all over Asia.

Chao arrived a few minutes early and ordered his first drink before Hal arrived. Hal was still not there after fifteen minutes and Chao was well into his next round. As he downed the drink and thought about leaving, he saw Hal enter the bar with a woman.

Hal waved, but Chao focused most of his attention on the woman. She was breathtakingly gorgeous and was conspicuous in displaying it. Her long dark hair was punctuated with blonde streaks. She wore spiked heels that rose to a short, tight dress, topped with a pronounced cleavage. She had blue eyes and blue fingernails and a birth spot on her cheek. Her large hoop earrings finished her look.

When Hal brought her to the bar to meet their host, she flashed Chao a dazzling, perfect smile outlined with bright red lipstick over full lips.

"Please forgive me for being late," said Hal. "My cousin Alissa called. She just arrived from out of town and asked if she could come to dinner with us. I hope it's all right."

With difficulty, Chao briefly took his eyes off the woman, glancing at Hal.

"Of course," he said. "I am Chao. It is my pleasure to meet you."

"It is wonderful to meet you as well," said Alissa. "'Carl' says that you're going to make each other a lot of money in the coming years."

"I hope he's right," said Chao. "Shall we go to a table?"

"Yes, please," said Alissa. "I've traveled all day in these shoes and I'd love to get off my feet."

Hal walked to a circular booth and let Alissa slide in first. Chao and Hal flanked her in the booth. Alissa put her purse on the shelf above the booth corner as she slid in.

Hal looked to Chao and explained, "Our mothers were sisters. Alissa popped into town on business."

Chao looked at her, "What's your business?"

Alissa shrugged her shoulders and said, "Fashion design. Not quite as lucrative as my cousin's computer business. Hey, we can't all be geniuses."

"Where are you traveling from?" he asked.

"Singapore," said Alissa.

"I love Singapore," said Chao, "when I'm feeling well behaved."

"What about when you're feeling frisky?" asked Alissa.

"It depends on which vice I'm cultivating at the time," said Chao.

"Do you specialize in more than one?" she teased.

"Truthfully, I'm a slave to many. That's a story for another day. How about a drink?"

"Good idea. Let's all have Singapore Slings," she said quickly, before Hal could respond. "It won't be like the Raffles Hotel, but it will make me think of home and having 'Carl' come visit me."

"No thanks," said Hal. "I hate those sweet drinks."

"Please, 'Carl,' just one. Chao, you'll be a nice guy and have one with me, won't you?"

"Sure I will," said Chao, with a grin. "Come on, 'Carl,' be nice to your cousin."

The waitress came to the table and Alissa quickly ordered three Singapore Slings and placed her hand over Hal's face before he could speak. She giggled as he wiped her hand away from his smiling mouth.

"She bosses me around, just like when we were kids. It is wrong, because I am her senior."

"By only two days," she said quickly.

"You should still respect your elders, Alissa."

"I do. I ordered a drink for you out of great respect." She laughed again. She turned to Chao.

"What do you do besides try to make deals with my cousin?"

"I work for many cousins," said Chao. "I broker relationships between western companies and mainland industries. My brother and I have been doing this for many years."

"You don't look that old," said Alissa.

"I try to keep my stress levels down," said Chao. "It helps you stay young."

"That's very useful to know," she said, and changed the subject. "How often do you come to Singapore?"

"Usually about three times a year," he said. "How often do you come to Hong Kong?"

"About once a month," she said.

"What kind of clothes do you design?" Chao asked.

"Lately, it's mostly for babies and kids. Asian moms want to keep up with the west with all the cute clothes. We've been behind in that market for a long time."

"Who do you work for?" he continued.

"I freelance. I have designs being made by several manufacturers in China, Singapore, Malaysia, and Vietnam. I'd like to find work in South Korea and Japan. It's harder for me to break in there; they're already too western, but I keep trying."

"Always keep trying," affirmed Chao.

She turned toward the bar, "Look, 'Carl,' here come our drinks. You can say you did one nice deed for the day by humoring me with this."

The waitress placed the drinks on the table and left.

"I'll give you my business card," Alissa said. "Would you hand me my purse?" She pointed to the corner shelf above the booth behind Chao and he turned to reach the purse. When he did, her right hand hovered over his drink. Hal watched closely. There was barely a splash as she discharged a small vial of liquid into Chao's drink.

Chao turned back to her with the small purse in his hand. "Thank you," she said, taking it and fishing out a business card.

"This is me. You should look me up the next time you come to Singapore. It's a wonderful place. I'll show you a good time." She hoisted her glass and giggled, "To Singapore Slings and to sweet drinks everywhere."

They all drank and eventually drained their glasses. Alissa gestured to the waitress to bring them another round. When the drinks arrived, 'Carl' complained, although he started to drink it anyway. Chao did likewise, supporting Alissa's choice. Alissa responded to Chao's support. She seemed very interested in Chao's business and continued to ask him questions. Chao spoke about it for several minutes until his train of thought began to wander and he was challenged with trying to be coherent.

Alissa turned to Hal and whispered in his ear, "It's time."

"Okay."

With that Hal spoke. "Hey, I have to make a call," he said. "I'll be back later. I'll take care of the bill tonight."

"Okay," said Chao, as Hal slid from the booth, walked to the bar, and put cash on the counter.

Alissa smiled at Chao and put her hand on his thigh beneath the table.

"Did you like the Sling?"

"Oh, yeah," said Chao. "I like your hand, too."

She moved her hand up to his crotch and slowly rubbed him there.

"Oh yeah, I really love the Sling."

Alissa continued to massage her new friend.

"Are you feeling good?" she asked.

"Amazing," he said. "It was a good drink."

"You bet," she said. "Do you want to feel even better? We can go somewhere." She applied more pressure with her hand beneath the table.

"Can I make you feel good too?"

"I hope so," she laughed.

He laughed too, and said, "Oh, yes, let's go." He added, "I like being with you. We should go to my place and put on some music."

"Okay, let's have a party," she said. "'Carl' already paid the bill."

"That was nice of him. Should we wait?"

"No. His business calls always take too long."

She maneuvered Chao to the street. The large dose of Ecstasy still had not taken full effect but it would in a few minutes, and she hurried to maneuver him to the street before he started vomiting or stumbling.

On the busy sidewalk, she took his hand and pulled him to the side of an alley in the crowded low-rise area. A white van with a hotel logo and "Airport Shuttle" written on the side was idling in the alley. The van pulled forward closer to the sidewalk when they approached.

The passenger side window dropped and Hal looked out, asking, "Do you need a ride?"

"Look," said Alissa, 'It's 'Carl.' Let's hop in."

Chao was distracted by the many people on the street, and followed her lead. She guided him into the van. He sat in the club seat behind the driver as the van pulled out into the traffic. Chao's headrest was like an exaggerated race car driver's, with padded side panels to cradle his head.

No one spoke in the van except Alissa. She was not in a seat, but instead knelt on the floor in front of Chao.

"Let's keep the party going," she said and lowered his pants zipper and started to play.

"Oh yeah," said Chao.

Her hands released his leather belt buckle and then the hook on his pants. She loosened them and started to pull them down. He helped.

"Are you feeling good?" she asked.

"Better and better," he said, as Alissa kept up her activity below. "Wow, the lights are incredible tonight." As an afterthought, he added, "Do we have any music here?"

After several blocks, they pulled off on a side street and the van slowed. Chao was more interested in Alissa's activities than the activity behind him. Another passenger, hidden from Chao in the back seat, passed a wide, heavily padded, nylon belt over his head. It gently rested on his waist. The belt was suddenly pulled tight and Chao's arms were immobilized.

The van turned off the street, down an alley, and through a large open bay door into a mechanic's garage. The garage door shut behind the van as soon as it entered. The van parked and Chao looked around.

"What's happening? Where are we?" asked Chao, confused, yet not particularly alarmed.

"It's all part of the party," said Alissa. "Let's do a little coke."

"Sounds weird, but okay. You're in charge."

Alissa was now at his side with what looked like a nasal aspirator from a child's medicine closet.

"When I tell you, sniff in," she said.

"Okay, cool," he said.

"Now," she said, and he took a deep breath through his nose. The white powder in the aspirator was discharged.

"Wow," he said, after a few more breaths to clear his nose.

"You want another?" she asked.

"Sure," said Chao slowly, slurring his words. She gave him more of the powder.

Chao closed his eyes, feeling the effects of the cocaine hits.

"Okay," said Alissa quietly, to the man in the back seat. "Give me the 'epi.'"

The man in the back handed her two syringes. Each had a capped small gauge needle.

Alissa took the syringes. Chao's pants were down below his knees and his knees were spread. She lifted his man sack and injected the adrenaline shot into the upper inner thigh on each side.

"You feeling okay, Chao?"

"Yeah, feeling okay. What was that pinch down there?"

"Birth control."

"Oh, okay."

They waited, watching him. Chao struggled to say, "Hey, my heart's beating out of my chest. That must have been good stuff."

"First class," she said. "We're going to do nitrous now."

"This might be a little too much, don't you think? I'm really tripping now. Wow."

"No, not too much for you, baby." She looked to the man in the back seat and said to Hal, "Open the door and windows, please."

The man in the back seat handed her a plastic facemask with a tube coming from it.

"Chao, I want you to take a few deep hits of this. You'll feel amazing. I'll play with your boy downstairs and make you feel good."

Chao was in and out of consciousness now. He said nothing.

The man in the back seat placed the gas over Chao's face. Chao initially took it quite easily, then started to struggle as his breathing became more labored. The man behind Chao easily kept the mask in place, with the padded side panels of the headrest limiting Chao's movement. Chao's struggling intensified briefly. After a few moments, it lessened, and then suddenly stopped entirely.

Alissa felt his neck for a pulse, "Okay, turn off the nitrogen. The fun's over here. I guess his little heart gave out."

"Too much to drink, a cocaine overdose, asphyxia, and an adrenaline rush might do that," said Hal.

"Yeah, too bad," said Alissa, as she left the van. "He was really enjoying that Ecstasy. He probably should have quit with that."

The man in the backseat loosened the padded belt and came around to lift and buckle Chao's pants.

With Chao still in the seat, Alissa turned to Hal. "Where's my 'go' bag?"

Hal left for a moment, and returned with a fabric travel bag from the garage office.

Alissa removed the wig, revealing her own short black hair, and took off her large earrings. Then she popped out the blue contacts and peeled the stick-on birthmark from her cheek. She extracted a small case from the fabric bag and walked to the bathroom, returning a few minutes later without a trace of makeup on her face.

"Is this my burn bag?" she asked Hal, looking at the large paper bag in front of her.

"Yes."

She picked up her other discarded items and removed all her clothes, except her panties, and put them in the bag.

She stood in front of Hal rubbing her breasts.

"If I never see another push-up bra, it will be too soon," she said.

She reached in her bag and retrieved a plain white bra, a casual blouse, and a pair of slacks from her bag. After re-dressing, she put on a pair of casual slip-on shoes. The effect was a modestly dressed, upper middle class young woman, probably a mother.

She pulled a garage rag off the countertop and sat on a stool. Reaching into her "go" bag, she found a bottle of nail polish remover. She opened the bottle and wet the rag with it. The other men peeled off the decal from the side of the van and replaced it with a decal for a plumber's business.

"I have to ask," said Hal, as he stood beside her, "Can't we do better than Singapore Slings in the future? I hate that drink."

"Sorry, Hal, but nothing does a better job at taste masking than gin, Cointreau and pineapple juice."

"Yuck," he said.

She sat removing her nail polish, and didn't argue further.

"He seemed like a nice guy," she said, gesturing over her shoulder with her head. Chao, slumped in his captain's chair, was now very pale and lifeless.

"He was all right," said Hal. "We think he stole a lot of DoD secrets, although we can't be sure. Pauling was just waiting for him to step out of line one more time."

"I guess he did," she said in a nonchalant way, to no one in particular.

Hal let her clean another finger or two when he said, "I still think you enjoy playing with the guy's junk when you do your little routine."

She cleaned another finger as she answered, "Hal, of course, I do, but I haven't heard of a medical examiner yet who's found the puncture marks there. They don't like to look. Are you aware that when they do a post, they'll go over a woman's genitalia with a fine-tooth comb, sometimes literally? They leave the boy's equipment undisturbed. It's terrible sexism. It has to be addressed."

Hal had no response to that, and instead asked, "Where did you buy the drugs?"

"I picked them up this morning in Kowloon."

"Any problems?"

"No. It was my usual supplier."

"Good," said Hal. "What time is your flight?"

"12:30 to Narita."

"Are you going back to the States?"

"No, I have a morning connection to Heathrow."

"What are you doing?"

"I'm taking a cooking class."

"I bet it's in Tuscany."

"No, wrong. Lyon."

"Good for you. Call me in about three months. You'll probably have to come in to Langley for a while."

"Okay." She pointed toward the van. The other men were sitting Chao a little straighter in his chair to make sure his blood pooled in the right spots for later. "What time are you dropping him off?" she asked.

"Probably about two. We'll have plenty of time to clean the van before we ship it out."

"Make sure you find my business card and destroy it."

"We will."

"Where's the van going?"

"I think Australia. It should be loaded on the ship by 0800 tomorrow and on the water by 1300."

"Are you done after that?" she asked.

"No. I have another job here and then I have to go back to Hawaii. After that, I'll go away for a little chill time."

"Good. Nice working with you again, Hal."

"You, too," he said. "I have a car parked on the street. I'll drop you off at a cab stand near the Hilton."

Hal hesitated. "You know, I have to say this. Even though I know you're putting the drug in the drink, I watch your hand closely but I can't see how you do it."

"I know. I'm very good at what I do, Hal. That's why the Company likes me. I practice. You should see me do card tricks."

"I guess the magic is all about misdirection and distraction."

"It is. I hate to say it, but my magic act works much better when I'm wearing that damned push-up bra."

CHAPTER 30

It was Sunday night, about 9:00 pm, and the streets were not crowded. In fact, they were almost empty. Rain was in the forecast, so it was not surprising to see the woman walking down the sidewalk in a long raincoat. She was tall by Hong Kong standards. Her long black hair draped down her back from under her wide brimmed hat. She also carried a large shoulder bag. It was odd that she was wearing sunglasses, but no one was around to comment. There was little additional detail apparent, especially if viewed from a low-resolution city security camera.

Just before coming to the park district with its zoo and botanical gardens, the woman swung away from her course and tacked left to a small side street that was far darker, although she was not on it very long. After about half a block, she turned into an alley and walked past a large dumpster to a door. The stick in the door was crude, yet effective. After pausing to make sure no one was passing on the street behind her, and with her hands protected by light leather gloves, she pulled open the building's back door and entered a stairwell. She knew that Hal's people had disabled the door alarm and the alley security camera. There were no security cameras on the stairway.

Taking a big breath, she began to climb the stairs in front of her. Although she ran daily, the stair climb was still sixteen flights and on the sixteenth landing, she sat on the steps and rested. After catching her breath, she removed the wig, her shoes, and her gloves. She combed out her red hair slowly, careful to not let any hair leave her brush. She applied more lipstick, and slipped on a pair of pumps from the bag. From the large bag, she pulled out a smaller purse, slung it over her shoulder and left the larger bag with the hat, sunglasses, gloves, and wig on the landing. Opening the door to the hallway, she was careful to hold the door handle with a Kleenex. She walked to Jun's apartment and tentatively rapped on the door. He opened the door slowly, and wordlessly let her in.

"Am I interrupting?" She knew the answer, as Hal had informed her that the last of his company had left an hour earlier. She ignored her own question. "I heard the news on the television and I had to come over to tell you how sorry I am. Your doorman let me come up. I know how much you loved Chao."

Jun nodded weakly at her. It was clear he had been crying. "I told him to stop using those drugs," he said quietly, and with difficulty. "He wouldn't listen to me."

"I'm sure you tried to help him," she said.

"I did," he said, suppressing a sob. "He was my only relative in the world besides my Uncle Quan. I need to send word to Quan. He lives alone on Lantau and has no phone or neighbors. I'll have to drive out there tomorrow to tell him. It will break his heart."

"I'm sure, "said Rorke. "I'd be happy to drive out there with you if you need company."

"Thank you. I appreciate the offer," said Jun. "You are too good to me. I may call you." He started to cry openly. "I feel that I let him down, as the responsible member of the family. I feel that I should have done better."

"You can't beat yourself up, Jun. You told me many times that Chao loved his wild living."

Jun said nothing, and Rorke added in a quiet voice, "I'm sure he died happy."

He looked at her and said softly, "Yes, I'm sure he did." He sighed and asked, "Would you like a drink?"

"Only if you're having one," Rorke said.

"In that case, I will," he said.

"Here, you sit down," she said. "I want to bring it to you. You need a little pampering today. What do you want?"

"How about a glass of the port you'll see on the bar top. I had some earlier."

Port, she thought. Perfect. She stood and walked to the bar, stopping to kiss him on the top of his head as she walked by. "You relax, I'll take care of everything tonight."

She poured the port and a glass of white wine for herself. The sedative flowed easily from the small vial and the bottle fit easily back in her pocket when emptied.

She handed him the drink and stood behind him to rub his neck.

"Tell me what you most loved about your brother," she said.

Jun turned to her again, choking back tears as he worked to tell stories of his little brother. He told her about how he counted on Chao to comfort his mother after their father had died and about his brother's ambition and his zest for their business. He talked about Chao's continued optimism and his unfailingly sunny outlook on life.

Jun finished the first glass of port and didn't object when Rorke offered to fill a second glass. She had a second vial.

Halfway through the drink, he became incoherently emotional and was teetering on falling into a near permanent drug-induced sleep.

She stood and said. "Finish this glass, and I'll put you to bed. You've had a terrible day."

He looked up at her. She thought he looked so needy, so weak, so vulnerable. She also remembered the broken man her father had become after the Chinese government crushed him years ago.

He drained the glass as she instructed. She helped guide his head to the couch pillow and lifted his feet. After a few minutes, he was snoring heavily.

Rorke went to her purse at the sound of his deep, rhythmic breathing, and pulled out a pair of latex gloves. She took the wine glasses, wiped them and washed them, making sure all traces of powder were washed off the gloves. She wiped down the Port bottle and everything she had touched in the room. Although there was a perfectly good reason for her latent fingerprints in the room, the fewer the better.

With Jun still deeply drugged, she went to his desk. The stationary and pen he had used for his investment wish list were still in the top drawer. Before starting her work, she went to him and pressed his hand to the pen and the paper. She would do it again when she finished.

From her purse, she pulled Jun's investment plan and began to write, using his characters as references. She thought to herself that by any standard she was an excellent forger, and could do it in multiple languages with multiple alphabets. From her purse, she withdrew a prescription bottle of Xanax that had been filled for a patient named Liu Jun when the brothers were in Bangkok on business a year before. After writing, and re-finger printing the pen and paper, she placed the bottle of pills on the lamp table.

When she finished, she read over the letter several times. As suicide notes went, it was pure gold. From the dead or nearly so, in his elegant suicide note, Jun wrote of his love for his brother and of his brother's wonderful attributes, many of which he had shared with her just a little while earlier. He wrote about the great responsibility he felt for his younger brother, since Jun was the older brother and head of the family. He wrote of his own failings. He had let his parents down by allowing Chao to stray all these years. His terrible shame and guilt were now overpowering, due to his brother's untimely end and legacy of overdosing on a bench outside of his after-hours club. Without his brother, Jun had no family, few friends, and nothing to live for anymore. He had to do the honorable thing.

She finished her work and was still admiring it when a single knock hit the apartment door. She opened the door to Hal Chen and two other men. One of the men carried a long tube coiled in his hand.

"You'd better load the stomach quick before he's dead. Be careful and go slow, I don't want any sign of trauma."

The man propped Jun up while his colleagues snaked the wide tube into his mouth, down his esophagus, and into stomach. His colleagues helped load several of the pills down the tube and, with a large syringe, used water to push them along.

Rorke turned to Hal.

"You're in the apartment downstairs?"

"Yes. I've been living there off and on for a couple of months."

"I assume you'll stay there until people go to work tomorrow morning."

"That's been my pattern."

"Okay. I'll need about an hour to pack my things and make it to the airport. Make sure his fingerprints are on the railing."

"Of course."

"Can you reconnect the alarm and the security camera after I go, but before Jun leaves us?"

"Sure."

"Also, don't let him hit anyone on the way down," said Rorke.

"No worries," said Hal.

"When you're done here, we're almost home."

"Yes," said Hal, and then he added, "There's a Rolls parked on the street just below us. I think it would make a pretty good target."

"That sounds like fun," Rorke said. "Just make sure it's empty." She looked at the men and turned back to Hal. "I'll see you in Honolulu."

She let herself out of the apartment and went down the hall to the stairwell. She would walk down the sixteen floors.

CHAPTER 31

W hen Sloan arrived in Honolulu, he was still half drunk. He hadn't had a drink on the trip until the layover in Narita. After that, it was an easy slide. The first vodka was good and the next several were better. The vodka made the news he carried seem lighter and farther away. He didn't eat the airplane breakfast. He was consumed with the thought of finding a bottle. Realizing that might be a challenge due to the early morning hour, he asked for a few "travelers" from the flight attendants before deplaning.

There were no liquor stores on the arrivals side of the terminal, and Sloan walked with the passenger flow to clear customs. His bag was transferred to the island hopper to the Ho'olehua airport on Molokai, and he carried nothing except a small leather case with papers. He found the island hopper gate at the Honolulu terminal, too lost in his thoughts to enjoy the amazing island views on the short flight from Oahu.

After arriving on Molokai, he reclaimed his bag, found his car on the lot, and drove to the package store near his home that opened early. He bought a quart and two pints of vodka and went home to think about what he should do. He drank through lunch and did not make it to dinner, passing out on his couch. When he awoke at 10:00 pm, jet lagged, hung over, and still high, he decided what he would do, what he must do. He found the bottle, took a few drinks and tried to sleep.

His conscience did not surrender easily to the peace of sleep. He was tormented by thoughts of the rice shoots and how they popped up so quickly beyond where they had been planted. The realization that there was no guarantee the rice would stay confined to China also tormented him. The image and memory that haunted him most was the recollection of the children he had met on a joint USDA-State Department visit. That trip had been to Cambodia to assess the results of an aid program. Previously, the kids had been malnourished, then their lives had been changed with the gift of U.S. agriculture, specifically U.S. rice.

He remembered the children who had learned his name and took great delight in saying it. The kids were by then well fed, and followed him around happily. They laughed and laughed with him. It had been one of the best days of his life.

Sloan tossed and turned for another six hours before deciding that sleep was futile. He left his bed and took a long shower. After eating toast for breakfast, he picked up his papers, and both pint bottles. Sloan walked out to his car and began the drive down the quiet, two-lane road between the scrub palms. No other cars were on the road at that early hour. When he arrived at the USDA quarantine station, most of the staff had not yet come to work. He entered his code at the gate and drove in as the motorized gate parted.

In the enormous greenhouse, only two of the staff were at work tending various plants. The office area was empty and the door to the seed closets was closed. Sloan waved to the staff when he arrived and shouted a response to their welcome back greetings.

In his office, he placed his leather case on the desk, walked to the seed closet, unlocked the door, and entered the room. Locating the vault where Buddy's seeds had been stored, he opened the drawer. It had been wiped clean of any plant material. It all made sense to him now.

When he looked at the facility's written logs, all pages referring to Jerome's plants were missing. As he searched the files on his computer, there was no trace of Buddy's seeds ever having been at the USDA. They'd scrubbed Buddy's rice completely out of the records. The only remaining evidence of Buddy's rice ever having been at the USDA was sitting on Sloan's desk in the leather case. There he had carried the copies of the logs, the hardcopy printout of the seed history, the description of the growth characteristics, the protein analysis of the plant, and the USDA report of the theft. It was all there. It was all that was left of the records, and no one knew about it but him.

He tried to remember what had prompted him to duplicate the USDA records of the rice. Initially, he copied a few reports to evaluate them further at home after hours. When the amazing growth and protein production data of the rice strain started coming in, he was so excited that he copied the records as a historian might, to preserve an epic event for later posterity. Finally, it became his private habit, and when the seeds were stolen, a small voice inside told him to continue what he was doing, and to keep it completely secret. He obeyed that small voice and no one knew of the dossier he still retained.

Sloan fumbled through a few unrelated e-mails even though he could only focus on the dossier in front of him. From time to time, he took a pull from the pint bottle when he was sure no one was near. By lunchtime, the bottle was empty and he felt the need to eat. Rather than lunch at the usual place nearby the facility, he drove toward the village and the small strip mall near there. He knew of a public telephone that was still there next to the rusting cluster of shops. He parked his car and fingered the number he'd looked up earlier. As he readied to make the call on the public phone, he opened the other bottle and took a long drink before punching in the number.

The strip was largely empty. However, Sloan looked at the few shoppers suspiciously while he entered the number and while the phone was ringing. When the voice on the other end answered, "Associated Press Bureau, Honolulu," he finally felt the dull pain in his head subsiding. It was a welcome wave of relief that improved over the thirty minutes of the phone call. It was not the healing absolution of the confessional, although he believed he was coming closer to that. What he was doing was important. It was necessary. It was for the good of the world. It had to be done, and he was glad he could do it. Yes, the government would eventually handle the situation, but this would make it happen more quickly. It had to happen quickly.

Sloan agreed to meet the bureau chief the next day at 3:00 in Honolulu, not far from the airport. They would meet in a park, not in an office or a restaurant. Sloan would arrive first and they agreed on what he would wear so the reporter could easily find him. The horrible secret would be exposed to the sanitizing light of public opinion. It would all be made right. He felt free. He could profess to himself, and to anyone else, that he was not part of this terrible enterprise. Sloan hung up the telephone and drove to the package store for another pint and another quart. There was a risk. He knew that. But after the news was out, what could they do? It had to be done and it had to come out in the open to save the millions and millions of innocent people at risk.

Sloan drove home and heated a frozen meal. He had a few more drinks to help him sleep. All he could imagine was the rapidly spreading rice plants in multiple places in China and the looks of the children and their parents with advanced cancer. He downed more drinks to blur that image.

Sloan had looked forward to being home again, and being able to fly his cherished plane. He woke early and was greeted by another beautiful Hawaiian morning. He ate a modest breakfast on his patio enjoying this gift of a perfect day. After breakfast, he put on the blue shirt and red tie as they had discussed, and picked up the soft leather case containing all the documentation he needed to prove his story.

The airport was a short drive from his home and the roads were wide open. The trip took just ten minutes and even though he would be a few hours early for the meeting, he decided to take off mid-morning.

He parked his car in the airport lot and walked, proudly, as he always did, to the tie-down area of his small high wing Cessna. He again checked the contents of the leather case. He was preoccupied and did a hasty pre-flight inspection of the plane. When he entered the cockpit, he confirmed the fuel tank was full, as he had left it a few weeks earlier. The rest of the cockpit pre-flight was uneventful and he started the engine. It purred like a contented kitten and he checked with his tower and with Honolulu control for the short trip across the channel. He took out a fresh pint bottle and had a deep drink. He was happy, and steered the plane out onto the taxiway toward the end of one of the two runways. As excited as he was to be flying again, he was even more excited to be talking with the reporter. He again looked to be certain the papers were in the case before take-off. Consumed with his meeting and with the take-off procedure, he had no reason to look behind one of the hangers as he taxied out. Had he looked there, and noticed Hal Chen watching him, it might have saved his life.

Sloan ran up the engine and began the take-off roll down the runway. He used only about half the runway before he was airborne and headed seaward, gaining altitude for the flight across the channel. About five minutes over the channel, his problems began. He heard a loud bang at the same time his left aileron became unresponsive. The plane turned violently. He smelled gas and saw a pool of liquid on the floor of the right seat. Distracted by the liquid, he fought for control of the small plane. It happened very quickly. He felt another detonation and saw a flash of light. Suddenly, he had no command of the plane at all. It fell into a steep dive, dropping out of the sky at a terrifying rate. None of the flight controls responded. The plane spun rapidly and the sea rushed toward him. He crashed nose-first into the channel. Parts of the broken plane lay on the surface for a few moments before they exploded. The many pieces then sank into the deep Kaiwi Channel. In the end, Sloan felt no pain at all.

CHAPTER 32

Her car pulled up under the canopy. Rorke exited the back seat and aimed a radiant smile at the doormen of Buddy's building as she entered. She walked to the security desk and directed her attention to the heavy-set man sitting there.

"It's a nice surprise to see you, Ms. Rorke. We were not expecting you today."

"I know, Marcus. This is very spontaneous. I just landed in Hawaii an hour ago, and wondered if by chance Mr. Jerome is available."

"You're in luck, Ms. Rorke. He arrived from Texas about twenty minutes ago. Let me call up and see if he can see you." Rorke thought to herself that the idea of luck was a bit overrated. Pauling knew exactly where Buddy was at any given moment. His arrival that afternoon in Honolulu was no surprise.

Marcus pressed a button on the electronics panel in front of him and spoke into his headset.

"Paku, this is Marcus. Let Mr. Jerome know that Ms. Rorke is here and she'd like to stop up to see him."

Marcus waited for a minute, listened, and then looking up at Sam, he said, "He's delighted you stopped by. Please go right up."

"Thank you," said Rorke. She walked around the console and shook Marcus's hand. When she did, her eyes went off his to scan the screens on his side of the desk. The only active video feed at the time framed the entrance foyer to Buddy's apartment. There were no monitors active inside the residence area.

Sam smiled at Marcus again and walked to the elevator banks, past the large man posted outside of the private elevator to Buddy's apartment. The big man stepped briefly inside the carriage with her and slid his thumbs over the security reader. The light of the reader turned green and the guard pressed the up button before returning to his post. The doors closed and the lift started to move. When it reached Buddy's floor, Paku was standing in the entrance hall to greet her.

Paku led her to the terrace where Buddy stood to greet her in his Hawaiian shirt and blue jeans.

"What a wonderful surprise," Buddy exclaimed. "You know I must be living a virtuous life to be blessed with a beautiful red-haired angel showing up on my doorstep twice in the same week. You're looking good, honey; you smell good, too."

"Thank you, Buddy."

"Let's sit out here," he said, gesturing to the terrace seats. He had a grin on his face and asked, "Is it too early for you to have a drink? It's about 8:00 o'clock in Houston. I believe we're on the safe side of the 5:00 o'clock fence."

"Sure, why not?" she said.

"Good answer. Hey, did you see that new Sir Winston oil on the wall?"

"I did notice it. When did you buy it?"

"Just last week. Do you like it?"

"It's a different kind of landscape than what you see from this terrace."

"Sure, but let's not hold that against him. He didn't live in Hawaii. I like it."

"That's all that matters, Buddy," she said quietly.

With that, Paku walked into the room with a clear drink on ice for Buddy and glass of white wine.

"Is this all right for you, Ms. Rorke?" Paku asked, as he presented the wine.

"Yes, thank you, Paku."

Buddy waited until Paku left the room. "Now, what brings you here?" He sounded more businesslike.

"I'm following up on your earlier announcement."

Buddy lowered his voice to a whisper. "You mean that Shelly's protein causes cancer?"

"Yes, that," she said, following his lead to whisper.

"What about it?"

"It's kind of an unpleasant topic, isn't it?"

"You bet. It's annoying as hell to think Shelly beat me again, although this one cost him a lot more than it cost me. What about it?"

She hesitated before asking, "Can we talk about something else for a minute?"

"Honey, you can do whatever you like. If you want to change the conversation away from rice, I don't mind talking about something else—anything else, as a matter of fact."

"Do you have any cameras in your bedroom?" she asked.

"Cameras in my bedroom?" he repeated. "Now, that's a very interesting question, Sam. Why do you want to know that?" He looked directly at her with a little smile forming on his now happy face. "No. Hell no. The only record of what goes on in there is right here, and nowhere else." He tapped his head.

"Absolutely no cameras are allowed in the bedroom. I don't ever want to think of the boys downstairs watching me in there. You also might like to know that the cameras throughout the rest of the house are only active when we have a business group in here. When I'm entertaining or home alone, no cameras are on." The smirk on his face widened. "Now, why are you asking about cameras in my bedroom?"

She undid another button on her blouse, then removed the clip from her hair and shook it out.

"Why don't you give Paku the night off?" she whispered.

Buddy grinned, thinking about how he'd like to see the evening ahead progress. "Oh, he'll be out of sight once he cooks dinner in a little bit. I sure hope you can stay. I don't know what he's cooking tonight. I'm sure it'll be a helluva meal. It always is."

"I'm not hungry, Buddy."

"Yeah, but you will be. We'll have a great sunset tonight over Diamond Head followed by a fabulous Paku dinner. After that, he'll go, and it'll be just you and me in this little ol' apartment."

"No. I mean I want us to be alone right now." There was no room for doubt in her demand.

Buddy pondered it and said thoughtfully, "Well, I guess the boys downstairs could bring us a little carry out for later." He yelled out, "Paku, come here." A few seconds later, the house-man arrived.

Buddy looked at him and said, "I want you to take the night off. Go down to the Royal Hawaiian and blow off a little steam. Have a good meal made by someone else."

Paku turned to leave.

"Make sure they give you the company rate," Buddy yelled after him.

After they heard the door close, she said, "Buddy, would you show me your bedroom?"

"Oh yeah. Third door on the right down the hall, and I'm right behind you."

They stood and walked down the hallway.

"Bring my purse, please," she called over her shoulder.

Buddy turned and picked up the bag, following her.

She walked ahead of him and was sitting on the large bed in the room overlooking Diamond Head when he arrived.

"Sit here with me," she said.

He happily did as he was told.

"Would you hand me my purse?"

"Sure." He passed the large bag to her and she fished inside it.

She moved quickly. She abruptly stood and turned to face him. Rather than see it, he heard the hammer cock of the pistol and felt the cold, hard, short revolver barrel on his forehead. She was no longer smiling.

"Buddy," she said evenly, "I don't want any more of your flirtation bullshit. I have important business to discuss with you. I want to tell you how to save your life and I hope you'll pay close attention."

Buddy was still in shock, trying to process what was happening. He was having difficulty forming words, only managing to stammer out, "Wh-what the hell is going on here? Okay, you got my undivided attention, Sam."

"All right. Now I'm going to put my gun away and we're going to talk about your very big problem without any bullshit."

She put the gun back in her purse.

He watched her closely. "What's this all about? Who are you, really? Are you a cop or a government spy?"

"Never mind who I am. Let's talk about you."

Buddy was quiet, still trying to process what was happening. "Okay, no bullshit. You say I have a big problem?" he asked nervously, not taking his eyes of the bag. "What's my big problem?"

"It's a huge problem," she said.

"Yes? What's that?" he said seriously.

"Your rice was stolen from the USDA."

Buddy seemed to relax when she told him her news. "Sam, that's no big deal. That's not a 'huge problem.' I don't know why anyone would want to do that. It's a failed project. We shut it down. It's okay, though. That rice has no value to us anymore. You had me worried there for a minute. Now, let's stop talking business since we've got that out of the way."

"No, you don't understand," she said slowly and firmly. "Your rice was taken to China."

Buddy shrugged his shoulders at the news. "They're welcome to it as far as I am concerned. What do I care?"

"Now I want you to think about this, Buddy," she said, slowly. "Your cancer-causing rice is a highly invasive plant. As far as we've determined, it's growing in at least three different areas of China and almost certainly in more by now. Your rice plant is practically indistinguishable from all the other rice in China, except that it grows like a weed."

She waited while he processed what she had just told him.

"Sam, just who are you?" He shrugged. "Yeah, I guess that could be a big problem. They're going to have to dig up those fields and burn all that stuff."

"Yes, they will—that isn't going to happen for a while. It's going to take time."

"What do you mean?"

"Listen to me, in plain English, now, Buddy. No one is going to say a word about this. The rice is going to continue to grow in China until the diplomats can sort all this out."

"No, seriously? How can you not stop it right away? We gotta stop it."

"The timing of that decision is well above my pay grade. We're not saying anything for now."

Buddy was stunned. "How can you do that?" he finally managed.

"We didn't do anything. They stole the rice."

Buddy considered her response. "It doesn't matter who stole it. You gotta stop 'em."

"In time, I'm sure we will. For now, let's concentrate on your problem."

"My problem? What's my problem? I keep asking. I have no problem. I don't want that rice anymore."

"No, Buddy. You have to understand that you're the guy responsible for potentially destroying China's primary food source and causing cancer for its entire population."

"The hell I am!"

"No, you are. If word of this ever leaks out, that you were the man behind this rice bioengineering project, it won't be pretty."

"What are you talking about?"

"I'm thinking that if the Chinese government learns where this rice came from, your life won't be worth very much. I can't even imagine how many assassination squads would be dispatched from the MSS to track you down."

"What's 'MSS?'"

"It's the Chinese Ministry of State Security, and I can tell you that their people make our CIA guys look like boy scouts."

Buddy was beginning to squirm. "That's not fair!"

"No, Buddy, it's not fair, but that's the way it is."

Buddy was quiet, with sweat beading on his forehead. "I wasn't trying to do this. Hell, I only wanted to jerk Shelly around for beating me at golf."

"I'm sorry about that, Buddy. I think your only hope is to keep what you did very quiet or you're probably—no you're definitely—a dead man."

"I swear, no one knows about this."

"Are you sure you didn't tell Shelly?"

"No, hell, no. I told you. I wouldn't give him the satisfaction."

"What about the scientists we met in San Francisco?"

"They don't know what happened at Shelly's company. They're working on corn now." Buddy stood and began to pace.

Sam's tone softened as she watched him. "Buddy, for what it's worth, the PRC will never admit to the truth. Soon, you may hear about rice blight or an insect infestation of the Chinese rice harvest. You certainly won't hear them say that eating their rice will cause cancer."

"Is that supposed to make me feel better?"

"Maybe. It may lessen the threat of the cancer-causing plants being traced back to you."

Buddy was thoughtful and said, "Yeah, I guess it does."

"You might be okay if you can keep your mouth shut."

"I can certainly do that," he said earnestly. "I can keep this secret." He took a few deep breaths and added, "I think I'm going to have to hire Paku some reinforcements."

"If word gets out about this, Buddy, fifty Pakus won't be enough to save your skin. Hell, we might even kill you ourselves if you talk."

"Who are you?" he asked. When she didn't answer, he continued, "Well, I'm definitely not going to talk." He looked at her. "Would you really do that?"

"Good," she said, ignoring his last question. "If all your people are in the dark, and you can keep your mouth shut, you may just come through this alive."

Buddy stayed quiet while he considered her words.

A little later, she added, almost sweetly, "I'm not going to be wife number four and I'm not going to be your girlfriend, however, I will try to help you stay alive."

"Well, I'll do my part. I suppose that's a good start."

He paced a little more and then he turned to her, "I guess I'm okay with your plan, but I wonder, if we're Americans, and we can allow this terrible thing to go on, what are the bad guys doing?"

CHAPTER 33

Before he left Hong Kong, Franco tried to call Pauling five more times on the emergency number. Each of the calls went to voice mail and Pauling did not return any of them. By the time he reached the cruise ship, Franco had resigned himself to the fact that he would not be able to speak with the old man and he tried to stop thinking about him.

On the cruise ship, it took no time for Franco to adjust his routine. He found the five-star pampering the perfect distraction from his recent revelations. In his first two days on board, he sampled all the restaurants and bars the medium-sized ship had to offer. By his observation of the other passengers, he was the only single man, not counting the two gay couples. There were a good number of single women, although only one or two within a decade of his age and they didn't seem at all interested in him. That was fine, since he was not looking for romance, only for decompression.

Franco could still not fully believe the events of the last week. He thought he knew Pauling well, and he could never imagine him orchestrating a threat as large as the one the Admiral seemed to have unleashed on the Chinese people. Franco considered himself to be a faithful sailor who had always relied on the chain of command. While there were times he questioned it, he had never disobeyed it. It had served him well. But this was all too overwhelming.

One of the activities he most enjoyed on ship was spending time in the passengers' computer room. Not wanting to compete with his fellow travelers for an unoccupied terminal, he made it the first stop of the day, before his workout, breakfast, or sun up. He was particularly interested in Hong Kong news and scanned two online English language Hong Kong papers.

He had a clear idea of what he was looking for in their local news. On Monday, he scanned the Hong Kong city section of both publications. The story that caught his eye in the tabloid paper was barely mentioned in the traditional broadsheet publication. The story was about a distraught businessman, living in a luxury Hong Kong high-rise building, who leapt to his death after receiving notification that his younger brother and business partner died by a drug overdose. The businessman left behind a suicide note, but there was no known next of kin, although authorities were still looking. The most exciting part of the story was that the jumper demolished a new Rolls Royce parked on the street below the jumper's apartment.

The paper claimed they had a reporter who had read the suicide note. By the reporter's account, it was a heart-breaking note detailing the older brother's failure in taming the destructive behaviors of his wild younger brother. The note described the jumper's shame for both his brother's end and for being unable to help him. Of equal importance to the story was that the destroyed car was owned by a high-ranking member of the Myanmar junta. However, the owner of the Rolls was not yet available for comment.

Except for the Rolls Royce angle, this was exactly the end he might have expected Rorke and her team to arrange for the brothers. If done well, it was much cleaner than having the authorities wondering about a missing body. As Franco thought about the story, he began to think long and hard about Rorke, and later about Pauling, and finally about Sloan. He hoped Sloan had returned to sobriety and that he was trusting Pauling to deal with the rice problem. Franco scanned his e-mails and seeing nothing except spam, departed the computer room. While there had been no doubt in his mind earlier, the current story further illustrated the enormously high stakes of the game they played. He hoped Sloan understood this, too.

On Tuesday, Franco returned to the computer room as was now his pre-dawn habit. The tabloid had a juicy story for their readers. The Rolls Royce, demolished in the early Monday morning fall, had full photo images and a background piece on the high official who owned it. In addition to the automobile, the official was leasing an apartment in the building where the suicide occurred. Four women from Thailand occupied the apartment and were apparently supported by the official for his use when he came to Hong Kong. Neither the official nor the Myanmar government was available for comment. Of note, there was no additional mention of the businessman or his brother.

On Wednesday morning, Franco saw that the Rolls Royce story was still alive with more investigation into the Thai women and the official. There was no further mention of the jumper, so the story no longer interested him. However, there was another story about a peasant farmer who died after apparently stumbling upon a cobra on his subsistence farm in southern Lantau. The story extensively discussed the dangers of venomous snakes in South China and printed a ten-year retrospective of all the serious snakebites that had occurred on the island. The rest of the article detailed how to avoid snakes and how to behave if a snake was encountered.

Franco again thought about Sloan. He realized that the circle of information on the rice story was tight and that the only loose threads outside of Pauling's control were Sloan, Buddy, and himself. He prayed that Sloan was behaving, and began taking a new and special interest in any passengers on board who seemed to be paying too much attention to him.

Thursday's news was of no special interest to him and his e-mail was also boring, with nothing worth reading. However, Friday morning brought a communication that Franco had been dreading, although half-expecting. He had somehow known that he would see it, but wanted to wish it away nonetheless. The letter was from a former Navy friend, a SEAL who Franco had worked with when he first met Sloan in Chicago. The Navy friend was retired and living in Oahu and he sent Franco an item from the Honolulu news. He knew Franco would care about what happened to Sloan because of working with him in the past. The SEAL had no idea about their most recent association.

The online link to the Honolulu papers only mentioned that Paul Sloan, a former decorated Marine pilot, died in an apparent malfunction of his single engine aircraft while crossing the Kaiwi channel. The Coast Guard search of the waters found only small scattered fragments of the plane. By the time the Coast Guard arrived on station, the debris field had spread widely, and there was no likelihood of finding any survivor or any useful insight into the accident. The National Transportation Safety Board's final ruling on the accident would not be available for months, although it was speculated that fuel starvation, pilot error, or equipment malfunction would be the most likely reason for the accident. Franco assumed that the Honolulu control radar record of the flight and its rapid final descent would probably go missing.

In the e-mail, his friend wrote that the Coast Guard hadn't spent much time on station searching the probable crash site because of the rough water and the low likelihood that anything could be found. The channel was up to 2000 feet deep and the expense of a deep recovery dive was not warranted. His friend wrote that part of what wasn't published in the newspaper was that an empty vodka bottle was found at Sloan's tie down spot at the Molokai airstrip. A few people at the airport also saw him drinking prior to the flight that morning.

Franco re-read the email and the newspaper link several times. It did not bring him any closer to knowing what to think or how to feel. He was angry and disappointed in Sloan, and angry with Pauling, Rorke, Chen and whoever else was involved in Sloan's death. In truth, Franco was just a little bit afraid for himself. He wasn't drinking and wasn't threatening to go public with this terrible news, yet he knew he was a loose thread in an otherwise seamless fabric of concealment.

Franco stayed in his cabin for most of the day. He would be disembarking in the morning, and he used the coming arrival for an excuse to do nothing except pack and think about the events of the last few weeks. The more he thought about them, the more frustrated he was that he could not make sense of them or of much else in his life.

When the ship arrived in Singapore, his luggage did not need to be checked, since he carried it out on his back. The cruise line arranged the airport transfer and he had no delays at the airport. That was fortunate, because he had no energy to do anything. He spent the day in the Singapore airport waiting for the overnight flight to Christchurch. The plan for the rest of his life flashed in front of him and, with some regret, he realized there was nothing on it.

CHAPTER 34

I t was about 10:30 local when Franco's plane rolled out of its landing in Christchurch and began its taxi to the terminal. The gate was ready, and it looked like there would be no delays for his connections to Invercargill and then on to Stewart Island. Franco felt his pocket for his passport and readied himself to collect his bag and go, when the captain announced that when they came to the gate, all passengers would have to remain seated for a few minutes. Franco began to feel uneasy after the announcement. Those feelings heightened after the plane came to a complete stop and the air-bridge mated the cabin. He saw the co-pilot walking down the aisle to his row.

The co-pilot looked down to him and said, "Mr. Franco, would you please come with me, sir?"

Franco weighed his options and realized there was nothing to do other than to follow him. He collected his bag from the overhead and walked after the co-pilot. When Franco came to the cabin exit door, he was greeted by two large senior enlisted military from the New Zealand Army.

One said, "Please come with us, Commander."

Franco was not sure whether to follow them, to call the police, or to try to run. There was no choice to make. He quietly followed them. The three made their way through the security door circumventing the customs route. A battery cart was parked there for them. One of the men drove, another stayed in back, and Franco sat in the passenger seat.

"What's this all about?" he asked the driver.

"I don't know, sir," said the driver, as he weaved around the concourse passengers.

"Am I under arrest?"

"No, certainly not, sir. We're military, not police."

"Where are we going?"

"Someone needs to see you. We're taking you to him."

"Who is that?"

"Don't know, sir," said the driver. "He's out at one of the far hangers—the Operation Deep Freeze hanger, you know, the military re-supply hanger for those blokes who go to the Antarctic."

"Maybe your new orders are for the Antarctic, sir?" said the solider from the back of the cart. "Wouldn't that be a shock?"

"Yes, Sergeant. That would be a helluva shock," agreed Franco, thinking there were perhaps fates worse than being sent to the Antarctic.

"Well, let's hope it doesn't happen," said the soldier.

They drove to the far end of the terminal and onto a large elevator that took the cart to the tarmac level. After flashing his identity credentials to the security guard, the driver brought the cart through a double door that led outside to the aircraft. They drove the cart close to the buildings and away from the airplane traffic. Away from the terminal, the airliner traffic diminished and they made their way past a row of hangers until they came to one outside of which a large business jet was parked.

A large man in a suit stood at the bottom of the jet's stairs when the cart pulled up.

The driver announced to Franco, "We're here. Good luck, sir. Stay warm."

Franco thought about Sloan.

"Thanks," he said, and walked up the stairs, not knowing what to expect, and wishing he were armed.

When Franco entered the cabin of the big jet, the old man was sitting and smiling at him.

Franco looked at him and immediately said, "You didn't answer my calls. Why not?"

"Easy answer," said the Admiral. "I didn't want to talk with you."

Franco said nothing, and just waited for the Admiral to speak again. "We did okay, Franco," he said.

"No," Franco said. "I think I let you down with Sloan, sir."

"Nonsense. You didn't. He came back to the U.S. without having said a word about the project. You did your mission."

"Are you sure he didn't make any calls or write to someone?" asked Franco.

"Unless he was engaging in spy tradecraft and had letter drops pre-arranged, he didn't communicate a word of the secret. We monitored the rest of his communications."

Pauling seemed proud of the fact when he said it. It prompted Franco to say, "Yes, I figured you did. Is that why you killed him?"

Pauling's warmth vanished. He hesitated before responding. "Although Sloan was once a fine man, his judgment was lost to alcohol. He was en route to speak with a journalist about the events you observed. That dumb Texan did our professor no favors by discussing the animal toxicology results with him. Sloan couldn't handle the information."

"Do you think I can?" asked Franco.

The Admiral took a deep breath. "Franco, if I didn't think you could handle the information, I wouldn't have called you in the first place."

"Yes, sir."

The Admiral seemed to brighten a little after the topic of Sloan was out of the way. "Do you realize that there are only four of us, five with the Texan, who really know what's going on? There are just five people in the entire world who know that the entire rice supply of China will soon be polluted and will cause cancer for the whole population. Just five people who can potentially kill a billion and a half people and change the course of the world history and the balance of power forever. Since the Chinese supply rice to North Korea, it's a double win."

"Yes, sir," said Franco, nervously. In all the years he had known Pauling, he had never seen him like this.

"Listen," Pauling continued, "there are only three of us who know all the key details."

Franco finally asked, "What about the NSC and the White House? What do they say about this?"

"They don't know anything about it, yet."

Franco was incredulous. "What do you mean? How... how could you do this?" he stammered.

"Do what? Pull off the secret?"

"No! How could you send cancer causing plants to China?"

"I didn't send them there. None of us did. They took them. They stole them like they've stolen missile guidance technology, fighter plane designs, nuclear power plant engineering, and weapons enrichment plans. We didn't give it to them, and I'm tired of having the Chinese rip us off."

Franco could not believe what he was hearing. "What agency is involved in this?" he asked.

"Just us," said the Admiral. "It's not even the agency, only Rorke and Chen. No one else knows. Langley has no idea."

"What are we, you, going to do about it?"

"Before I tell you that, Franco, let me tell you a story, from an old cold warrior." Franco waited while the Admiral collected his thoughts. "Did I ever tell you my Dad was killed by the Chinese communists?"

"No, sir," said Franco, now very nervous.

The Admiral continued, "I grew up not remembering my father at all. My older brother had a few vague memories of him. I had nothing."

"Yes, sir."

"It was when the Chinese first invaded Korea—a colossal intelligence failure that we didn't see them coming. It was November of 1950, and my Dad was in the hill country near Usan as a junior officer in the 8th Cavalry Regiment. I didn't know much about it for years, until I was old enough to read, and then I learned it was very gruesome. I eventually ran into a survivor who said my father went down in the first wave. The entire regiment was overwhelmed with a surprise attack, and they were chopped up in little pieces at the start of the Chinese invasion."

The old man looked out the window of the jet, not making eye contact with Franco. It was an uneasy pause, and Franco didn't know how to respond.

"I'll tell you this," the Admiral said finally, "I'll never be in love with the Chinese communists, because they killed my Dad."

"Yes, sir. We both know you are a mean, miserable, son of bitch with a long memory."

"Yes, I am, Franco. Do not forget that fact."

"When do you share all this with the NSC?" Franco asked.

"Well, everything is coming together soon. You want to have it in a nice bundle before you turn it over to the politicians."

"Sir, how will it be presented?"

"I've had all the Texan's research documents translated into Spanish. I think, if we tell it right, that a pretty convincing story will be that the Cubans were working on this killer rice with the help of the Russians. The documents will be full of ill intent for the Chinese. We may try to implicate the Iranians as well. I haven't completely worked that out."

"Will the Chinese buy it?"

"Like everything in life, Franco, it's all about salesmanship and presentation. I think if we arrange for the right middleman to show this to the Chinese, it could work. The cover story would be that they found it on a Russian spy as he was transiting their country back from Cuba. Maybe we find a Syrian that can bring it to the Chinese, maybe not."

Franco was silent.

Pauling started talking again. "There is one thing that is tragically ironic. The ChiCom's Red Army makes a lot of money on their various businesses in China; cigarettes are one of them. They may be a little reluctant to believe that there is still another reason, and a powerful one, to stop smoking. The scientists think that lung cancer with the rice and smoking will come on in a matter of a year as opposed to when it will happen in non-smokers."

"Where it may take several years?" asked Franco.

"Yeah, that's probably right," said the Admiral.

"But it will happen?" persisted Franco.

"That's what they say," agreed the Admiral, almost cheerfully. "You know the Chinese communists are not animals like the North Koreans are. Well, some are—although their society as a whole is nothing like their neighbors. What I'm saying is, even if they need to import 100 percent of their rice for a few years until they can be sure none of this cancer rice is still around, they'll do it. If they're forced to choose between spending billions to catch up with us to close their military technology gap or billions buying food for a starving nation, they'll buy the food. And they'll have to buy a lot of it from the U.S. No one else has the capacity. That's what I'm counting on."

Pauling paused for Franco to respond. When he said nothing, the old man continued, "This is going to fundamentally change our balance of trade with the PRC. Because of this stolen rice, we'll be able to pay down the markers the Chinese have on our debt."

Franco said, quietly, "Admiral, this is a terrible thing you're doing."

Pauling did not immediately speak. He stood and walked about in the cabin a moment before turning back to Franco.

"Three points," he said. "First, the history of using starvation in conflicts between nations is a long one. It's even in the Bible as one of the Lord's tools—see Ezekiel 5. That's total war there. Starvation is obviously an ugly tactic because it hits non-combatants hard, yet there's no doubt that it's effective. From any of the sieges of the ancient walled cities, to MacArthur's island campaign in the Pacific, to the current senseless control of tribes in the Sudan and Somalia, it's a useful, albeit a non-discriminating weapon."

Pauling looked intently at Franco as he continued. "Second, remember we didn't do anything actively except to remove spies and thieves. We have a long history of doing that. When George Washington hanged Major John Andre, everyone was upset, although they understood the argument. That's all I've done here. For the rest of it, the Chinese have done everything to themselves."

"And third, yes, it's a terrible thing. And it's also true what they say—payback is a bitch."

"The PRC will suspect we're involved and that the Cuban story is bullshit," Franco countered.

The Admiral replied. "That may be even better, so long as they can't prove it. Think about it. They may think twice before ripping us off again."

Franco sighed. "Sir, how does the story end?"

"Franco, I'm not sure." Then he added, "Isn't it amazing that only three little people control the fate of the world? If we just do nothing, if we are all hit by that proverbial bus today, the amazing events that will play out will be due entirely to the fault of others trying to take things that didn't belong to them."

Franco said nothing, letting the implication of those words hang in the air for a while. "Should I be concerned that your red-headed assassin will try to screw up my life?"

Pauling said, "If you're talking about Rorke, unless you pissed her off with something I don't know about, I don't think so. You're just not a threat to this operation, Mike. Let's be clear. Even if you wanted to talk to someone about this, you don't know anything for sure. That was by design. You don't know the names, or places, or times. I'm sure you could come up with a theory, and maybe a few facts with a little investigation, although it would likely take you several months to build your case and longer to find an audience for your story. Convincing the Chinese that eating rice is bad for their health—now that wouldn't fly without a lot of supporting data that you don't have. If you did upset some people about lung cancer, their army operatives would likely kill the story or kill you because you'd screw up their cigarette business. As it stands right now, it's a big country, and you don't know where they planted all the bad plants. You're not on the inside, Franco. I didn't want you in, and because of that, Rorke has no unfinished business with you."

Franco thought about the Admiral's assessment of the situation. "Sloan had enough credibility to be a risk?"

"As a former Undersecretary of Agriculture with possible documentation on the project in his possession? Yes, he had credibility."

Neither of them said anything else about it until Franco spoke. "You would have killed Sloan anyway, even without the call to the reporter."

The comment was made quickly, and it stopped the conversation. Both men were uncomfortable. Both knew there was no more to be said about Sloan.

After a few seconds, Franco spoke again. "What will you do about Buddy?"

"Rorke talked to him and convinced him that if word ever got out that he was involved in this, he'd be a dead man. That is certainly not an exaggeration. The Chinese would not let this pass without a punishment. Buddy will keep quiet about this with the hope he won't be blamed for it."

Franco nodded. The Admiral looked out the window. "Your ride is here. It's time for you to go. I assumed you'd prefer your own flight back rather than going commercial. The Royal Kiwi's have provided a King Air for your trip, if that's okay with you."

"Yes, sir," said Franco meekly. He felt exhausted as he struggled to understand how all this was actually happening.

The Admiral stood, and Franco followed his lead.

"Don't look so glum. This will all work out fine. It's an incredible thing we're doing. Trust me: it's all going to go very well." The Admiral handed him an envelope and said, "Here's your check. Don't spend it all in one place."

"Goodbye, sir."

"Goodbye, Franco. I'll know where to find you if I need you again."

Franco wanted to protest; instead, he simply said, "Yes, sir." He turned back to the Admiral. "When are you going to tell the Chinese?"

"Don't worry. It will be handled just right." He pointed to the door. "Go. You did your job."

Franco walked to the cabin door and saw the King Air parked across the tarmac. More important than his plane, his attention became riveted on Rorke and Chen, standing at the bottom of the jet's steps.

He descended the steps. Rorke's unblinking eyes showed nothing. Franco looked closely at those green eyes that had earlier seemed so beautiful. They were expressionless, cold, and frightening.

Franco walked past Rorke to his plane without speaking, thinking about what he had learned that day.

CHAPTER 35

The flight back was smooth, picking up clouds on the approach to Stewart Island. It was raining again, and despite the low ceiling, the pilots amused themselves with an aerial tour of the island. As they made the wide circle, Franco thought about how insignificant and secluded it was. It might be a good place to sit out a war.

There was no one else on the airstrip when he landed. The pilots kept the engines running as he deplaned and walked off the taxiway. The turboprop's engines revved higher as soon as he cleared the backwash. He was lost in his thoughts as he stood watching the King Air disappear into the clouds over the far end of the runway.

He phoned for a cab and the taxi arrived ten minutes later. Franco knew the cab driver by face from the restaurant and from walking around in Oban. Even if Franco had not known him, the driver would have recognized Franco, who was a local curiosity, if not a celebrity, as the American who came to Stewart Island for an extended holiday.

WILLIAM CLAYPOOL

Although the driver was interested in hearing about Franco's trip, Franco was not in a sharing mood. In fact, he was still in shock from the events of the last two weeks. The world was an unsettled place for him. The idea that only three people could destroy a country and could do it anonymously was simply too hard to grasp.

He daydreamed through the short drive home, and mostly blocked out the chitchat of the driver. He felt as if he might cry. His fear, anger, and disappointment all distilled down into a vast feeling of emptiness. The values and respect he thought he shared with Pauling were no longer certain. It was all so terribly wrong, all so horribly sad.

Franco paid the driver, walked to his house, and stepped up on his porch. The rain had lessened on the drive although he did not expect it to stop. He walked to the door and turned the knob. He hadn't locked it when he left. The door opened and the room was as he had left it.

When he walked to his bedroom, he saw that things had changed. The bed was made differently and there was a new pillow on the bed. A woman's toiletries were on the dresser and in the small bathroom. He looked in the closet and Ani's clothes were hanging there. She was back.

Franco did not know how he felt about the return of his room-mate. His future was uncertain in every way, and he was not sure she could help him bring it into focus. It was now mid-afternoon and he had missed lunch with the trip down from Christchurch. He put on a coat and hat and walked the short distance into town to his favorite restaurant.

Immediately on entering the restaurant, he saw her. She was in a booth reading a book. She faced him as he came in the door.

She looked up from the book and watched him come to her. He walked to the booth and sat across from her. He felt no ambivalence as he looked at her. He was delighted she was there.

"You're back," he said. "It's great to see you. You look beautiful."

"I never really left," she said. "You're the one who's back—and you still look cute."

"Yes, I'm back and I'm through working with Pauling."

"Haven't you said that before?"

"Yeah, well, this time I mean it," he said firmly.

She reached over the table and held his hand. "How was your trip?" she asked quietly.

"You don't want to know."

"It was that bad?"

"Let's not talk about it."

"Okay," she said, and waited for him to continue.

"I missed lunch," he said. "Let me order my food. Do you want anything?"

"No thanks. I ate," she said.

He walked to the bar and greeted the bartender. He ordered lunch and returned to the booth. "How have you been? Did you miss me?"

"Okay, thank you, and yes, I've missed you." She squeezed his hand a little harder.

He looked at her closely before he said, "I'm finished with the old man. Are you still working for Pauling?"

"Would you believe me if I told you 'no'?"

"Probably."

"Would it matter to you?"

He also thought about the question before answering. "No. I don't think it would at this point."

"Well, I'm not," she said.

"Good. I believe you. So, you're unemployed?"

"Yes, like you."

"I'm not unemployed," he countered. "I'm retired."

"Oh, I'm sorry for misstating it. What are you going to do now that you're 'retired?'"

He thought a moment, and then said, "I think I'll have lunch."

"Do you see anything more strategic on your horizon?" she asked.

"No. I have no idea how the future will play out," he said truthfully.

The barman walked over and brought a beer and Franco's lunch platter—fish, rice, and a salad.

Franco thanked him and turned back to Ani, "Let me eat lunch and we'll try to work that out." He scraped the rice off his plate, and was grateful for his food in a way he had never been before. He looked at the lovely woman in front of him, gazed out the window through the trickling rain, and wondered when the sun would shine again.

SPECIAL THANKS

I am so grateful for the generosity of friends and family who have provided thoughtful input to this novel throughout its multiple iterations. By name, thank you to Emily, Peter K., Peter C., John, Alex, Tony R., Garrett M., Denny W. and Joe B.. I thank Linda Cashdan and Carol Bleistine for their invaluable editorial input. Thanks especially to Mary Packer at Meadow Lane Press for her ongoing support and expertise in bringing this manuscript into print. Thanks always to Cissy for her unwavering confidence and patience.

ABOUT THE AUTHOR

William Claypool is a graduate of the University of Notre Dame and has had a long career as a biological research scientist and as an executive in the pharmaceutical industry. Additionally, he has held faculty positions at the University of Illinois at Chicago, the University of Pittsburgh, and the University of Pennsylvania. He lives outside of Philadelphia.

CPSIA information can be obtained
at www.ICGtesting.com
Printed in the USA
BVOW06s1827201117
500927BV00015B/172/P

9 780986 063787